I0715555

JOSHUA JUMPER

A Story of Strength and Survival

HOPE

To all those who are struggling through hard times. May you find the strength to persevere and hold onto the hope that brighter days are ahead. Although the journey may be tough, every challenge is an opportunity. Your resilience and courage are inspiring. Keep moving forward, and hold onto your hope as you move toward the light at the end of the tunnel.

Chapter 1

It was a chilly September morning as Adam rode the bus to school. The school year had only just begun, and he'd already had enough. As he'd always done, he hid in the front-right seat so none of the other kids could see him. He crouched low, making sure his head didn't poke up over the top of the seat. With his head just high enough to peek over the bottom of the window, he watched as the bus drove past all the houses. When the bus neared the school, Adam grabbed his backpack off the floor and slowly slid it on, all the while trying to stay hidden.

The duct tape holding his backpack together kept sticking to the raggedy blue sweater he wore most days of the week. The pack was beginning to become more gray than green now, and he tried to peel the tape off his sweater without making enough noise that the other students would notice it. Once Adam got it on, he turned toward the aisle, leaned forward, put his hands on the seat to push off, and turned his head around to watch for the exact moment the bus would stop so that the instant they got there, he'd be able to get off before any of the others got up.

They arrived at the school, and Adam got off the bus and rushed toward the doors of his junior high. As he looked through the glass doors on the side of the building, he didn't see a place of learning. Every day when he arrived at school, Adam saw a place of torment.

I know that everyone there either hates me or doesn't even know I exist, Adam always told himself.

He walked across the junior high's faculty parking lot as quickly as he could to keep the other kids from picking on him—a desperate attempt he had to make every day. His heart began to beat faster with every stride he took. Step by step, Adam sped toward the door, hoping no one would notice him. Fear filled his eyes as he thought of who might be coming from behind. He increased his pace, almost running in an attempt to avoid his usual bully. Unfortunately, his efforts were in vain.

Suddenly, Adam felt his heart jump. Derek caught up to him and grabbed the handle of his backpack, jerking him to the ground. The tape holding the handle on wasn't strong enough. Derek threw it to the side as it tore from the backpack. He was much bigger than Adam, who only weighed seventy-five pounds and didn't stand a chance against Derek's massive size.

Adam lay on the ground in fear. He wondered what was coming next. He expected Derek to kick him. But to his surprise, Derek walked past, laughing with his three friends. Adam's eyes glistened as they filled with tears. The other kids walked past, some intentionally bumping into him, others kicking him. He took a deep breath, put both hands firmly on the cold asphalt, picked himself up, and ran the rest of the way to class.

When he got there, Adam sat at his desk in the back corner of the room. He tried unzipping his old, worn backpack, and the zipper got stuck several times. When he finally got it open, he pulled out a green spiral notebook and a number-two pencil and set them on his desk.

The classroom was empty. The bus had arrived half an hour early. Adam had a class with Derek later in the day, but since they didn't share first period, he could spend that time hiding in the classroom. While the other students hung out in the halls and talked to their friends until the bell rang, Adam had no one to talk to and knew he'd only be made fun of or tormented by Derek if he waited outside. Instead, he sat quietly at his desk and pondered his future. He put his left elbow on the desk, rested his head on his hand, and thought about that beautiful day when he would leave for college. He wasn't happy as he did, though. He knew that day was still far away and feared he wouldn't live long enough to get there.

Adam listened to the chatter in the halls. As the noise grew louder, he knew more children were arriving. Kids would be coming into the classroom soon enough, ending the only genuinely peaceful time of his day. He looked behind him at the clock on the wall above the wooden cabinets with black pendant pull handles. The time was twenty minutes after seven. In only five minutes, the first bell would ring.

As the classroom began to fill, he kept his head hung low, never looking up at the disgusted expressions on the faces of the kids as they stared at the freak wearing the same dirty clothes he'd had on all week. He tried to no avail to block out the thoughts of their piercing glares and pulled his tattered sleeves down farther in an attempt to cover up the bruises on his arms.

The bell rang and Adam focused his gaze on the blackboard, fighting the urge to look away for fear of making eye contact with anyone. Mrs. Kendall walked in and picked up her lesson plan book. Adam breathed a sigh of relief as he felt the attention of the others shifting to her. When she looked at him with the same concerned look she always did, Adam dropped his head to the notebook on his desk. He knew she'd seen the bruises and the cuts. He also knew she'd ignore it as she always did.

The class was State History, and Mrs. Kendall spoke about the California gold rush of 1849. As Adam listened, he wished he'd lived back then. He daydreamed of being able to run across the country in search of gold and fortune, leaving everything and starting over in a new land where no one judged him. Instead of the loser everyone despised, Adam would be the rich man all the townspeople envied. He'd be the man everybody wished they could be rather than the miserable kid nobody liked. He regularly fantasized like this to drown out his thoughts of misery.

The two boys seated next to him began to laugh. Adam tried to listen to the teacher but couldn't get the boys out of his head. He knew they were laughing at him. His hands clenched into fists and when the teacher spoke, he could only focus on half of every sentence. His mind kept returning to the boys.

The sound of the bell ending class made his heart jump. As always, to avoid people on his way out, he waited for everyone to leave before getting up, keeping his head down and his right hand on his forehead to avoid eye contact with them as they went.

Once the room had cleared, Adam stood up, grabbed his backpack, and headed for the door. His eyebrows rose with fear as he approached it. His strides slowed and he wished he didn't have to face that dreadful hallway. He stopped at the doorway, took a deep breath, and stepped out. He kept his head down as he walked to his second-period class, looking at the checkered black-and-white floor tiles, avoiding the awful stares of the other students.

As he approached a junction where two hallways met, he took a sudden right turn. His next class lay straight ahead, but Derek and his three friends were standing in a circle just outside of it. Adam took a long detour, arriving in the same hall from the other side and hiding from Derek by following behind a large boy going into the same classroom. Once inside, he walked straight to the back of the room and sat in the seat farthest from the door. This prevented the others from walking past him and picking on him.

Adam couldn't avoid Derek for all of his classes, though. Later, he arrived at his biology class and took his seat. Adam took biology because he thought the subject sounded interesting. Derek only took the course because he was required to take a science class. To make matters worse, two of Derek's friends, Davis and Brandon, also took the class. Adam was just glad Derek's other friend Miles also didn't have the class. Then Derek would have had his entire gang.

Adam was fortunate that Mr. Peterson's assigned seats kept Derek and his friends at a good distance. This allowed him to concentrate on the class most of the time. But when Derek got bored, he found ways to torment Adam anyway.

As Mr. Peterson drew mitochondria on the board, Adam thought he saw something fly in front of his face. It was too fast to tell, so he brushed it off as a fly or just his imagination.

"Can anyone tell me the purpose of the mitochondria?" Mr. Peterson asked the class.

Adam knew the answer but didn't raise his hand.

"It makes ATP. It's the powerhouse of the cell," Mr. Peterson said after no one answered.

As Mr. Peterson turned back to the board, Adam felt a sting on the back of his neck. He turned and saw a rubber band on the floor. Then he saw Derek pointing and laughing. Adam turned away and tried to concentrate on the lecture.

Another rubber band skimmed Adam's cheek, followed by a hit to the back of his head. He looked back at Derek and saw him reaching for another in his backpack. Adam realized Derek had a whole bag he intended to fire.

Adam was struck by dozens of rubber bands before Mr. Peterson finally saw several on the floor. He questioned the class, but no one dared be the one who tattled. Derek didn't dare fire another shot, allowing Adam to finish the class in peace. When class ended, Adam bolted out the door before Derek and his friends could catch up, just as he did exiting the bus.

At lunchtime, Adam stood in line in the cafeteria. He was last, as always, so he could stand back and away from the other students. As the line progressed, Adam inched forward, always keeping at least five feet between himself and the kids ahead. He stared intently at his shoes, looking at all the mud and red bloodstains on the sneakers that were two sizes too small.

Gazing downward, Adam didn't notice Derek sitting on a table just to the left of the line. He didn't see it when Derek pulled a piece of cherry bubble gum out of his mouth and rolled it into a ball in his fingers, watching and waiting for Adam to come closer.

Derek tapped his friend's arm with the back of his hand and pointed to Adam's feet. As Adam stepped forward, Derek threw the gum, and Adam stepped down on it. Laughing with his friends, Derek held up the gum wrapper, taunting Adam with it.

Adam turned away, staring at the tiles on the floor to his right, fighting the urge to look up. His right hand balled into a fist and he wanted to attack Derek to get revenge, but he knew it would result in another beating.

After getting his lunch—a repulsive slice of pepperoni pizza with a stale roll and chocolate milk—Adam sat by himself in the corner of the cafeteria, eating slowly. Despite the awful taste, Adam just enjoyed having anything to eat.

He was halfway done when a boy sat down across from him. "Good pizza?" he asked caustically, a smirk on his face. Adam said nothing and continued eating. "What's with the backpack? That thing's more duct tape than backpack now. Why don't you just get a new one like a normal person? What, you want to see if you can make it through all twelve years of school with only one backpack or something?"

Although he looked up occasionally as the boy insulted him, Adam made sure to never make eye contact, but being ignored was starting to anger his tormentor.

"Why are you such a freak?" the kid snapped.

Adam clenched his jaw as he chewed his food but never looked up. The bully snapped his fingers in Adam's face.

"Hey, I'm talkin' to you! You're really weird, you know that?"

Wanting to get away, Adam ate faster, taking large bites and chewing quickly.

"Seriously, what is wrong with you?" the kid asked as Adam pushed the last piece of food into his mouth.

Adam crumpled his paper plate and headed for the door, forgetting his milk carton. His cheeks were bulging and he chewed his food as he walked, keeping his head down, staring at his worn-out shoes.

As he reached the cafeteria doors, he reached for the handle. His exit was interrupted by his forgotten chocolate milk carton hitting him in the back of the head. He closed his eyes and took a deep breath as his fist tightened around the door handle. He put a hand on the back of his head and heard the boy laughing with his friends behind him. The thought of turning around and confronting them crossed his mind, but Adam just exhaled and pushed the door open.

He continued down the hall with his head low, holding his backpack with his left hand, his right fist clenched angrily. Students weren't allowed in the halls during lunch, but Adam couldn't stand to be in the cafeteria for another second. He rounded the corner into a seldom-visited hall where he wouldn't be caught, stopped at a bank of lockers, put his back against them, and slid to the floor. He set his backpack on the ground, put his arms on his knees, and rested his head on his forearms. His eyes began to water, but he held back the tears. He looked up at a nearby clock and saw it was 12:24. Six minutes until lunch was over. Adam put his head back down, closed his eyes, and waited for the bell.

Chapter 2

Adam sat there for what seemed like a day before the sound of the bell finally came. He rubbed his eyes and slowly got to his feet. He picked up his backpack, slid his arms through the straps, and headed to class.

He arrived early. Only the teacher was there. He went to his desk and sank into his seat. Ms. Weldon watched as Adam put his head down on his desk to avoid seeing all the other kids as they came to class, but she assumed he was just tired, never wondering what was actually going on.

Ms. Weldon lectured the class, and although Adam watched, he paid no attention. His mind was elsewhere, still thinking about what had happened at lunch—not *that* it had happened, but that it *always* happened.

Eighth grade had just begun. Adam had already suffered through two years of junior high. It was his last year here, but he knew how long the year would be. And afterward, there were still four more dreadful years of high school.

Will it be better? Will I make some friends there? Will the kids here forget about me when we get there?

Adam hoped for the best, but two years of hoping the next year would be better had whittled away his optimism. Still, high school had many more students, and hope for the future was all Adam had. Maybe there would be someone there who'd like him. A best friend who would stand up against the bullies with him. Perhaps even a girl.

He refocused his attention on the teacher. His fantasies faded but stayed in the back of his mind. They helped him forget about the reality of his current life so that he could enjoy the class.

As the last bell signaled the end of school, Adam packed his books and grudgingly began the journey home. When he arrived at the exit doors that led out to the buses, he stopped. Instead of walking outside, he went into the nearest bathroom, stepped into a stall, and closed the door. Because he didn't own a watch or a phone, he began counting to keep time. Anytime Adam finished his classwork early, he used the clock on the wall to practice perfect timekeeping. After exactly seven and a half minutes, he exited the stall and headed outside to his bus.

The extra time he waited allowed everyone else to get on the bus before him. Adam climbed onto the bus, crouching low to stay hidden, and sat down, unseen by anyone but the driver. As the bus drove off, Adam began to relax. When they reached the first stop, he closed his eyes and rested in his seat.

When the bus pulled up to stop number five, he opened his eyes and watched as Derek got off, stopping for a moment to look at Adam, but he wouldn't dare touch him with the driver sitting right there.

They came to a slow halt at stop number eight. Adam grabbed his backpack and stood. His heart began to race again as the driver opened the doors. Slowly, Adam exited and walked reluctantly in the direction of his house, dreading his arrival the entire way. He stopped in the driveway and stared at the front door.

Most children who have such a hard time at school look forward to getting home, arriving at that place of sanctuary away from the heartache and torment of the other kids. Not Adam. For him, there was no place he called home. This was just another place of suffering.

He walked to the front door, held the knob, and turned it slowly. He began to open the door, listening for any sounds from inside and attempting to be as quiet as possible. He stepped inside and crept up the stairs, skipping the steps that creaked. At the top, he stopped and listened for the sounds of someone entering the hall. Even though the empty driveway let him know he was alone, he was still vigilant out of habit. Silently, he went into his bedroom and closed the door.

Sitting on his bed, he let out a sigh of relief. He opened his tattered backpack and began doing his homework. There wasn't much, as he usually finished most of his work at school, but today the math teacher had given the class an extra-long assignment.

While most kids hated doing homework, Adam enjoyed it. It gave him the chance to lose himself in his work, distracting him from his life. It was quite relaxing. He worked thoughtfully on each problem, not trying to rush it, making sure every answer was correct. After finishing each question, he solved it twice more. He didn't have an expensive video game console like the other kids or even any cheap toys to play with, so he used homework to pass the time.

Suddenly a pounding erupted downstairs, and Adam's heart hammered along with it. The front door opened and Adam's father stumbled into the house. It was barely five o'clock, and although most people hadn't even shown up at the bars yet, his father had already been there for hours. Adam listened for him to come upstairs but breathed a sigh of relief at the sound of his father collapsing onto the couch and passing out.

As he finished his homework, Adam kept an ear out for his father to awaken, occasionally stopping to watch the door. A slight smile appeared as he completed checking the final problem for the last time, and Adam closed his school books and packed them back into his backpack. He reached for the top handle and remembered Derek had torn it off earlier that day. Instead, he picked it up by a shoulder strap and set it by his bed so that it was ready for the morning.

With his homework done, he decided to go to the kitchen for some food. Slowly, he opened his bedroom door and checked left and right before moving toward the stairs. Tiptoeing down, he stopped halfway and watched his father sleeping on the couch. Adam knew his father was usually so drunk he could bang a drum on his way down and he wouldn't be heard, but that didn't stop Adam from being careful. Upon reaching the bottom, he hooked around the railing and went into the kitchen, watching his father the entire time.

There wasn't much to eat in the fridge, so he checked the pantry: bread and peanut butter. He took a knife from the drawer and spread peanut butter over two pieces of bread without using a plate to avoid more dishes. When he finished making the sandwich, he put away the bread and peanut butter, rinsed off the knife, and put it back in the drawer.

He took the sandwich to his room and sat on his bed to eat. He ate slowly, making it last, savoring every bite, knowing there wouldn't be any more food for the rest of the night. When he was finished eating, he lay back on his bed and closed his eyes.

Adam imagined the future. College. Oh, how grand it would be. A time when he'd no longer have to sneak around his own home. A time without fear. He wondered which college he should attend.

One very far away, or one just far enough to get away from all this?

Hours passed, and Adam watched as the clock struck nine. He got off his bed and went to brush his teeth, creeping down the hall. Afterward, he rinsed off his toothbrush and put everything away. He didn't have any floss, so brushing would have to be good enough.

He moved to leave but his foot slipped on some water on the floor, and he fell forward, striking the door. His heart filled with terror as the sound echoed throughout the house. He stopped and listened, hoping the alcohol would keep his father from waking up. He heard no sounds coming from downstairs.

Opening the door a crack, he stuck his head out to peek down the hall when a giant hand came swinging down and smacked the side of his head. Adam stumbled back into the bathroom, holding his cheek as he hit the floor.

"How many times have I told you to keep it down while I'm sleeping!" his father screamed as he threw the door open and charged inside.

"I'm sorry," Adam cried, "it was an accident!"

His father picked him up by the back of the neck. "No, *this* is an accident!" he screamed and threw Adam into the hall.

Adam hit the wall and immediately dropped to the floor, curling up into a ball. He began to cry as he was picked up and thrown down the hall.

In a desperate attempt to escape his father's drunken rage, Adam jumped to his feet and took off at a sprint for the stairs. He was only two steps down when he felt a quick jerk on the collar of his shirt.

"You want to go down the stairs? Fine! Go downstairs!"

Adam's eyes widened in horror as he was pushed forward and rolled down the stairs. He screamed when he hit the bottom and clutched his arm in pain.

"Stop screaming, you little girl!" His father picked him up, ready to toss him again, but he halted at the sight of Adam's left arm. The broken bone bulged out of his left forearm, and now his father began to worry. "Oh, stop crying like a baby. It's not even that bad. I'm sure it'll pop right back into place."

Adam's father pressed his palm against the protruding bone, causing Adam to clench up and fall to the floor.

"I suppose you think you need to go to the hospital because of this. Alright, fine," his father said, picking Adam up off the floor. "Get your stupid shoes on."

Stumbling back up the stairs, Adam went to his room to get his worn-out shoes. With his good hand, he forced his feet into the shoes he had outgrown long ago.

"What's taking so long!" his father screamed up the stairs. "Let's go!"

"I'm coming," Adam cried back.

"Well, hurry up and quit wasting my time! Do you really think this is how I want to spend my night?" As Adam walked slowly down the stairs taking one step at a time, his father shouted, "I don't care what's wrong with your arm! When I tell you to hurry up, you'd better start running!" He grabbed the front of Adam's shirt and pulled him down the last few steps. Then he opened the front door and pushed Adam outside.

Adam paced slowly to the car in the driveway while his father stumbled behind him. Adam stopped at the back door on the passenger side to put some distance between them.

"What are you waiting for, you idiot?" his father snarled as Adam lingered at the door, waiting for him to unlock it. "Get in the car!"

His father got the key into the lock and unlocked the car. Adam slinked into the back seat. Falling into the driver's seat, it took his father several attempts to put the key into the ignition and start the engine.

They backed into the street, knocking the neighbor's trash cans over in the process, and sped off to the hospital. Adam struggled to buckle his seatbelt with only one arm but was greatly relieved at the sound of the click as they swerved down the road. Even with his nap, his father's blood alcohol remained well above the legal limit, and Adam jumped as the car clipped another garbage can on the curb. He watched behind them as it rolled down the street, hands gripping the seat, fearing for his life.

Adam turned and looked out the back window when he heard the sound of sirens ringing from behind. A police car raced up from behind with its lights flashing, flooding the interior of the car. Still, his father would not pull the car over.

Fearing the worst, Adam double-checked that his seatbelt was secure. His heart raced as the police car pulled close and then veered to the left and sped up. A sigh of relief escaped Adam's lips as the police car sped past, but he couldn't help thinking that it might have been better if he hadn't.

His life might be terrible, but would a foster home be any better? He didn't know what they were actually like. All he could think of were the orphans who'd grown up to be criminals out of necessity on a crime show he'd seen years earlier. As bad as things were, Adam still looked toward the future and his escape to college. He didn't want anything to ruin his chance of that.

The car clipped the curb when they arrived at the hospital parking lot. His father parked the car almost sideways, taking up two spaces. "We're here!" he shouted. "Get out of the car."

Adam unbuckled his seat belt, holding his broken arm away to avoid it catching, and opened the door. As he stepped out of the car, his father began shouting again.

"Well, go on, then! Go inside and get your stupid arm fixed! I'll come in when I'm good and ready!"

The ER was virtually empty when Adam went inside. A loud thud behind him sent a shiver down Adam's spine as he thought of his father entering behind him. A sigh of relief escaped Adam's lips when he realized it was only the sound of the automatic doors closing. The woman behind the admittance desk was half-asleep. As he approached, a passing nurse gasped when she saw his arm.

"Oh no! What on earth happened to you? Why are you here all alone? Here, come with me, young man. Right this way, right this way!" She showed Adam to a bed and helped him onto it. "Now wait here. I'll go get a doctor," she said and sped away, leaving Adam alone.

Holding his arm, Adam looked around. He spotted some medical tools on the table and began to wonder what they did with them. He still hadn't decided what he wanted to be after college and wondered if being a doctor was a good idea.

Moments later, an ER doctor entered the room with the nurse following. "Alright," he said, "let's take a look at that arm." He took Adam's hand and began examining his arm. "So tell me, how did you break your arm?"

"I…uh…" Adam thought about his answer and finally said, "I fell down the stairs." After all, it wasn't a lie.

"Really? And how did you do that?"

Adam took in a deep breath as he contemplated his answer. "I tripped as I was running down the hall." He bit his tongue as he resisted the urge to tell the rest of the story.

"Okay," the doctor said. "But what are you doing here alone, then? Where are your parents? Why aren't they with you?"

Adam was starting to grow annoyed with the line of

questioning. "He dropped me off so he could park the car and I could come in quicker," he begrudgingly replied.

"So he should be here in a minute, then?"

"Ya, probably, I guess," Adam replied, not wanting to give a definite answer. He didn't know if his father was going to come inside or not.

"Well, let's get started while we wait for him, then," the doctor said. "Your arm is definitely broken. As you've probably noticed, the bone broke the skin. The break is small, but we'll need to disinfect the wound to ensure you don't get an infection." He turned to the nurse and said, "Can you please bring in the antiseptic solution and sterile gauze? We'll also need to get him in for some X-rays and contact orthopedics."

"Radiology said they're ready whenever he can come in," the nurse said when she returned a few minutes later, handing the doctor the supplies. "I also called orthopedics and let them know the situation, but his dad still hasn't come in."

"We can't do much until we contact his parent or guardian," the doctor said. "Do you know where your dad could have gone?"

Adam knew where he was all along—passed out in the driver's seat in the parking lot. He simply hadn't cared enough to bother coming in. "He's terrified of hospitals. He's probably waiting in the car because he doesn't want to come in," Adam lied, wondering why he was still covering for his abusive father.

"I'll go check the parking lot," the nurse said. "I can't believe he'd let you come in here all alone and never come see you."

As the nurse left, the doctor turned back to Adam and smiled. "I'm sure she'll just be a minute. Let's get this broken arm cleaned up. If your dad still isn't here by then, we'll head out to the waiting room so when the nurse finds him you can head straight to radiology together."

Adam sat quietly in the waiting room when the nurse came back inside and approached him. She forced herself to smile politely. "Your father will be in shortly. Just wait here for him, and we'll get you out of here."

Luckily, his father had sobered up enough to be able to walk a straight line after spending a half hour passed out in the car. As he approached, the nurse who woke him glared at him. "Right this way, sir," she said with a fake smile and showed him to the front desk.

Adam's father didn't bother to even look in his direction as he walked past him to the front desk. Adam tried not to touch his forearm as he watched his father fill out paperwork. The gauze was putting pressure on it, which was irritating Adam. He knew if he touched it, it would hurt much worse.

Neither Adam nor his father said a single word to each other on the drive home. When they got there, Adam went to his room, laid down on his bed, and closed his eyes, trying to sleep. He rolled around as he tried to find a comfortable position with his new cast.

His father went straight for the kitchen. The sound of clinking glass echoed up the stairs, and Adam knew he was already drinking again. He pulled the blankets over himself, trying to ignore the sounds of the blaring TV downstairs. Still groggy from the anesthesia used for the surgery, he fell asleep.

*   *   *

It was morning, and Adam was already late for school. He knew it would have been normal to miss school the day after breaking your arm, but he didn't think it was likely his father would inform the school of what had happened.

The school would probably call. Adam worried that would

cause more problems. It was bad enough he was going to spend several months reminding his father he had follow-up appointments with the surgeon who'd fixed his arm.

Unfortunately, there was nothing Adam could do about that now. He had no choice but to wait and see. He knew his father would probably avoid him so soon after breaking his arm. He also knew the nurses and doctors didn't believe his story about falling down the stairs, even though they had no proof of his father's abuse. Still, it gave Adam hope. His father couldn't risk sending him back to the emergency room anytime soon.

Chapter 3

Adam scratched his arm where the cast had been. It had come off the day before, and after months of wearing it, it was taking some getting used to.

Adam had been eagerly awaiting this day for two reasons. First, he wanted to be able to focus on school. Although he'd fractured his non-dominant side, a broken arm was distracting when he tried to take notes in class. He wasn't going to let his father's abuse be the reason he fell behind. It wasn't going to stop him from getting into college and never seeing his father again.

Second, Adam loved the anonymity of not wearing a cast. He already felt the constant piercing gazes of the other children. A broken arm was unique and made Adam stand out even more. Now, he felt invisible by comparison.

A sharp stinging sensation shot through Adam's right ear, causing him to jump. He looked up from his paper but didn't turn around. He already knew what it was. Derek was in this class. After moving to the seat directly behind Adam, Derek had reached forward and flicked him in the ear. Mr. Peterson still had assigned the seats, preventing Adam from sitting safely in the back corner. Although Adam stuck to his assigned seat, Derek and many other classmates started ignoring the rule shortly after the school year began.

Adam stared straight ahead angrily. Again, the pain shot through his ear. Derek had begun flicking him repeatedly. Refusing to turn around, Adam watched the teacher intently. After a minute of nonstop flicking, Adam tried to return to his work, but the pain in his ear was becoming more intense, and it was too much for him to concentrate.

Derek showed no signs of letting up, so Adam sat forward in an attempt to create some distance. Derek simply moved forward with him. As the teacher turned to face the class, Derek sat back in his chair, acting casually.

The reprieve was short-lived, and as Mr. Peterson turned back to the whiteboard again, the flicking resumed. Adam packed his papers into his backpack and moved seats. If Mr. Peterson hadn't noticed Derek moving seats, Adam should be able to get away with it as well. It angered Derek, but he didn't dare draw the teacher's attention by following him.

With Derek now a safe distance away, Adam was able to spend the rest of the class period in peace. When the bell rang he packed his papers, and after waiting for the others to leave, he exited the class, passing swiftly through the halls to avoid any confrontation with the other kids. He sped around everyone, never slowing down until he saw something that forced him to change his course.

When he saw Derek headed in his direction, Adam turned and stepped into the bathroom. There were other boys already there, so Adam casually went into a stall to avoid their attention. Once inside, he waited until he felt the hall was clear.

He didn't want to be late for class, but he knew that if Derek caught him, he'd be even later. As he always did, Adam began counting to himself to track the time. After a full minute, he left the stall and pushed open the bathroom door to look down the hall. Derek was gone. Relieved, Adam went to class. No one bullied him this time, and he sat comfortably and calmly in his seat, enjoying the lesson. This time he took his notes in peace and filled his paper as fast as he could write.

At the end of the day, Adam climbed onto his school bus. He was the first on board. All the other students had stopped to chat with their friends before getting on. Since Adam didn't have any friends to talk to, he took the opportunity to take his seat up front where the driver's presence would protect him as the others got on.

As another school day came to an end, Adam readied himself to endure another night at home. The driveway was empty when he got there and he smiled knowing his father wasn't home yet. He happily stepped through the door into the empty house.

He went into the kitchen and poured himself a bowl of cereal; he wanted to eat before his father arrived so he could hide upstairs when he got home. He sat at the table eating his Rice Krispies, thinking about his future again. He pictured himself onstage in a high school gymnasium, wearing a graduation gown, crossing the stage to shake hands with the principal and collect his diploma. Diploma in hand, he arrived at a bus station, stepped on board, and took a seat. As the bus pulled away, Adam sat happily in his seat and never looked back.

When he was finished eating, Adam washed the bowl in the sink and put it back in the cupboard, hiding any evidence that he'd been there. Then he went into the living room and sat down on the couch, popped his feet up on the coffee table, and set his backpack down beside him. Pulling out his books, Adam began his homework, beginning with algebra. Anytime he got stuck on an equation, he searched vigorously for the solution, and a small smile would come across his face when he solved the problems.

He moved on to his history homework next, but before he could begin, a car pulled into the driveway. He rushed to the window and looked outside, relieved to see only the neighbors pulling into their driveway across the street. He sat back down and began to study again.

Adam enjoyed history. It allowed him to travel to far-off lands in times when none of this existed. He could go to places where great kings and heroes triumphed over their enemies and brought justice to their people. As he continued studying, Adam grew more comfortable, and he forgot about his own life. He wondered what could have been if only he'd been born in a different time and place. He could have helped Alexander the Great conquer the world or fought with the Spartans at Thermopylae. He might have been a great general who led his army to distant lands to conquer evil and bring peace to the region.

Another car pulled up outside. Adam hurried to the front window and saw his father in the driveway. The car was parked crooked, and he knew his father had already had a couple of drinks. Grabbing his backpack, Adam ran upstairs to his room and continued his homework on his bed.

As he worked, he glanced over at a picture on his dresser. Climbing off his bed, he picked it up. It was in a stained wood frame, a photograph of a beautiful woman with long blond hair and green eyes. Her hair glistened in the sunlight, and her smile would light up a room, but the picture only brought tears to his eyes.

It reminded him of a time when his life was better. He thought back to his ninth birthday party. Balloons and other decorations filled the backyard. There was a folding table set up, holding the gifts. A dozen other kids were there, all of them his friends. The woman in the picture came out of the house carrying a cake.

She set the cake on the table and Adam ran over and held her hand. "Mom! Mom!" he said excitedly. "Come look at this!"

He dragged his mom to one of the games. The purpose was to toss a small bean bag into a hole in a board without crossing the line. Eager for his mom to see, Adam began throwing the bean bags. Every one of them landed on the board without falling into the hole.

"Dang it!" Adam exclaimed. "I had it before."

His mom laughed. "Don't worry, I'm sure you'll get it next time," she said and went back inside the house.

Adam played happily with his friends and they all took turns tossing the bean bags into the hole. Trying again, Adam made two out of the three tosses. His friends cheered for him. Soon they spread out to the other games.

He moved to a game of horseshoes. "You go first," one of his friends said, handing Adam the shoes, and he took them and put his foot on a line spray-painted on the grass. Adam held a horseshoe to his face and looked at the stake. He swung his arm a few times before he tossed it. The horseshoe turned backward and hit the stake, landing beside it.

"Oh, so close!" his friend said. "You'll get it next time."

Adam lined up his second shot. Taking a deep breath, he made the toss. The horseshoe hit the top of the stake and spun as it slid to the ground.

"Oh, great shot!" another friend yelled, patting him on the shoulder.

"Yeah, nice one," said the other, holding up his hand.

Adam gave him a high-five with a big smile on his face and got ready for his third throw. Now overly confident, he missed the stake completely, tossing the shoe over and into the grass behind.

"Well," his friend said, "at least you got one."

The other boys took their turns as Adam watched. Afterward, they moved on to other games. Adam approached a dartboard hanging from the fence with another boy playing it.

"Here, take a turn," the boy said, pulling the darts from the board and handing them to Adam.

Adam tossed the first dart, hitting the top edge of the board. He turned to the other boy and smiled, bringing the second dart up. His next throw struck the same spot. His third dart dropped below the board and penetrated the wooden fence. The boys laughed together.

His mom stepped back outside and came over to watch. Adam called her over. "Mom!" he said excitedly. "I hit the dartboard!"

"You must be a natural at darts," she exclaimed. Adam urged her to play, and she took aim and fired, missing the board entirely. "I guess I'm not as good as you are," she said, then added, "You enjoy your party. I've got to get back inside."

Tears ran down Adam's face as he put the picture back onto the dresser. Finally, he set it face down and went to his bedroom door. As he always did, Adam listened for his father in the hallway and crept to the bathroom. He brushed his teeth and sneaked back to his bedroom. Once he was safe inside again, he looked again at the picture frame but fought the urge to pick it up.

He lay in bed face down, his eyes still watery, thinking about his mom. He began to drift off to sleep, but his heart jumped when a loud blaring noise awoke him. The sound of the TV roared from downstairs and filled his room. By now, Adam was used to this common occurrence, but that didn't make it easier for him to fall asleep. He lay awake to the sound of fake laughter from the TV audience. After two hours, Adam finally fell asleep, the television still blaring.

He woke to the TV still screaming from downstairs. That meant his father had slept on the couch, and Adam would have to sneak past him to get out the front door. Silently, he got ready for school. Before he left, he looked again at the picture on his dresser, fighting the tears. Then he sneaked out the door.

Chapter 4

Adam always enjoyed the brief walk to the bus stop. It was peaceful and calming. Birds chirped in the trees, and he passed a cat sleeping on the front porch of a neighbor's house.

He turned suddenly, startled by the sound of loud clinging metal. A tin trash can lid came rolling down the driveway of a house, and the trash cans shook as if something were rummaging around inside of them. He sighed in relief when he saw a raccoon tail in one of the trash cans. Adam continued to the bus stop.

His heart was still racing when he stepped onto the bus. His small chance to relax instead left adrenaline pumping through his veins. Derek was sitting at the back of the bus. When he saw him, Adam's heart sank. Even though it was rare, every day he hoped Derek wouldn't be there.

Adam took his usual seat up front, and when the bus arrived at school, he charged for the door and bolted into the school. He weaved between the other kids and made his way safely to class.

Later in the day, in the class he shared with Derek, Adam wrote ferociously in his notebook, trying to pay attention to Mr. Peterson's lesson. Occasionally he'd look over at Derek, who was staring at him with a sinister smile.

The look worried Adam. He couldn't get the idea out of his head that Derek was planning something. Usually, Derek would point and laugh with his friends, but now he was staring. His eyes were on Adam more often than not, and Adam began nervously tapping his foot. Still, he didn't stop taking notes.

When class was over, Adam waited for the classroom to empty before leaving. As he passed through the doorway, he felt his body lift off the ground as Derek and his friends, who'd been waiting for him, pounced.

They carried him across the hall into the boy's bathroom and threw him on the floor. Derek stepped toward him, and Adam felt a deep pain in his stomach as Derek's foot plunged into his abdomen.

Gasping for air, Adam tried to catch his breath, but Derek's foot returned for another blow. Adam tried to drag himself back out into the hall, but a heel to the calf quickly stopped him. He grimaced in pain as his leg was crushed under the weight of the bully's foot.

Taking hold of a sink pipe, Adam curled his body around it in an attempt to protect himself. Derek bent down and began punching him in the ribs. When they grew bored, Derek and his friends left the bathroom. Realizing they were gone, Adam loosened up and let go of the drainpipe. He rolled over and looked around, double-checking that they'd gone. He snatched up his backpack and darted out the door.

Running down the hall, Adam sprinted to his next class, trying not to be late. As he turned the corner, he spotted a teacher and began walking to avoid getting in trouble for running in the halls. Walking as quickly as possible, he sped down the hall. Rounding another corner, he switched to a sprint and ran through the classroom door, landing in his seat just as the bell rang.

After school, Adam retreated to his room, rubbing his hands on his ribs. He took his mom's picture off the dresser and held it close. He wished she was still there. His emotions began to build, and soon Adam was crying uncontrollably. Rolling onto his side, he pulled the blanket over his head and curled into a ball, hugging the picture.

*   *   *

Adam's mom opened the back door, stuck her head outside, and announced, "Alright, everybody, come inside! It's time for cake!"

Excited, Adam and his friends dropped everything and ran into the house. Kids piled in through the sliding door and scampered into the kitchen. Gathering around, the kids urged Adam to the head of the table. He sat down and the rest filled in the chairs around him. The kids were all talking and laughing as Adam's mom finished the cake on the counter by putting in the candles.

"Alright, everybody," she said, picking up the cake, "it's ready." She carried the cake to the kitchen table, and all the kids stopped talking as she set it down in front of Adam. "Okay, we just need to light the candles."

The kids sat silently but anxiously with big smiles on their faces as she lit the candles. Some gripped their seats to contain themselves. Adam sat at the head of the table, kicking his legs as they dangled from the chair, his arms spread out on the table, the cake between them. His eyes sparkled as the light from the candles reflected off them. He was so happy. His friends were there spending his birthday with him, and most importantly, his mom.

His mom loved him more than anything in the world, and he

adored her completely. When she was around, Adam felt as if nothing in the whole world could bother him. As far as he was concerned, no one on earth was more wonderful than her.

"Happy birthday to you," Adam's mom sang, waving her arm in a conducting motion, and they all joined in, singing.

Adam watched his friends as they sang but listened to his mother. Her voice echoed through the room, soft and beautiful. When the song came to an end, everyone looked at him. He took in a deep breath and then sucked in a little more to be safe. His cheeks bulging with air, he looked at his mom and blew out the candles. He pushed out every last bit of air he had on the final candle, but he put out all of them.

Everyone cheered, clapping their hands and throwing their arms in the air in triumph. "Good job!" and "Way to go!" they shouted.

"So, what did you wish for?" one of his friends asked.

"Yeah, what did you wish for?" another echoed.

"Now, now, you know he can't tell you that," his mother told them. "Because then his wish won't come true."

She began pulling the candles out of the cake, handing one to Adam and passing the rest to his friends so they could lick off the frosting. Then she cut the cake into even pieces except for one, which was twice as big as all the others. She gave that one to Adam.

The end of the party drew near, and cars began pulling up in front of the house as parents came to pick up their kids. Everyone moved into the living room and said goodbye to Adam. One by one, they all left, until finally only he and his mother were left in the house.

"So, did you have fun?" Adam's mom asked him.

"Yes, thanks for the party, Mom," he replied, wrapping his arms around her waist.

"I'm glad you enjoyed it." She put her hands on his shoulders. "I wasn't sure how many kids were going to show up. I'm sure glad we had enough games and cake for everyone. A lot more were here than I expected. You must be really popular."

"No, Mom," he told her in a sarcastically complaining voice. "I'm not popular."

"Sure you are," she continued. "In fact, I bet you're the most popular kid in the entire school."

"Mom…I told you, I'm not."

"Okay, whatever you say, Mr. Popular."

She went to the kitchen to clean up, and Adam went to play with his new toys.

*   *   *

A sharp, deep pain pierced Adam's side like a knife entering his flesh. He opened his eyes wide like a frightened child as he shot awake from his sound sleep. The corner of the picture frame was pressed into his injured ribs, stabbing his bruised flesh.

He pulled the blanket off and slid his shirt up. His ribs had turned a dark bluish color like a rotten piece of meat. He applied pressure against his side with his palm but immediately withdrew as his body seized up in pain.

As carefully as a police officer defusing a bomb, Adam removed his shirt, making sure not to touch his ribs or move in such a way as to cause further pain. He tossed the shirt into the hamper and opened his dresser drawer. His heart filled with dread as he realized he had nothing else to wear and would have to put back on the same shirt he'd just gone through such anguish to take off.

A sense of rage washed over him. He yanked the top from the laundry basket and threw it on without any regard for the pain. He soon regretted that decision as immense agony replaced his anger. He dropped to his knees and buried his face in the mattress as he gripped the blanket in his fists.

Slowly, he began to take deep breaths, letting the pain subside. As he started feeling better, he loosened his grip on the blanket and picked his head up off the bed. He opened his eyes, sucked in one last big breath of air, and stood up.

In his emotional state after the beating from Derek, Adam had forgotten to brush his teeth before bed the night before and knew he had to this morning. Brushing his teeth and getting ready was difficult with his body in such pain, but he managed to get out of the house without waking his father. At one point, he dropped his backpack, and the sound echoed throughout the house like a scream in a canyon. Fortunately, it didn't wake his father.

At the bus stop, he anxiously waited for the school bus to arrive. He was safe from his father for now but realized Derek might have more planned for him today. Adam knew managing to escape or hide would be pretty unlikely in his current condition. His only hope was that Derek wouldn't be at school today. Only then would he know he was safe.

The bus pulled around the corner. The old engine was loud, roaring through the streets with an aggravating thunderous rumble. Adam stared at it like an ill omen. Who was onboard? What would they do to him today? Something even worse than yesterday? He could only wonder, and that was the problem. Not knowing seemed worse than anything they could do to him.

The brakes squealed like a ravenous crow as the bus came to a stop. The door opened, and Adam reluctantly walked up the steps with great despair. He looked around the corner, and there was Derek.

Why? Adam wondered what had made him think that today

would be a good day. Hopefully, Derek would just leave him alone today. He'd already tormented him more than usual, so Adam thought the possibility was high.

Adam turned away, avoiding eye contact as Derek looked at him. He took his usual seat up front where he was safe, but in his rush to avoid Derek's glare, he sat down too quickly and his bruised body howled in pain. He sat forward, resting his arms on his legs to keep his back away from the seat. He realized he would have to do this all day, resting on the desk and not leaning back at all.

Luckily, today was Friday, and he would only have to pull this off for one day. Nothing was broken, and while the bruises would still be there on Monday, they should heal enough by then to reduce the pain significantly. Adam just had to make it through the day without incident.

When the bus got to school, he ignored the pain and moved quickly, knowing the pain would not compare to anything he'd have to endure if Derek caught up to him. He moved through the halls like an animal racing through the woods, avoiding other students like one would dodge tree branches. He made it to class without incident. Later, in a class he shared with Derek and his friends, they seemed not to pay attention to him at all.

At the end of class, the boys left the classroom while Adam stayed behind. Were they really gone, or just waiting in the hallway again? At the door, Adam peeked out like someone hiding from an ax killer in a horror movie. The coast was clear. Adam let out a deep breath. The rest of the morning went just as smoothly.

After finishing lunch, Adam slipped quietly out the door in the back of the cafeteria. He wanted to sneak to his next class before everyone else finished eating—something he usually wouldn't do because the school had rules about being in the halls at any time except between classes, but Adam was willing to risk it today.

Almost there, he thought to himself. Today was turning out to be a good day. He felt as if nothing could bring down his high spirits today. He was wrong.

Passing the same bathroom where Derek and his friends had beaten him up the day before, Adam felt a strong push on his right shoulder as he was shoved inside. There they all were: Derek and his friends, back for more.

Derek stepped in front of the others and took hold of Adam's bag straps, throwing him onto the tile floor like a shell fired from a cannon. Adam flinched in pain as he rolled across the hard ground, but Derek took no mind to his suffering and plunged his foot callously into his sternum.

With a quick gasp, all the air was pushed out of Adam's lungs, and he found he couldn't take another breath. Quickly, he realized that breathing didn't seem to be his biggest concern as they started pummeling him back-to-back.

To protect himself, Adam reached out and took hold of the pipe he had before and pulled himself toward the sink. He wrapped himself around it and angled himself with his legs facing Derek in an attempt to at least have them direct their blows toward his thighs and away from his back. His plan worked, but as their feet pulverized the backs of his legs, it started to seem worse than his ribs.

He didn't intend to, but Adam began to inch his legs away from them, exposing his back. It may have seemed worse as they pounded his thighs, but Adam quickly learned he was wrong as they started in on his ribs again. The pain was unbearable. The lights went dim, and Adam began to see stars as he struggled to maintain consciousness.

With all the strength he had left, he forced himself away and charged for the door on his hands and knees. If he could just make it into the hallway, it would force them to let him go. However, his attempts were in vain, and before he made it even a few feet, Adam felt a shin smack his ribs like two cars in a high-speed collision. He dropped to the floor and the room went dark again.

When Adam opened his eyes, the bathroom was empty and he was alone. Why was he here? As he started to stand up, the pain surged back into his body. Now he remembered. Suddenly, he realized class had already begun.

Ignoring the horrendous agony, he jumped to his feet, grabbed his backpack, and ran out the door. Every step felt like another kick from Derek and his friends. His muscles tightened and the bruises in his legs roared, but Adam never slowed down. He knew what would happen if he was caught in the halls so long after class had started, and that would be worse than anything Derek dared do to him.

He was almost to his classroom when he heard the most horrifying sound ever. "Why are you in the hallway?" a voice yelled from behind him. "Class started twelve minutes ago, so don't act like you're just running a little late!" He made quotation marks around the words. "I've heard that one before, and it's not going to work on me."

Adam turned around and saw Mr. Pendleton yelling as he walked toward him. Adam had never been in his class before, but Mr. Pendleton was known for being a stickler for the rules.

Adam knew he was in trouble. "I was just…" he began but stopped, trying to think of an excuse. He knew turning Derek in would only make him more driven, and it wouldn't stop the real problem.

"Don't even bother. I don't want to hear it. I don't care about your excuses. Follow me. We're going to the principal's office."

Mortified, Adam followed as they marched to the front offices.

"Take a seat right there," Mr. Pendleton said, pointing to a bench next to the door to the vice principal's office. "I'm going to tell her how you didn't want to show up to class today."

Adam felt dead inside. Soon he would be anyway, so it seemed fitting to feel this way. He sat down, no longer bothering to care about his bruises.

Why? Why did this have to happen? Adam asked himself.

When they called home, it would be the worst thing that could happen. Indeed, this was the end of Adam's life.

Chapter 5

As he sat on the bench outside the vice principal's office, Adam's heart raced like never before. He knew what was coming after they called his father, how horrible it would be. The feeling of dread was immense. Adam hadn't felt this bad in years. Not since the car accident, the night his life changed for the worse. The longer Adam spent on that bench, the longer he had to think about it, and the worse his stress grew.

The office door opened and Adam heard a woman's voice telling him to come inside. Mr. Pendleton was standing in front of the vice principal's desk, watching Adam enter the room.

"You can leave now," the vice principal, Mrs. Thompson, told the teacher. "I can take it from here."

Adam faced Mrs. Thompson. She was a small woman, five foot one at the most, but she was still several inches taller than him. With how terrified Adam was to see her, those inches felt like ten feet.

"As you should know, we don't tolerate tardiness at this school," Mrs. Thompson said in a stern voice. "However, I've looked at your record, and since this is your first infraction, I've decided to let you off with just one day's detention. If you report there immediately after school, it will be like this never happened. I'm not even going to put it in your record."

Adam was ecstatic. He couldn't believe what he was hearing. He knew he would have to walk home from school, but as long as he could sneak into the house without his father hearing, he would be fine. He would even sleep outside tonight until his father left the house, if necessary. But at least he wouldn't find out about this. Could Adam be this lucky?

The answer to his question came too quickly. "Of course, I've called your father and let him know that he'll need to pick you up when your hour of detention is over. You can head back to class now. You've already missed enough, and we wouldn't want you to miss anymore."

The vice principal said these things with a smile on her face as if she'd just done Adam a favor, but Adam wasn't at all happy about it. He left the office just as depressed as ever.

His pace was slow as he moved, and his feet dragged on the floor. Shoulders down and head hanging, Adam slumped his way to class. When he arrived and sat in his seat, he slid down, creating a low posture, arms crossed and staring blankly at the desk in front of him.

The teacher was in the middle of her lesson. Usually, if Adam didn't know what was going on, he would have been frantically reading the board trying desperately to figure out everything he'd missed. This time, he didn't care. He kept staring at his desk, not listening to a word. After all, what was the point anymore?

Adam knew he was dead as soon as school was over. These were quite possibly his last few hours alive. Many kids had said things like "I'm dead" or "My parents are going to kill me," but Adam knew this could be the literal death of him. His father most likely wouldn't intentionally kill him, but where would he stop?

How drunk would he be? Would it be too late by the time he finally decided to stop beating Adam? As far as Adam was concerned, the answer was definitely yes.

The bell rang, and Adam picked up his bag and headed for his next class, no longer worrying about remaining unseen on his way. What was the point in that now? Any more problems he had with Derek would be nothing in comparison.

No longer excited to reach the end of the day, each bell brought Adam closer to his doom. With every second that passed, Adam grew more depressed as his fate drew nearer. As he sank farther into his seat, he thought about how he only had one class period left in the day. At least they'd given him detention. That was a good thing now, as it gave him an extra hour of life. He had one more hour before he had to face him.

This time, in an attempt to distract himself, Adam tried to pay attention to the teacher, but it was no use. He stared but the words never entered his brain. In one ear and out the other they went as his mind kept pushing back to what was coming when he got home.

Adam rubbed his arm, remembering the time he'd broken it, how much it had hurt when his father threw him down the stairs and his bone snapped. But at least that was the end of it. Sure, his arm was broken, but at least that made him stop. Adam wondered what kind of injuries he would have to endure for his father to stop this time. A broken arm? A leg? Or a no longer beating heart?

During Adam's last class, he stared at the clock. Each tick of the secondhand pounded like a mallet banging against a gong. If only he could just stop the seconds from passing and never go home. The sound of the final bell made Adam feel as if his heart had stopped beating. The bell seemed to keep going, taunting him, a high-pitched squeal that wouldn't stop.

Adam headed to detention. Though he had never been there before, he knew where it was because he'd seen Derek and his friends there so many times after school. The window to the room was on Adam's route to the bus, and if he cut across the grass, he could catch a peek inside. Occasionally he would do this in hopes of knowing Derek wouldn't be on the bus ride home, but now he realized Derek might be in there with him.

He stopped at the door, his hand on the knob, hoping that when he turned it, the room would be empty, or at least free of Derek. He didn't dare to look through the window. He was afraid he wouldn't have the courage to open the door if he saw Derek.

He opened the door. Derek wasn't there. The room was vacant except for some scrawny kid Adam didn't know. Based on the kid's small size, Adam figured this was probably his first year in middle school.

The teacher entered as detention began, and Derek still hadn't shown up. Adam released a small sigh of relief that Derek wouldn't be bothering him today. That was a small comfort at best, but it was still better than none at all right now. As the large, burly, balding man sat at his desk, Adam turned and faced the clock. It was exactly one hour until he couldn't stay here anymore. Only one more hour that Adam had to live.

Tick-tock…tick-tock.

The sound of the clock pounded in Adam's head. He just sat and stared at the wall at the front of the room, chin dropped, arms hanging down at his sides. You were allowed to do homework during detention, but that didn't matter to Adam. What was the point in getting his homework done now? He would never have the chance to turn it in.

As the time passed, Adam grew more anxious. His depression was turning into fear as his impending death approached. He brought his arms in and folded them. He felt as if he might just get up and run out of the room screaming and was trying to calm himself down to prevent that from happening.

The teacher stood. Adam stared at him, hoping it wasn't true, that he wasn't about to say what he knew was coming. "Alright, detention is over for the day. If this isn't your only day, be back here at the same time on Monday."

Adam looked at the clock. It was time. He stood and walked begrudgingly toward the parents' pickup site, staring at his feet as he went. His last few moments of life were only going to be the sorrow of knowing his painful demise was already here. Not only was he so young, but he hadn't even really lived since he was nine years old—since the night of the car crash.

The front doors of the school looked like the gates of hell leading him toward his eternal damnation. Still, he had no choice but to step through and meet his fate. The devil was on the other side of that glass doorway, and there was nothing for him to do but say, "Hello."

As Adam pushed the doors open, they seemed remarkably heavier than usual. He felt fragile as he stepped outside. There it was, the car—an old beaten-up piece of junk parked crookedly on the curb behind a pickup truck.

His breathing grew fast and shallow, and every step he took was slower than the last. Wanting just to run away and disappear forever, Adam turned his gaze up the street. But where would he go? How would he survive? That would be no way to live. At least this way, he had a chance of making it to the day he left for college. Even as slim as that chance seemed right now.

Chapter 6

Adam pulled gently on the door handle when he reached the car. The rusted metal ground together as he forced the door open. He sat in the worn seat, clicked the seatbelt, and slid toward the door, putting as much distance between him and his father as he could.

He sat quietly, waiting for whatever he had coming. Confusion came over him as the gears clanked into drive and the car started rolling down the street. His father was silent; the only sound Adam could hear was the squealing of the engine as the heap of metal worked overtime to get them back to the house.

Adam tilted his head and looked at his father's cold, expressionless face. What was going through his mind? Adam could only wonder. Was he not going to do anything to him?

They stopped in the driveway. Adam didn't dare move. As his father got out of the car, Adam sat perfectly still on the edge of his seat. He watched as his father went into the house; not once through the entire ride had he even looked at Adam.

None of this made Adam feel better. He knew this might just be the calm before the storm.

Adam crept up the stairs to his bedroom. His father sat on the couch with his shirt open and a bottle of scotch in his hand. The TV clicked on and started playing a paper towel commercial. Adam was glad to use the sound of the yelling salesman to cover his ascent to his room. Maybe if he kept quiet long enough, his father would forget the whole thing ever happened.

Lying in bed, Adam pulled the blanket over his head and hid underneath. The waiting and wondering seemed worse than what might be coming, and Adam almost wished he would just come upstairs and do it already. It was better to get it over with anyway.

He listened to the television. Was he still watching? Or was the sound simply covering up the sound of his father's steps on the stairs?

The answer came with the eerie sound of his father's drunken stumbling up the stairs. The pounding of his sloppy footsteps went side to side as he struggled to find his balance. But was he coming to Adam's room?

The answer was yes.

Adam's bedroom door flew open with such immense force that it rattled the nails in the hinges. His father fell into the room and rested his hands on Adam's bed to keep himself upright. Adam jumped from the bed and curled up in the corner next to his dresser, burying his head in his legs as if trying to pretend none of this was happening. Adam knew what was coming next and that it was unavoidable. He just wanted to pretend it wasn't.

Despite his hopes, the inevitable still came. A giant hand clutched his leg and ripped Adam from the corner. Adam tried to stay curled in a ball as he was dragged across the floor. The carpet burn was terrible, and to make things worse, it was right on top of his bruised ribs.

Another hand came down and took hold of Adam's arm and threw him across the room. He slid across the bed corner and fell onto the floor on the other side. Adam was thankful that the bed broke some of his fall, but his mind quickly went back to the pain as an open hand smacked across his back.

His father picked him up and slammed him down on the bed, punching Adam repeatedly in the stomach as he yelled in an incomprehensible drunken rant. With each strike, the agony became worse as the pain from every punch built on top of the last.

As bad as this was, though, it could have been much worse. Adam realized his father was holding back. There were no punches to his face, which meant he didn't want to leave marks or break any more bones. Whether this was for Adam's sake or to avoid getting caught, it didn't matter. Adam was just relieved to know he wouldn't take it too far.

The incoherent shouts grew quieter, and the blows began to slow down. The beating was coming to an end. Finally, his father stopped and stared blankly ahead. His breaths were heavy but few as he gazed oddly at the wall. He no longer seemed angry. He seemed depressed. Adam watched as his father staggered to his bedroom door, mumbling under his breath.

When the TV got louder, Adam got up and closed the door, knowing his father wouldn't hear it. He touched his stomach to determine the amount of damage done. The pain was awful, but not as bad as his ribs. Adam shivered at the thought of what would have happened if those had been the focus of his father's beating.

How awful this day had been. Two beatings, detention, and the time he'd missed in class. At least Adam could take solace in the fact it was over now. It was time to let his wounds heal, to give his bruising a chance to subside.

Adam knew he couldn't let this happen again. Although he couldn't possibly avoid all future attacks, he needed to keep them from happening so frequently. He needed time to heal. If he was late for class one more time, it would go on his record. Passing out again was unacceptable.

It was springtime now. There were only a few months left in the school year, which meant there were also only a few months left of junior high. Soon, Adam would be starting high school.

Although he'd still be going to the same school as Derek, maybe Derek would forget about him with so many more people to pick on. Even without Derek, he still had his father to worry about, but at least he was always drunk and easier to avoid. As long as Adam stayed quiet and out of the way, his father wouldn't beat him every day.

Adam took solace in the dream of leaving middle school. It had been months since he'd been beaten so severely, but his hope of letting his bruises heal was in vain. Hardly a day had gone by without his father or Derek doing something. As used to the beatings as Adam was, and the more his tolerance for pain grew, his emotional strength was diminishing quickly.

The days dragged on. As Adam sat on the bus once again, he checked his planner to see what homework he had to do tonight. It hit him as he ran over the days that today was April 24th. Today was the day that had changed everything. Today was the day that had ruined everything.

Adam had been the happiest kid on earth. Every day he would wake up knowing that today would be a great day to be alive. There was always a smile on his face from the moment he woke up until the moment he went to sleep. Until that day. Until April 24th, when he was only nine years old. The day he stood alone outside the soccer field. The other kids had all been picked up after practice. Adam was the only one left. His mother had never been late before, and Adam had no idea why she hadn't shown up yet.

Derek walked onto the bus, snapping Adam back into the real

world in a hurry. A deep breath escaped his lips as Derek passed by without incident. Safe again, Adam delved back into his state of deep thought.

Adam never stopped thinking about that awful day years ago that had brought his world crashing down around him. Off the bus and into the house, Adam was in a hurry to get his homework done. He knew what would come later that night, and there wouldn't be much of a chance of doing homework then. Today was guaranteed to end badly.

Math, science, English—he hurried through his homework, leaving no time between questions, not giving himself a chance to get distracted thinking about something else…about that day.

Finally done with everything, he slid his books back into his bag and crawled under his bed. Typically, Adam considered the chance of a five-minute beating to be too low to spend hours crammed in a tight space trying to conceal the sound of his breathing. After taking beatings for so long, he could stand that now. But not tonight. Tonight, not only did he know the beating was all but guaranteed, but he also knew it was going to be more than a mere five minutes. April 24th always came with a worse night than any other day.

Hours passed as Adam waited patiently in his concealment. Yet as uncomfortable as it was, hiding didn't bother him tonight. The fear of what would always come on this day made being under the bed seem peaceful in comparison.

Eventually, the inevitable arrived. The front door of the house swung violently open. The walls shook from the door crashing into the doorstop. Already drunk, his father stumbled through the door.

Adam focused his attention on keeping quiet as he heard his father head straight up the stairs. When he got halfway up the stairs, there was a bang. The sound of more stumbling footsteps came, and another smash echoed through the house. Adam wondered what was going on, but his curiosity didn't outweigh his need to remain silent.

Minutes passed, and Adam was still hiding safely under his bed with no unwelcome intruders smashing through his bedroom door. By now, he'd figured out what was going on. His father was too drunk to make it up the stairs. Every time he tried, he would get about halfway up and then fall, sliding back down.

Adam was safe from his father's hands but not from the sounds of his screams as he desperately tried to crawl up the steps. "YOU KILLED HER!" he shouted. "IT'S ALL YOUR FAULT! IT SHOULD HAVE BEEN YOU! IF ANYONE DIED THAT NIGHT, IT SHOULD HAVE BEEN YOU!"

There it was. Adam's yearly reminder of why his father hated him so much. He usually didn't bother to say why. He'd just take out his misery on Adam. But on April 24th, he always gave the reason.

Adam thought back to that day waiting with his friends by the soccer field. One by one, the others were all picked up by their parents until Adam was left alone. He heard a loud noise a couple of blocks away, but he didn't know or care what it was.

Soon he heard the sound of sirens blaring down the road. An ambulance rushed past him in the direction of all the commotion, and Adam's curiosity got the better of him. He left the soccer field and walked to see what was going on.

As he walked, Adam continued to look for his mother's car. Since she would be coming from the direction he was walking, he knew he'd find her. As he went around the corner, he found a bunch of police cars blocking the road around an ambulance and a fire truck.

This is why she's late, he thought. *These people are blocking the road.*

He considered going back to the soccer field. If he had to go around the barricade, he wouldn't see her. Still, Adam's curiosity was in charge, and he wanted to see what had happened before going back.

Hesitant to go where he wasn't supposed to, he crept past the police cars, trying to get a peek at what had happened. There were shards of metal and broken glass on the ground. Moving past the police cars, he saw a car on the other side of the fire engine. It was so much worse than he'd expected. It hardly resembled a car at all after being crushed so badly. There were so many broken pieces everywhere that Adam wondered how anything could remain of the car's body.

By now, he'd forgotten that he needed to head back. Finding his mom was the last thing on his mind at this point. All he cared about now was finding out what had happened.

Moving around the fire truck, Adam saw another car. It seemed as if this car had no hood. The front end was crushed back to where the windshield used to be.

Adam's thoughts went back to his mother, but he decided to take one last look before going back to the soccer field. There was a loud grinding sound coming from behind the ambulance. Walking around it, he saw a minivan. It was long and narrow from having been crushed on both sides. The firemen were using the jaws of life to cut the driver's door off the vehicle.

Fascinated by the massive tool, Adam watched intently. The van was so mangled that the color was the only distinguishable feature about it—and something about the van seemed oddly familiar.

Finally, the door fell to the ground with a loud clunk, followed by a searing screech as the firemen pulled it away. A hand hung out of the now-open doorway. Blood dripped from the fingertips.

The paramedic checked the body for vitals, turned to the others, and shook his head. Everyone gathered around and began to pull the body out of the driver's seat. Some hair came into Adam's view and he realized it was a woman. Still and quiet, eyes wide and sad, Adam watched as they pulled the lifeless body out and laid it on a stretcher.

A cold, dark, awful feeling swept over him. In his entire life, he had never felt like this before. The bloodied face fell sideways, facing Adam. There was so much blood, but Adam still knew. Her face wasn't glowing with the happy radiance he was used to. Her hair was no longer flowing. Instead, it was heavy and red, the blood making it fall flat. She was barely recognizable, but Adam could still tell it was his mother.

His knees began to shake. He didn't try to run to her; he lost the ability to move. His shaking legs gave out beneath him, and Adam fell to the ground. He didn't cry. In complete shock, Adam lay motionless on the concrete.

Everything around him started spinning as his mind tried to ignore what he'd just seen. It was as if he wasn't breathing and his heart had stopped beating. Adam no longer knew why he was sad. His mind went blank, and he became utterly oblivious to his surroundings.

The paramedics loaded his mother's body onto the ambulance. Adam didn't notice when they drove right past him. Ten minutes earlier, Adam had been the happiest kid you could ever meet. Now he could barely comprehend the horror his life was about to become.

Adam woke from the dream, still hiding under his bed. He turned his alarm clock off and climbed out from underneath. As he got ready for school, he listened for any sounds that his father was still there. Would there be the clanking of dishes in the kitchen, or the sound of snoring as he still lay passed out on the stairs?

Adam hoped his father had woken up and managed to go to work.

Quietly, Adam left his room to see if his tormentor was still there. He crept his head around the corner and looked down the stairs: nothing. Relaxed, he went downstairs and looked out the front window to see his father's car gone.

Adam walked happily to the bus. For the first time, he'd managed to make it through the anniversary of that dreadful day without getting attacked by his father. He had 364 days before he had to worry about that again, and next year he would be in high school. Hopefully by then, Derek wouldn't add to the problem.

Although he'd avoided the beating from his father, he still couldn't get his words out of his head. "YOU KILLED HER! IT'S ALL YOUR FAULT!" Adam kept telling himself it wasn't true, that none of it was his fault, but deep down inside, he blamed himself for his mom's death.

If she hadn't been coming to pick him up from soccer, she'd be alive today. If only. If only Adam had played some other sport. Why soccer? He'd never even played it before, and he certainly hadn't played it since. Were those few hours spent on the field worth his mom dying?

His guilt was all the more reason Adam needed to get away. It wasn't just the beatings, the bullying, and the torment from others. The longer he stayed, the more he tormented himself. If he could only make it for another few years, through the end of junior high and high school, he could finally be free. The only question now was: Would high school be any better?

Chapter 7

On his first day of high school, Adam woke up with a smile on his face. For the first time in a long time, he had high hopes for a good day. Cheerfully, he hopped out of bed and sneaked quietly to the bathroom to brush his teeth.

He grabbed his rugged backpack and threw the torn straps over his shoulders. A bag held barely together by duct tape was no way to start high school, but Adam didn't care. Today was a fresh start, and nothing was going to bring him down. He was going to a new school, one large enough that he should be able to easily avoid Derek. Maybe Derek would even forget he existed.

Today, Adam thought, *I can finally stop worrying about being bullied and start focusing on school.*

With his complete focus on school, Adam would easily ace all of his classes, get into college, and leave forever. He could move across the country and never think about this place again—or Derek, or his father, everything. All that now stood between him and everything he hoped for was four years of high school. Even without Derek's constant abuse, Adam would still have his father to worry about at home, but he thought that should be easy compared to what he'd already endured.

Ready for school, he headed out his bedroom door and down the stairs. He moved silently as he went, but only out of habit—he was too excited to be afraid as he walked out the front door.

Safely outside, Adam practically skipped to the bus stop. When the bus arrived, the door swung open and Adam stepped on. Derek was nowhere to be seen. Adam's spirits sprang even higher, and he took a seat in the middle of the bus. There was no need to hide next to the driver now. Adam didn't know if Derek would still be getting on the bus later, but he was too excited to start high school to care.

Sprawled out in his seat, Adam enjoyed the ride to school. He stared out the window at the autumn colors on the trees. He felt so carefree that he couldn't even be bothered to notice the other kids commenting to each other about his backpack. Even if he had, nothing they said would bother him. Years of middle school had numbed Adam to any insult. Nothing they could say would compare to what he'd already endured. He looked forward to the eight hours of peace and safety he'd enjoy on school days.

The bus rolled to a stop along the curb in front of the high school. There were already three buses lined up. Adam smiled at the sight of the buses, knowing they were there because this school had a lot more students, furthering his assumption that he'd be able to spend his years here hidden from Derek, who Adam hadn't seen get on the bus at all that morning. His smile widened even further as his eyes took in the building. The school was massive, big enough to accommodate over two-thousand enrolled students.

Adam inhaled deeply as he stepped through the front doors of the school for the first time. The smell of the halls was virtually the same as it had been in middle school, yet the scent was distinctly more pleasing to him. Gone were the odors of crowds of kids, cleaning chemicals, and cheap cafeteria food. This was the fresh scent of a new start.

Adam's first class was physics. He reached into his pocket to recheck the room number: E-123. Remembering back to the description of classroom numbers in the school pamphlet, he looked for hallway E on the first floor. Taking a guess, he turned right. When he passed room D and got to C, he knew he was going in the wrong direction, so he turned around and passed through the main lobby, arriving at hallway E on the other side. The 1 indicated the classroom was on the first floor, so he started down the hall, scanning the doors for number 23. He chuckled to himself when he realized his first high school class was in room "1-2-3."

He entered the classroom but didn't look for an empty seat in the back like he had in the past to prevent Derek from throwing stuff at the back of his head. Instead, he took a desk in the center front row in front of the board. Adam was ready to learn, knowing there was no way Derek would be in a physics class—now that he was in high school, Adam was taking classes a bit too advanced for someone like Derek. The fact that these were classes Adam preferred to take was a bonus.

Adam continued to each class without incident. No Derek, no torment from anyone. The kids in Adam's classes were a lot like him: eager to learn and more concentrated on their academics than picking on other kids. If anything, they'd be the ones who got picked on. Still, Adam managed to stand out. All of the other kids were well dressed, exceptionally so for the first day of school—but Adam still wore ragged clothes, and his pants were up to his ankles as he'd outgrown them over the summer.

His clothes weren't the most notable thing, though. What made Adam stand out from the other kids was his backpack. If anything were to draw attention his way, it was that backpack. Although attention was the last thing Adam wanted, he decided not to worry about that. Right now, he had too much hope for high school to be concerned with such things.

No longer confined to the cafeteria for lunch, Adam ate on the lawn in front of the school. The warm sun combined with a gentle breeze created the ideal temperature, making this perfect day even better. He calmly chewed away, unlike his old middle-school habit of swallowing chunks to get them down faster before anyone could mess with it.

Suddenly, Adam's head rang. A sharp, gnawing pain shot from the back of his head up to his forehead. He looked behind him and saw a pine cone rolling away. He had no idea where it had come from. He looked up; he wasn't sitting under a pine tree.

Then a cringing thought sprang into his mind. He turned again to look behind him, and there he was. Derek. The last person on earth Adam wanted to see right now.

He couldn't even manage to avoid him for one day. Adam had hoped that Derek would forget about him now that they were both in high school. He thought maybe Derek would find new friends who would convince him to stop. Derek had found one new friend—and added him to the group of three from before. Now there were four others with him. His numbers had increased.

Adam picked up his lunch and rushed back inside the school. He hurried into a bathroom and hid in a stall, feeling as though he was on the verge of a panic attack. His heart raced, his palms began to sweat, and the world was spinning as if he were about to black out.

Hyperventilating, Adam fought the urge to scream. If nothing else, he couldn't risk Derek being within earshot to hear it. Still shaking, he finished his lunch while sitting on the toilet.

Once again, he had to be worried about Derek. When he finished eating, Adam stepped slowly out of the bathroom, checking both ways to see if Derek or his friends were anywhere in sight. He made his way swiftly through the crowd of students, always keeping a watchful eye.

Luckily, by now Adam had gotten down the layout of the hallways so he could get to his next class quickly…on the first floor, anyway. But when he reached where he expected to find hallway L was, it wasn't there. He double-checked and realized it was on the second floor, so he backtracked, looking for the stairwell.

When he got to the second floor, he got turned around again and had to double back. There was no time for stealth now. Derek or no Derek, he couldn't be late on his first day. He rushed down the hallway and found the classroom just in time. He sat down, safe in knowing Derek wouldn't be in a geometry class but stuck in a more remedial class.

At the end of the day, on his way to the bus, he paced the halls, checking for Derek along the way. When he got onto the bus, he immediately learned why he'd been lucky enough not to run into Derek—he was already on the bus. Evidently, Derek's mom had given him a ride that morning. Adam could now expect to see him on the bus twice a day, all year long. How would Derek ever forget Adam existed now?

Someone had already claimed the front seat, forcing Adam to sit in the third row. Derek and his friends were only four rows back. Adam hunched up against the window and set his backpack beside him for additional cover. He had been in that position many times before and had spent years growing accustomed to Derek's torments. For a brief time, he'd allowed himself to hope it was over. Now that hope was gone, and with it, Adam's tolerance for abuse.

When the bus arrived at Adam's stop without incident, he stepped off quickly and continued to the horrors that awaited him at home. When he got there, he snuck upstairs and sat on the floor between his bed and the wall, concealing himself from the view of anyone opening the door. He started his homework immediately. He needed to get it done before he lost the will.

When he was finished, he kept studying. It was a coping mechanism to keep his mind occupied. His life wasn't any better or worse than last year. Now that he realized it would be the same for another four years, his ability to handle it was gone. He tried to keep his mind on the end goal: college. Even though he was closer to that goal, it still seemed like a lifetime away.

Chapter 8

September was drawing to a close. Adam hadn't managed to make it through a single day without running into Derek, both on the bus and in school. The dream of being forgotten by Derek was dead.

Every day he had to endure Derek's bullying made him lose more and more of his sense of self. He felt like he was no longer living his life but just watching it happen. Every bit of control he might have held over his life before was now lost.

Adam sat on the floor on the far side of his bed with his head against the wall, staring blankly at the other side of the room. He hadn't moved in over an hour. He couldn't see the point. Two more hours passed. His books lay spread out across the floor. He'd pulled them out hours ago but the will to work had left him. Adam had always finished his homework right away, but not this time.

Finally, he pulled himself up and put his books back into his backpack. He wished he cared enough to do his homework. He set the backpack against the wall and climbed into bed with his shoes still on. He didn't have the motivation to take them off. What was the point?

Adam lay in bed tossing and turning. As tired as he was, he

couldn't fall asleep. After an hour, he finally kicked off his shoes, still leaving them under the blankets. At 1 a.m., he finally dozed off.

He woke to the sound of the alarm just as tired as he was when he crawled into bed. He stumbled to the bathroom and scrubbed the film he hadn't bothered to brush last night. He threw water on his face to wake himself up and stared at himself in the mirror as water ran off his chin. His hands gripped the counter, his body tensing. He didn't dare make a sound, but he could feel the screams coursing through his body. Eventually, the feelings subsided and Adam left for school.

Halloween was approaching quickly. Adam's ability to hold on was fading. He had been getting all his homework done, but the days he had any will to do so were growing further apart. The only thing that kept him going was the occasional glimpse of hope when he thought about college.

Once he started, working was a great distraction. But Adam was like an old car. Once he started moving, he had to keep his momentum or risk breaking down and stopping. Sometimes, this helped him get his homework done faster. As he could feel the demons creeping up inside him, Adam worked harder to keep them suppressed, knowing that if he slowed down, they would take over.

Downstairs, the television was blaring. Derek and his friends had stolen his lunch and he hadn't eaten anything all day. His stomach was screaming but he couldn't get to the food with his father between him and the kitchen. He waited, but the sound of the TV wouldn't stop. Now Adam had lost his ability to obtain basic sustenance.

Turning his head to the closet, Adam saw his old tie. It was a black tie he hadn't worn since his mom's funeral. He sat motionless, staring at the tie until finally, the roaring sounds of the TV clicked off. Adam listened as his father went to bed and it was finally safe to eat.

Slipping downstairs, Adam crept into the kitchen. He made one peanut butter sandwich, then another. When he finished, he poured himself a bowl of cereal, trying to consume an entire day's worth of food in one sitting. When he finished, he washed the plate and bowl and put them back in the cupboard, making it seem as if he hadn't used them. As if he didn't exist.

That idea—not existing—was becoming more than a survival mechanism for Adam now. It was turning into his genuine desire. He spent so much time trying to make it seem as if he wasn't here that he wondered what would happen if he went away forever.

When his stomach was full, Adam went back upstairs and climbed into bed. Although it was too dark to see it, Adam lay staring in the direction of the black tie.

At school, Adam sat in class, staring at the whiteboard. His eyes were focused, but his mind was elsewhere. His ability to focus was continuously diminishing. Every day, it was becoming harder to focus. The negative aspects of his life were consuming him. He was safe in class now but knew Derek was still out there.

When the bell rang, he reluctantly got up from his desk and began his stealthy trip to his next class, walking alongside crowds to hide his movements, peeking around corners, and moving quickly to reduce his exposure. His techniques helped. Sometimes he would slip right past Derek, hidden behind a crowd walking the same way. Today, Adam's luck wasn't as good.

Suddenly, the group Adam was walking behind turned, leaving Adam exposed. Derek was just ahead, talking with his friends. Adam bolted in the opposite direction but was spotted just as quickly. His speed was no match for theirs, and it didn't take Derek and his crew long to close the distance and catch up.

They surrounded Adam and forcefully guided him into the bathroom. Each of Derek's friends took a limb, holding Adam in the air as Derek approached. He pulled up Adam's shirt, exposing his stomach. Adam squirmed wildly, but it was no use. Miles and Brandon held his arms tightly, and he had no chance of breaking free.

Derek reached into his pocket and took out a thin rubber band. He wrapped it around his thumb and index finger and put his hand on Adam's stomach. He pulled upward on the band, reaching maximum tension, and released it.

A sharp sting pierced through Adam's skin, leaving a bright red mark just below his sternum. Derek repeated the process relentlessly, not even stopping when the rubber band broke the skin and drew blood. It was only after hearing a teacher's voice in the hallway that they finally dropped Adam to the floor.

Adam pulled himself up, took a paper towel from the dispenser, pressed it against the wound, and rushed to class, maintaining pressure with his hands. When he got to class, he took off his backpack one arm at a time, keeping the other on his stomach. Adam kept this up, taking notes with his right hand and holding the paper towel through his shirt with his left. Although it hurt immensely, the wound was superficial, and the bleeding stopped after a few minutes. Adam discreetly slid the paper towel into his backpack.

After the incident with Derek, the surge of adrenaline gave Adam a boost of energy and motivation that allowed him to excel for the remainder of the day. But when the final bell rang, the rush ended. His strength plummeted, and his feelings of hopelessness began consuming him more than ever. Staring out the window of the school bus, watching as it rolled closer to just another place of torment, he felt utterly defeated.

At home, Adam crept to his room, sat on the floor between his bed and the wall, and tried to do his homework, but he wasn't able to concentrate. He finally gave up, put his books back into his backpack, and went downstairs for a bowl of cereal, hoping some food might increase his ability to focus. He ate the cereal in his room and afterward washed the bowl and put it back.

This time, it was easier to concentrate. But more than the food in his stomach, it was the excitement of managing to make it to the kitchen and back twice without being caught by his father. He burned through his homework and started reading ahead.

He got thirsty and went downstairs for a glass of water but drank too quickly and spilled half of it onto his shirt and the floor. Although it didn't take him long to clean the mess up, it wasn't fast enough. Before he could finish, his father burst into the kitchen and the screaming started.

"You can't even manage not to make a mess on the floor? What, are you an idiot? Now you're wasting paper towels! Do you think those things are free?"

His father shoved Adam to the still-wet floor and kicked him in the ribs. Adam slid in the water, soaking it up with his shirt.

"Oh, look at that!" his father said. "I guess you didn't need to waste paper towels, did you? Moron!"

Adam picked himself up off the floor as his father walked out of the kitchen. He finished cleaning the floor and went back up to his room. Lying in bed, Adam started to think about how he couldn't do this anymore. He turned his head and stared at the tie in his closet again.

Minutes went by. Adam got up and pulled the tie from the hanger. He sat on his bed, holding it in his hands, contemplating. The sound of the TV started ringing through Adam's room, and as the noise echoed in his ears, Adam began to tie the tie. But instead of a standard Windsor knot, he tied one end into a circle. Then he got up and walked to the closet. He hung the tie over the coat rod and pulled downward, testing the rod's strength. After confirming it could support his weight, Adam tied the tie around the rod.

He stood in the closet, holding the tie. He spent hours staring through the hole, occasionally stepping forward, moving his face up to it. Each time, he stepped back, not quite able to convince himself to slide his head through. Eventually, he got back in bed, but he stared at the makeshift noose until he finally drifted off to sleep.

A month passed. Ever since he'd hung the tie on his coat rod, Adam had been spending two or three nights a week standing in the closet, thinking about putting his head through. Each time, he took a little longer to step back when he put his face to the tie. Each time, he got closer to sliding the tie around his neck.

At school, Adam's focus became less about learning and more about getting back to his closet as thoughts of his tie weighed heavily on his mind. One day, as he navigated through the crowded hallways, he turned a corner and was knocked to the floor. Derek and his friends had been coming from the opposite way, and Adam didn't have enough time to react as he went around a corner before it was too late. Derek rammed into Adam, forcing him onto his back.

A couple of teachers were in the hallway talking, and they watched as Derek moved on and Adam picked himself up, assuming he'd just tripped. Although small, the incident was enough to make Adam think about the tie in his closet again. These days, it didn't take a lot to bring his mind back there. Often, Adam would start to think about it for no reason at all. The idea of it brought him comfort. Knowing it was there allowed Adam to feel a slight sense of control over his life he hadn't had before.

When he got home that day, Adam went straight to the closet. This time, he immediately put his face up to the noose, not moving back. Still, he didn't slide the tie over his head. He stood there for an hour before finally moving to his bed, where he continued to stare at the closet.

At first, he ignored it. What was the point, after all? But eventually, Adam became hungry enough to venture downstairs for food. When he got downstairs, the front door burst open and his father came in holding an empty bottle of vodka he'd finished in the driveway. He threw the bottle at Adam but missed and it smashed on the floor. As the alcohol took effect, he stumbled over and fell onto the couch. Not wanting to waste the opportunity to escape before his father got back up, Adam ran back upstairs without any food.

Once again, a starving Adam sat in his room. He went back to the closet, this time immediately putting the noose around his neck. He leaned forward, putting a bit of weight on his trachea. He leaned forward more, now with enough force to make himself gag. He stood back up straight and started choking. He almost stopped after that, but then the rumbling in his stomach came back. This time, Adam leaned forward even farther, lifting his legs one at a time, trying to convince himself to pick them both up at once to cut off his air supply.

He repeated the process several times, stopping when he began to choke, but every time, he held it longer than before. The last time, his face turned bright red before he stood up straight. In the end, he gave up and climbed into bed with no harm done aside from a sore throat.

By the time December rolled around, Adam was spending more time in his closet than not—at least four or five days a week. It was cold now, and Adam sat in his last class of the day wearing a withering jacket with sleeves that were an inch and a half too short. The bell rang, and Adam charged through the classroom door for the school bus, moving at a near run to get out of the cold.

Of course, on the last day that Adam didn't want to stay outside longer than he had to, Derek and his friends emerged from behind the bus. Adam tried to get to the bus door first, but Derek and his friends positioned themselves between him and his goal. Even worse, they had no intention of getting on the bus before he left. Instead of tormenting Adam quickly and letting him get on, they surrounded him and forced him to the side of the school where no one could see.

Once there, they forced Adam onto the ground, each pinning an arm and a leg with their knees, allowing them all to punch him in the stomach and chest unhindered by Adam's attempts to resist. To make matters worse, Adam's jacket and shirt rode up in the struggle, exposing his back to the frozen ground. The frost-covered grass sent chills up and down his spine.

For several minutes, they continued beating Adam, occasionally pulling up clumps of grass and dirt and forcing them into his mouth. When they finally let up and walked away, Adam rolled over and spat the dirt out of his mouth.

Realizing he was going to miss the bus, he jumped to his feet and took off at a dead sprint to catch it. But when he got around the corner, the bus was already gone. Adam dropped to his knees in dismay. He'd have to walk home in the cold with a nearly worthless jacket. Now no longer in a hurry, Adam went back inside the school to warm up and wash the dirt off his face and out of his mouth in the bathroom sink.

He made sure to dry his hands and face thoroughly before going back outside. At first, he walked just as fast as he had on his way to the bus, but he couldn't maintain that pace for the entire walk. He slowed down but still kept a brisk pace. His legs were warm from moving, but his face and hands were going numb. He opened and closed his hands repeatedly to keep his blood circulating, but that strategy quickly stopped working. By the time he'd walked the six miles to his house, his hands felt as if they could break off with the slightest touch.

Adam slid his backpack off and put it on the floor when he got to his room. The strap sliding across his hand sent a stinging sensation up his arm. With his toes numb, he took off his shoes and climbed into bed, wrapping the blanket around him and curling up into a tight ball. As Adam's face began to thaw, the tears ran down his face.

When he regained the use of his fingers, Adam climbed out of bed and went straight for the closet. This time, he didn't plan on playing any games. He wasn't going to lean forward until he started to choke. He was going to go through with it.

He untied the tie and shortened it to a length where his feet couldn't touch the floor. Then he went down to the kitchen pantry and retrieved an old stool his mom used to use to reach high shelves. It seemed fitting to use her stool since her death had been the start of all his problems. He positioned the stool in his closet, slid the tie around his neck, and prepared to kick the stool out from under himself.

Despite his anger, following through was more difficult than he had thought it would be. Adam stood in the same position on the stool for hours but couldn't do it. Finally, he gave up, climbed into bed, and cried himself to sleep.

Chapter 9

It was almost Christmas vacation, but unlike the other kids at school, Adam wasn't excited. For him, there wasn't going to be a Christmas; no decorations, no presents under the tree, no tree at all. None of that mattered to him, though. He wasn't going to spend the next two weeks off school hiding from his father in his room. He'd spent nearly every night since the beginning of December standing on a chair in his closet, trying to build up the courage to kick the stool out from under himself. Adam had no intention of going back to school in January. He had no intention of being alive by then.

Once again, Adam climbed onto the stool in his closet. It began to rock back and forth. At this point, he thought, the stool might slip and he'd succeed by accident. As he stood there, images of everything wrong in his life flooded his mind: Derek, his father, and the death of his mother, who had been the only person who ever cared about him.

"Just do it, you pathetic coward," he told himself as tears streamed down his face.

His heart rate began to race. He put his foot on the edge of the stool and started to shake it violently. He wanted so badly to go through with it, but he just couldn't manage to. Giving up, he slipped the tie off his neck, climbed into bed, and wept.

"Why won't this just end?" he kept asking himself.

It was the last day of school before Christmas break started. Adam sat silently in the back corner of the classroom while all the other kids talked. There wasn't a lesson plan today. None of the teachers saw any point, knowing that the students would be too focused on their vacation to pay any attention. While everyone around him happily chatted, Adam sat waiting to go home and try again.

When the bell rang signaling the end of school for the rest of the year, Adam left school knowing it would be for the last time. He'd never have to come back, never have to see Derek again. The thought brought a slight smile to his face, the first smile he'd had in months.

Like he often did when he didn't have one of his friends drive him, Derek rode the bus. It was a slight annoyance, but it didn't bother Adam. When the bus pulled up to Derek's stop, Adam watched for the last time as Derek got off. Again, Adam smiled, possibly his last smile ever.

This time as Adam walked off the bus and up his driveway, he felt calm. Not only would he never have to see Derek again, but his father's car wasn't in the driveway. If he could manage to kick the stool out from underneath himself before his father got home, Adam would never have to fear him again. Just in case, he stopped in the kitchen and got some food before going upstairs so he wouldn't have to come down again. If he did succeed, at least he would get a last meal, even if it was only another sandwich.

His stomach full, Adam went to his closet and climbed almost happily onto the stool. As he stood in the closet preparing to end his own life, he realized this was the happiest he'd felt in years. He had regained control over his life again.

With his newfound happiness, Adam stood with the makeshift noose around his neck, rocking the chair back and forth like a game. Finally, he decided it was time and pushed forcefully on the edge of the stool.

Although he'd stepped into the closet intending to kill himself, when he finally rocked the stool far enough for it to come out from under his legs, he instinctively grabbed the tie with both hands and frantically tried to get back onto the stool. But it fell onto its side and out from under him.

As Adam hung choking, he tried to pull himself up, his feet swinging wildly. The idea of just letting go and following through with his plan never occurred to him. He tried to lift himself and pull his head through the tie, but the noose was too tight around his neck. Adam's face was turning purple as his arms began to lose strength and his body weight put more and more pressure on his throat. Things started to go dark as he struggled to breathe. He was about to lose consciousness.

Kicking desperately, his shin hit the leg of the stool and he managed to pull it closer. Even with it on its side, Adam was able to stand on it just enough to let go of the tie with one hand and loosen the noose. It slipped off his neck and he fell to the ground, curling into a ball and crying.

Adam was still lying in his closet when his father came through the front door. He heard him set his bottle on the coffee table and collapse onto the couch. Adam started crying again. This time, he was filled with regret.

Why? he asked himself. *Why didn't you just go through with it?*

He'd come so close to accidentally doing what he'd planned, yet he still couldn't let it happen. It would have been so easy. All he had to do was not try so hard to stop it and it would be over.

Climbing into bed, he realized how sore his neck was. His throat ached when he tried to swallow. As if trying to shovel down food to avoid his father wasn't bad enough, now he'd have to do it in immense pain. He drifted off to sleep with conflicted thoughts. Did he want to die or not?

As the Christmas break went on, Adam's throat began to heal. The redness and the pain that came with swallowing were subsiding. The end of the holidays was fast approaching, and so was the time when he'd have to see Derek again. Unless Adam succeeded in his plan to stop that from happening.

It took several days after nearly hanging himself before Adam built up the courage to try again. This time, when he went to put the tie around his neck, Adam hesitated. The redness and pain in his neck were beginning to subside, but they were still present. The fear he'd felt as he desperately struggled for life rushed through his mind. The fear didn't give back Adam his will to live, but it did make it harder to follow through. This time when he put the tie around his neck and stood on the stool, he focused on his balance. If Adam were going to kill himself, it wouldn't be by accident.

A few more days passed, and so did Christmas Day. Adam didn't run downstairs to find presents under the tree as all the other kids did. Instead, he spent his Christmas morning lying in bed with the covers pulled over his head, hoping his father wouldn't use the holiday as a reminder of how much he despised Adam's very existence. He didn't mind that he wasn't getting any presents. Not only was he used to it, but he also didn't see any point in receiving any. Adam planned on being dead by the end of the day.

Although he didn't care about getting any gifts, the holiday was a reminder of how horrible his life was. He thought about other kids from school spending time with their families while he had no one. His existence seemed pointless.

Adam stopped hesitating and pushed his head through the noose. He carefully maintained his balance on the chair, but this time he put his foot on the edge of the stool, toying with the idea of kicking it over. This time, he thought, it would be intentional. He wouldn't stop it when it happened. He planned on kicking the stool far enough forward that if he started to panic, he wouldn't be able to reach it again. Adam's yearning for death was driving out his fear.

Still, he couldn't bring himself to push the stool out from under himself. He may have had an immense desire for death, but he still wasn't capable of bringing it upon himself. Yet as the dreadfulness of school kept drawing closer, it seemed that Adam's capacity to follow through was increasing.

Adam spent New Year's Day in his closet. By now, he had started leaning forward on the edge of the stool, balancing it on two legs. Just the slightest increase in pressure and the stool would topple, and once again he'd find himself with nothing but the noose around his neck holding him off the ground.

Adam set the stool back down on all four legs. Taking a deep breath, he thought about having to go back to school, and he pushed the stool back onto two legs. Just as it was about to fall, he froze, unable to continue.

The thought of following through terrified Adam. But so did the idea of seeing Derek again. He knew he had to complete his plan before school started.

The night before the end of the Christmas break, Adam was more determined than ever. If he didn't hang himself tonight, he would suffer again at the hands of Derek. Not following through would only result in more suffering before he inevitably ended up in the same place, hanging from the curtain rod in his closet.

It was now 3 a.m. Adam had been pushing the chair back and

forth for hours. He was exhausted, but he refused to give up. If he did, he would have to go to school in the morning. He considered skipping school, but that would result in them calling his father, which would be even worse than facing Derek.

When his morning alarm went off, Adam pulled the noose off from around his neck and stepped out of his closet. The break was over, and he had no choice but to get on the bus and go back to school. Adam had failed in his plan, and now he had to face the consequences.

Adam's eyes were heavy. Not only had he been up all night, but his disappointment at going back to school was weighing him down even more. Still, he forced himself through his morning routine. When he was ready, he walked reluctantly to the bus stop. As the bus pulled up, he stepped on.

Adam froze in his seat as Derek stepped onto the bus. There he was. The person he'd hoped to never see again. Adam considered running off the bus and straight back to his closet, and he might have if he thought he could follow through with it. Instead, he stayed still. Perhaps if he could make it through one day without letting Derek get hold of him, he could get home and do it before having to suffer at Derek's hands again.

The day was off to a promising start. Adam managed to get his usual seat at the front of the bus, which he'd started doing again in case Derek was riding the bus that day. Meanwhile, Derek sat in the middle of the bus, well out of range. Although this didn't make Adam feel any better, the bus ride wasn't going to last all day. Adam would have to get off, and Derek would have many opportunities to find him—and after weeks of not seeing him, he knew Derek would be eager to do so. He could see it on his face.

When the bus arrived at school, Adam bolted from his seat. The bus driver remarked that he was far too excited to be back to school, but Adam didn't have the time to correct him. He made it inside and headed straight for his physics class, where he sat and thought about how to make it to his next class without running into Derek. He had to plan his route carefully.

At lunch, Adam hid in a bathroom stall, balancing a plate on his lap and eating dry chicken breast with his hands—he couldn't keep the plate still enough to cut the rock-hard meat with his flimsy plasticware. Chewing ferociously, Adam choked down his food so he could get to his geometry class before Derek left the cafeteria. Sadly, even though he couldn't enjoy it, Adam planned on this potentially being his last meal except for a quick bowl of cereal when he got home.

Adam walked peacefully down the empty halls. There was no need to rush. Derek and the rest of the school would be either in the cafeteria or off-campus for lunch. Although the first floor was still quite busy, the second floor was deserted, and he didn't need to worry about running into anyone.

When he got to his classroom, he took his seat at the back of the room. He was more than halfway there. He just had a few more classes to go before the day was over and he'd never have to see Derek again.

The bell rang, and kids started filing into the other seats. They were all saying hello to each other after not seeing one another all break. No one would say anything to Adam, but it didn't matter. Adam was all alone, and he knew it. There was no sense in caring anymore.

Everyone sat down, and class started. Adam focused on only two things: getting to his next class Derek-free and convincing himself to finish his task when he got home. There wasn't any point in listening to a word about geometry. He wouldn't be around to use it.

Being in an advanced class for his age, Adam was one of only a few kids in his grade in geometry. That was why his teacher made a particular point of announcing that a new kid, also in ninth grade, would be transferring to the class shortly.

Adam didn't hear a word of it, but he took notice when the new kid and an administrator walked through the door. He looked at them quickly and then looked away so he wouldn't have to make eye contact. Then he did a double-take. The teacher introduced Sara to the class. She had dark hair, mostly black with a hint of chestnut brown, and her blue eyes seemed to glow from across the room. She was the most beautiful sight Adam had ever seen. Without realizing it, Adam sat up straight for the first time in a very long time.

Chapter 10

Sara took her seat as everyone awkwardly stared at her. A couple of boys sitting ahead of Adam started whispering back and forth. Sara sat in the middle of the classroom. From where he was sitting, Adam could only partially see Sara's rosy cheek—but even from that angle, the corner of her eye seemed to shine with a sparkle of intense magnificence. For the duration of the class, Adam could barely take his eyes off her.

When the bell rang, Adam didn't rush out the door as he always did. He didn't know what to say, and he certainly didn't dare to do so, but Adam sat in his chair thinking about introducing himself to Sara. It only took a moment for him to miss his chance; half a dozen of the older boys in the class surrounded her, each eagerly trying to get their chance to say hello. Adam stood and slowly walked out the door.

When he passed into the hall, someone bumped into him and knocked him down. Three more people tripped over him, each one kicking him in the stomach. It was no accident. The one who'd knocked him down was Derek, and the others were his friends. They walked away laughing at their clever plan, making it look as if nothing had happened.

Other kids laughed too, but Adam wasn't concerned with them. Sara would be coming out of the classroom any second, so he picked himself off the floor and rushed away before she had the chance to see him, a pathetic kid lying on the ground.

For the rest of the day, Adam found himself wanting to listen to the lessons, regardless of whether he would be using them. He took several pages of notes in each class, getting practically every piece of information down. Even as he headed to the bus, he kept his newfound motivation. He still moved diligently, but he wasn't afraid of running into Derek. Adam didn't even care about what had happened earlier in the hall. He took his usual seat on the bus, and Derek glared at him when he walked past to the back of the bus.

At his house, Adam went into the kitchen, poured a big bowl of cereal, and then had seconds. He wasn't worried enough to rush. After downing the second bowl, he washed and put everything away as usual. Walking up the stairs, he realized his stomach felt fuller than it had in a long time. He'd had almost too much food.

When he got to his room, he stopped and looked briefly at his closet. He didn't think about it for more than a second before ignoring it and sitting on his bed. He pulled out his books and started his geometry homework.

Adam had taken no notes in geometry. He'd been too busy wondering about Sara to pay attention at all in class. So he pored over the chapter trying to figure out what was going on. Even without any lecture notes, he figured it out. After finishing his geometry homework, he started to work his way back through all the other courses.

Adam slept better that night than he had in a long time. For the first time in months, he didn't wake up halfway through the night. It wasn't just because he hadn't slept at all the night before; he just felt better. He woke up the following morning refreshed with new energy for life. Adam didn't know who this girl was, but he had to find out.

Typically, Adam only took showers when he knew his father wasn't going to be around. He didn't want him to hear the sound of the water. But this morning, Adam got out of bed fifteen minutes earlier than usual and took the risk of showering anyway. Hopefully, at this time of the morning, his father would be sound asleep and possibly still too drunk to wake up.

After he showered, Adam pulled a comb out of the drawer. He hadn't bothered to use it in years. His typical hairstyling technique was running his hands through his hair while walking to the bus. It was a safer way to spend less time in the house.

When the bus pulled up at school, Adam took off to get to physics class. He still had to move quickly to avoid Derek. At his desk, he got out his textbook and notepad and began immediately to think about Sara. He couldn't get the way her eyes shone out of his head. Even her dark hair seemed to glow. He just had to make it past lunch to see her again. No matter how scared he was, Adam was determined to talk to her.

The bell rang, and class began. A few minutes passed. Adam had just finished taking his first page of notes when the classroom door opened and Sara walked in. He lost his breath when she took a seat at the front of the room. His surprise at seeing her left him completely stunned, and her beauty left him mesmerized.

She hadn't made it to first period yesterday because she was stuck in the administration office. Today, she'd arrived late after getting lost on her way to class. Luckily, the teacher understood. Sara settled in her seat and pulled out her textbook, trying to figure out where they were in the lesson plan.

When Adam saw Sara taking notes, he realized he needed to get back to taking his own. Today, it was a struggle. He kept getting distracted by Sara's long flowing hair.

The class flew by, and before he knew it, the bell rang. Typically, Adam would consider this a problem because he had to get to his next class as fast as possible to avoid Derek, but this was his opportunity to talk to Sara. He jammed his books into his backpack, but when he looked over to Sara, she was gone.

Adam was disappointed, but he wasn't going to let it bring him down. He rushed out the door, still salvaging any time he had left to get through the halls before Derek found him. As for Sara, he'd just have to take the opportunity to talk to her in geometry, as he originally planned.

His following classes seemed to drag on forever. Adam kept his mind focused on his teachers and his notes, trying to forget how much he wanted geometry class to start. In his last class before lunch, it felt like he spent the entire hour watching each click of the second hand. When lunch finally rolled around, he felt as if he had been sitting in class for an eternity.

Adam avoided being spotted as he went to the bathroom at lunch to hide, afraid Sara would see him take his food in with him, killing his chances to get to know her would be gone before they even started. When he finished eating, he went straight to class. Maybe Sara would get to class early.

When he got to class, he took a seat up front and waited for lunch to end. After a while, he got up and went back into the hall. He'd thought up what he felt was the perfect plan to meet Sara. He would wait in the hall, and when Sara got there, he'd say hi, telling her he recognized her from yesterday, and show her where the room was. This way, not only did he have an excuse to talk to her, but most importantly, he would be the first one in class to talk to her today. Adam didn't want to wait until eager admirers surrounded her. He didn't even care about risking running into Derek in the hall.

Lunch ended, and the hall started to fill up. Adam leaned against a bank of lockers and waited for Sara. There were only a couple of minutes left until class started, and Adam worried she would be late. No matter how much he wanted to meet her, he had to be in class on time. The school might call his father if he wasn't. It wouldn't be the first time.

With only a minute to spare, Sara came walking around the corner. Instantly, Adam thought about changing his mind but forced himself to stick to the plan. He only had one shot at meeting her like this. He stopped when he saw she wasn't alone. She already had two boys from class walking on either side of her, and Adam watched in dismay as all three of them walked into the class, forcing him to follow behind them alone. The boys took the seats next to Sara, and Adam reluctantly went to his usual seat in the back.

Throughout class, Adam kept looking up from his notes to see the boys leaning over to make comments to Sara. He thought it may have been his own bias, but it looked as if while they were laughing at their own jokes, Sara would just smile politely and turn back to her notes with a look of annoyance as she tried to pay attention to class.

Watching her, Adam saw that Sara took almost as many notes as he did. Despite being distracted by her intense beauty, he was impressed. No one had ever come close to doing that before.

At the end of class, the boys walked Sara out the door and showed her to a class they weren't even in. Once again, Adam had missed his opportunity. He wondered if his chances had been ruined forever. Everything else in his life was horrible. Why should anything change? Maybe he should just go home and finish what he planned on doing after all.

That night, Adam had just enough motivation to get his homework done. If he ended up talking to her about class, he didn't want to seem like an idiot who wasn't up to speed. He studied for all his classes but focused mainly on geometry and physics.

Adam didn't bother to try talking to Sara in physics class. Just as he expected, she came in surrounded by boys trying to talk to her. The crowd was growing. Adam sat in the back corner of the classroom just as he always did and tried to ignore the way everyone kept leaning in to say something to her.

In his following classes, he no longer watched the seconds pass until he could see her again. He would probably never meet her, so what was the point? Instead of Sara, Adam would focus on school. He didn't realize it, but even though he felt he had no chance with Sara, the short burst of motivation she'd given him kept him from returning to thoughts of his closet. His mind was back on school.

The next day in physics class, Adam ignored everyone ogling Sara and kept his head buried in his notebook. But when the teacher took a break to turn the page in his textbook, Adam couldn't resist the urge to glance over at Sara. To his surprise, she was looking back at him. As their eyes met for the first time, Sara smiled and looked away, turning her attention to her textbook. Adam was in awe, staring at the back of her head as if he'd lost the ability to think. It wasn't until the teacher started talking again that Adam snapped out of his trance and remembered where he was.

The class went on, and Adam kept stealing glances at Sara, hoping to meet her gaze. Sara focused on her notes, and it seemed as if it had been a one-time incident. But when class ended and Sara turned to put her books away, she looked up and smiled at Adam again before zipping up her backpack and leaving. Three boys followed her out.

Chapter 11

Adam rolled over in bed and turned off his alarm. Sliding his feet off the bed, he stood up and looked at his closet. Although he didn't intend to put the noose around his neck today, the tie still hung from the rod. He wasn't ready to take it down yet.

Sara may have smiled at him yesterday, but he'd still given up on meeting her. People always surrounded her. Adam was never going to get the chance. He wouldn't have the nerve even if the opportunity were thrown at him, anyway. Maybe she hadn't been smiling at him. Maybe she was just laughing at the weird kid hiding in the back corner. After all, why would someone like Sara ever smile at him?

Still, her existence gave Adam a new sense of purpose. The chance of meeting her, no matter how ridiculous, put a small glimmer of hope back into his life.

Adam stared out the window of the bus on the way to school, still thinking about Sara. Never in his life had he seen anyone like her, and he knew he'd never get to know her. Trying to distract himself, he thought about school, reviewing his physics equations in his head. His need for distraction had resulted in Adam putting more time into his school work than ever before, which was helping him catch up.

As always, Adam rushed off the bus to avoid Derek. He could hear Derek and his friends following as they chased him into the school. Suddenly, a broom appeared from out of the janitor's closet. Adam's ankles caught the handle and he went tumbling to the floor. The broom hadn't been Derek's doing, just lousy luck.

Derek and his friends helped Adam to his feet, assuring the janitor he was alright. Knowing this was just an act, Adam tried to get away, but as soon as the janitor was gone, the boys forced Adam into the closet.

They pummeled him mercilessly. When Adam tried to reach for the door, Derek grabbed his arm and pushed him against the back of the closet. As Davis and Brandon pinned Adam against the wall, Derek grabbed a mopstick and jabbed the end repeatedly into Adam's stomach while Miles watched and laughed.

The boys eventually grew bored and left Adam, who fell to his knees. They had repeatedly knocked the wind out of him, and Adam struggled to breathe. He heard the ringing of the five-minute warning bell. Practically holding his breath, Adam climbed to his feet and staggered into the hall.

He grew lightheaded as he rushed to class, barely able to take in any oxygen. When he got to the door, he stopped and took a moment to straighten out his shirt and hair and finally catch his breath. He may have stopped expecting to meet her, but that didn't mean he didn't want to look as decent as possible in front of Sara.

She was in her regular seat at the front of the classroom, surrounded by boys, all trying to talk to her. She looked up and watched Adam as he walked past to his seat.

The bell rang, and class began. Adam watched Sara taking notes as the boys tried to distract her with their jokes. She would occasionally feign interest but kept writing.

As Adam expected, when physics class ended, Sara left with several boys surrounding her. He didn't have the slightest chance to talk to her, as he knew he wouldn't. He was never going to meet her.

The day dragged on, and Adam went from class to class. It was easier to concentrate in those classes since Sara wasn't there. He could take his notes without her in the corner of his eye, distracting him. She was the most beautiful thing he had ever seen. He loved watching her as she paid attention in class, even with everyone else trying to stop her from doing so. She was a remarkable sight upon which to gaze.

Walking between classes, Adam looked for Sara when he wasn't checking for Derek. She usually walked down the hall surrounded by boys, but Adam thought maybe he could find her on the rare occasion she wasn't. He knew the odds were against him, but he still wished for the chance, even if he never expected it actually to happen.

At lunch, Adam charged for the cafeteria and almost made it to the front of the line. There were only a few people ahead of him, and he expected to make it out of there before Derek got there. He gathered his meal on his paper plate, leaving behind the tray so he wouldn't have to return it, and went for the door.

He was only a few paces away from the exit when he slowed down and stopped. His sense of urgency vanished when he saw Sara enter from the door on the opposite side of the cafeteria. She seemed to float across the cafeteria like an angel before sitting down with her friends. She talked with them for a moment and then got up to get her food. Adam regained his focus and continued to the exit as people gathered behind Sara in line, blocking his view of her.

Just as he crossed the threshold into the hallway, Adam's plate fell from his fingers and to the floor.

"Way to go, butterfingers," Derek said after smacking Adam's plate.

Adam froze, but luckily, taking away his meal was all Derek had planned. His own lunch was too enticing, and he went into the cafeteria, leaving Adam to hide.

When lunch was over, Adam rushed to geometry class. This time, he looked at it as just another chance not to be able to talk to Sara. She would sit on the other side of the class, surrounded by boys, while he hid in the back corner. Thinking about her was pointless, but Adam still couldn't get her out of his head.

He watched as Sara walked into the classroom with a group of boys and sat down with them. Trying to ignore her, Adam pulled out his textbook and tried to read it a bit before class started. Just as he finished the first paragraph, he was interrupted.

"Hi," he heard from above him.

Adam looked up, utterly stunned to see Sara standing next to him. He wanted to respond but was at a complete loss for words as he stared into her beautiful eyes.

"So," Sara awkwardly continued when Adam failed to respond, "do you mind if I sit here?" She gestured to the seat beside Adam.

"Um," he muttered, trying to regain his ability to think and speak. "Yeah, of course you can." A giant smile broke across his face. He'd never had anyone sitting next to him in class, at least not by choice, and now he had the most beautiful girl in the world sitting with him.

"My name is Sara," she said, sitting down and extending her hand.

"Hi, Sara," Adam replied with a slight crackle as he forced the words out.

"So," Sara said with a smile, "do you have a name?"

The word "Adam" barely made it out of his mouth.

"I hope you don't mind me sitting by you," Sara continued. "I've noticed you sitting back here. You're always taking notes. You seem to be the only one in class who pays attention. I think it's cool."

Adam was astonished. She'd noticed him. He never dreamed that she would actually see him. After all, he spent most of his time trying not to get noticed. To someone like Sara, Adam should be completely invisible.

"Thanks," he said. "I've noticed that you bother to take notes as well."

"Yeah, well, I try, but everyone keeps bugging me. I don't know why."

Adam knew why. Every boy in the school wanted to talk to her. How could they not?

"I'm sorry," Adam said, too shy to tell her it was because she was the most beautiful girl in the world.

"I think you have the right idea," Sara said. "Sitting in the back so no one bugs you is smart."

"It does make things easier; I guess." Adam left out that he did it intentionally out of a desire to avoid as much contact with the other students as he could, not just to pay more attention.

"Well," Sara continued, "maybe I should sit with you from now on. I might as well, right?"

"Yeah," Adam replied. He was still smiling but trying to hide the full extent of his excitement, as he was secretly resisting the urge to jump up and down.

"Aren't you also in my physics class?" Sara asked. "It's first period."

"I think so," Adam answered, trying to hide that he knew from all the staring at her he'd done in that class. "I also have it first period, and I think I've seen you in there."

"Well, good. Maybe you can help me study for that class. Sometimes it can get kinda confusing."

"Definitely," Adam answered excitedly. "I mean, it's always nice to have a study partner." Adam didn't tell her that he didn't know if that was true since he'd never had anyone to study with before.

"Great!"

Adam and Sara listened to the teacher as they both scribbled in their notebooks. Occasionally, Sara would lean over to see what Adam had written and compare it to her notes. As the two of them paid attention, the rest of the class bickered, oblivious to the lesson.

Up front, the boys Sara had abandoned for Adam kept looking back at him angrily. Adam hardly noticed them. His mind was mainly on Sara, but he managed to force enough attention on the lesson to impress her with his notes. Luckily, Adam had already studied everything in great detail from the textbook. If he hadn't, he wouldn't have been able to understand any of it from the little attention he'd paid.

Eventually, the class came to an end. All the other kids jumped up excitedly and hurried out of the room, relieved by the end of a long boring lecture on quadrilaterals. Adam, on the other hand, had hoped it would last forever. The fifty short minutes weren't nearly long enough.

The classroom emptied out, leaving only Adam and Sara still in their seats. They took an extra minute to compare notes one last time before following everyone else out the door. As they finished, Sara turned to Adam and said, "Bye."

Hiding his dismay, Adam replied, reluctantly accepting that this moment always had to come. He finished packing his bag as Sara headed for the door. As she walked away, all the doubt rushed back into Adam's mind. Sara probably wouldn't sit with him tomorrow. The other boys she'd been sitting with would probably convince her not to. Or maybe she'd already realized it wasn't all that much fun to talk to him.

"Sorry I have to leave so quickly," Sara said, stopping at the door. "My class is on the other side of the school. If you get here first tomorrow, save me a seat, okay?"

"Okay," Adam said as she disappeared out the door.

With that, Adam again started to hold onto the hope he'd had when she first said hello to him. He finished zipping his backpack and rushed for the door. He moved quickly through the halls to his next class, zipping past the other students. This time, his speed wasn't an attempt to avoid Derek and his friends. It wasn't even about the need to make up time because he'd left class late. It was his excitement.

Adam felt an energy that he hadn't felt in years. Any other day, he felt drained when he got to class and was just happy to fall into his seat. Now he felt as if he would rather keep moving. If he'd had the time, he would have taken another lap around the school before class.

Chapter 12

Mrs. Whitmore wrote the assignment for the class on the board and took her seat. They had twenty-five minutes to write a 500-word short story about someone taking a trip which they'd trade with the person next to them to read and discuss until class ended. Adam started writing before the teacher had even finished giving all the instructions. He had two paragraphs completed by the time anyone else even put their pencil to the page.

For the first time in his creative writing class, Adam wrote a happy story. Usually, he couldn't help but write about misery and despair, holding back just enough that the teacher didn't feel the need to ask any questions. But today, his story was filled with joy.

Adam wrote about a man recently paralyzed in a car accident who'd heard of a woman at the top of a mountain with special powers. His wheelchair couldn't make it over the rocks, and so the man dragged himself up the hill with just his arms. The woman helped the man pull his dirty, broken body into a chair when he got to the top of the mountain. And then she told him she had no healing powers, crushing his dreams. As he began to accept that he would have to drag himself back down the mountain and live out his life in a wheelchair, the woman tripped and stumbled to the edge of the cliff. Suddenly, the man sprang to his feet and ran over to stop her from falling.

Even though he'd reached his word count, Adam continued the story on a separate page, telling how as the man thanked the woman for healing him, she told him he must not have been paralyzed and thanked him for saving her. But after walking back down the mountain, he returned every year to drag himself to the top again with just his hands to thank her for healing him.

Adam's spirits remained high for the rest of the day. As the final bell rang, he walked speedily toward the bus with a smile on his face. He barely noticed when Derek and his friends walked past his seat on the bus and made their way to the back row, and they never once crossed Adam's mind the entire ride home.

His father's car was nowhere to be seen when Adam got home. He was still at work. Adam swung open the front door and walked happily inside. In the kitchen, he made himself some food. Most days, he didn't bother to eat after getting home from school, and on the days he did, he'd stick to a single sandwich or bowl of cereal. Today, he spread peanut butter over two sandwiches and went to his room.

Sitting cross-legged on his bed, Adam opened two textbooks and flipped through them as he ate. He'd barely managed to glance at the pages before he finished both sandwiches. Despite having eaten twice his usual amount, his stomach was still rumbling. Adam usually only had one sandwich for dinner; he'd simply never cared enough to keep eating. Today, however, his spirits were lifted. As his stomach roared, Adam went back down to the kitchen for more. He thought about Sara as he made himself three more sandwiches.

When he had finished the fifth sandwich, which was more than

Adam had ever eaten in one sitting before, he read the current chapters for two of his classes. It had only been forty-five minutes since he'd swallowed the last bite, but Adam was already getting hungry again. He grabbed his plate and went downstairs again.

By now, he'd finished off the loaf of sandwich bread, so after rinsing off his plate, Adam went for the cereal. He started eating before he even put the milk and cereal box away, and he continued shoveling spoonfuls into his mouth as he picked up his bowl to go upstairs. Before he reached the living room, he heard the front door unlock.

Usually, Adam was attentive to the sound of his father's car pulling into the driveway, but today he didn't hear it at all. His mind was too busy thinking about Sara. Adam hid against the wall beside the open doorway separating the kitchen from the living room just as the door flew open and his father walked inside.

Luckily, Adam wasn't the only one who rarely bothered to eat after getting home. His father went straight for the couch and picked up the half-empty bottle of whiskey still sitting on the coffee table from the night before. Adam had no choice but to remain in place and hoped he would have the opportunity to go upstairs before his father came into the kitchen.

Despite this annoying predicament, Adam wasn't the slightest bit upset. His heart was racing, but it felt as if he was playing an exciting game and had just won by hiding before being seen. He stood there holding his bowl of cereal and thought about seeing Sara again tomorrow. In a situation that would typically terrify and depress him, Adam was still as happy as could be.

About a half hour later, his father finished off the bottle of whiskey and stumbled down the hallway to the bathroom. Adam took the opportunity and tiptoed upstairs. When he closed his bedroom door, he looked down at his bowl of cereal. It had turned to mush. Adam simply laughed and drank it down.

He sat back down on his bed and started reading again. He pored over his textbooks, transferring all the information into his notebooks. Without losing a speck of focus, Adam not only finished all of his assigned reading but got ahead in a couple of classes.

He looked at the clock as 9:04 clicked onto the screen. It was hours later than he'd expected, so he closed his books to finish studying for the night, but something stopped him. He reopened a book, flipped back a few chapters, then reached into his backpack and pulled out his old assignment sheets for physics class. He didn't feel like stopping, so he redid the homework problems he hadn't had the heart to care about before.

It was now 11:38. Time had passed without Adam noticing. Despite how exciting his day had been, he was too tired to continue with equations and complex calculations. He finally closed his physics book and packed up his backpack.

After getting ready for bed, Adam slipped under the covers. With a smile on his face, he finally drifted off to sleep.

The next morning, he rolled over to look at the clock. It was fifteen minutes past his usual wake-up time. A sense of urgency shot through him, and Adam flew out of bed. With Sara on his mind, he'd forgotten to turn his alarm on before bed.

Rushing to get ready, Adam threw on his clothes. He considered not brushing his teeth but didn't want Sara to think his breath smelled. He ran to the bathroom and slipped his toothbrush and toothpaste into his pocket. Looking at the wild mess on top of his head, he put his comb in his back pocket and bolted from his room.

Adam saw the bus rolling down the street as he opened his front door. He took off in a sprint and barely made it to the stop on time. He climbed onto the bus and sat down, ignoring Derek's taunts. It didn't affect Adam's mood today.

As they arrived at school, Adam looked back at Derek and his friends. He couldn't risk them catching him and doing something to make him look like an idiot in front of Sara. He could comb his hair and brush his teeth before class, but he couldn't do anything if they threw something on his shirt or did whatever they might have planned.

When the bus came to a stop, Adam got off running. He only slowed when he began to worry that Sara might witness him running away. He slowed to a brisk walk and looked around for Sara. He already had more than enough distance between Derek and his friends, anyway. As he opened the door, Adam made one last scan. Luckily, Sara was nowhere to be seen.

Once inside the school, Adam went straight to the nearest bathroom to hide from Derek. He also couldn't risk meeting Sara in the halls before he got ready. He went to the sink and looked in the mirror. His hair was even worse than he remembered before leaving for school.

He cupped some water in his hand and wet his hair. He ran the comb through it, trying to get it perfect. He was glad he'd see Sara in the first period of the day. This way, he could get his hair just right and not have to worry about messing it up before he saw her. He wanted it to be fresh.

When he finished combing his hair, Adam took out his toothbrush. He usually brushed pretty well, at least when he wasn't too depressed to bother, but today Adam did an exceptionally detailed job. He went back over each tooth five more times after they were already clean. He ran the toothbrush obsessively over his tongue to make sure his breath didn't stink. He brushed the roof of his mouth and the inside of his cheeks. He wasn't leaving anything to chance; he even put more toothpaste on the brush three times.

Before he left the bathroom, he combed his hair one more time. He wanted to be sure every strand was perfectly placed. He moved carefully through the halls, mostly to avoid Derek but also to avoid shaking any hairs out of place.

When he sat down at his desk, Adam took out his notebook and physics textbook and went through all of his notes, double-checking everything. He wanted to ensure there weren't any mistakes that would make him look foolish in front of Sara. He was trying desperately to impress her, and hopefully, the extra work he'd done last night would help.

The five-minute bell rang, and the other students began filing into class. Adam stared at his notes as he avoided making eye contact with anyone, but he kept looking up out of the corner of his eye to see if Sara had arrived. When she finally did, Adam gasped a little, sucking in a deep breath. He let the breath out slowly, not wanting Sara to see him panting.

Even now, Adam was too shy to make eye contact with her. He pretended to study, not noticing her, but he watched her through his peripheral vision, only flashing his eyes when he was sure she wasn't looking.

Sara finished her conversation with the two boys she had arrived with as the bell rang. The boys sat down up front, leaving a seat between them for Sara. They looked astonished and devastated when she didn't sit down and instead headed to the back of the room to sit beside Adam.

"Sorry," she said as she sat down. "They just wouldn't stop talking, and I didn't want to be rude."

"That's okay. I didn't think about it," Adam lied. "I was just looking through my notes."

"I think it's cool how motivated you are," Sara said. "Nobody else here seems to care at all. I'd rather hang out with you. I don't know why all these people keep trying to be my friend. I think I'm pretty boring. Why won't they just forget about me?"

That's a silly question, Adam thought to himself. She was the most beautiful girl in the world. It was blatantly obvious why all the boys in the school wanted to hang out with her. He wondered if she was really oblivious to the reason or just making conversation.

"I don't know," he finally said. "It's because you're just so nice." He wanted to but just couldn't bring himself to add, "And the most beautiful girl ever."

"Ah, thanks," she said. "I think you're nice yourself."

Adam blushed but couldn't think of anything else to say. Luckily, the teacher started talking, covering up his awkward lack of a response.

Just like in geometry class, Adam and Sara were the only two paying attention. They sat quietly together, jotting down notes and comparing them as the class went on. The teacher finished the lesson five minutes early, and the quiet chatter of the class turned into a roar for the remainder of the period. Adam and Sara continued to go over the lesson while everyone else talked about TV shows and weekend plans.

When the final bell rang, the class poured out the door. They already had their bags packed if they'd bothered to pull their books out at all. Sara packed her books, looking sad that her time with Adam was over. Adam hated the idea of parting with Sara, but he tried his best to hide it.

Walking out the door together, they walked to their following classes. Both were going in the same direction, so they walked together for as long as possible. When they finally came to the hallway intersection where they had to part, Sara stopped and faced Adam.

"Thanks for all the help in physics," she said. "It was a lot easier to understand when I'm going over it with you."

"Yeah, it was pretty fun," Adam said.

Sara giggled. "I don't know if I've ever met anyone who thought physics was fun."

Adam wanted to tell her that he thought anything would be fun if he were doing it with her but just couldn't bring himself to say it.

"Well, I guess I'll see you later," she finished. "Bye!"

With that, she turned and disappeared into the crowd. Adam was sad to see her go, but happy with how things had gone. Was his life finally starting to get better?

His classes following physics weren't nearly as good without Sara in them, and Adam found himself counting down the seconds until he saw her again in geometry. When lunch came, he hurried to the lunchroom to grab his food and get out before any of his bullies messed up his day.

As usual, he hid in a bathroom stall and ate his food. Today, he ate more slowly and carefully. The last thing he wanted was to get food on himself and look like an imbecile for Sara. His attentiveness paid off, and he managed to consume his food without losing any of it, finishing every last molecule. He noticed that he was hungrier today than he usually was, and he even considered eating breakfast in the morning before leaving for school from now on.

As soon as he finished eating, Adam took his toothbrush from his backpack and brushed his teeth at the bathroom sink, making a mental note to bring it with him from now on. Then he combed his hair, rechecked all of his shirt buttons, and left for his next class.

When he got to class, Adam quickly went over everything on the day's lesson plan. He was thinking about what Sara had said, and how she liked having him to help her understand the material. He wanted to be sure he knew every last bit before she got to class.

Sara finally arrived just as the final bell rang. All the boys who followed her into class made a not-so-subtle attempt to have her sit with them. They boxed her in and gestured to the desk in the middle of them, but Sara apologized as she slipped past them and made her way back to the seat beside Adam.

"Hey there," she said and put her hand on Adam's forearm to get his attention.

Adam's heart raced at the warmth of her fingers. Her hand was soft and smooth. He struggled for breath as he felt it glide along his skin. After what seemed like a lifetime, he managed to vocalize a "hey" back to her. It was an unconvincing attempt at sounding confident. Although Adam didn't know it, Sara found his bashfulness endearing.

"Why didn't I see you at lunch?" she asked. "I looked for you, but I couldn't find you anywhere."

"Oh," Adam started apprehensively, "I don't know. I didn't see you either."

"I guess you must have just been hiding," she joked, unaware she was being entirely accurate. "At least it was easy to find you here. If I didn't see you, that would have been upsetting. I would have thought my friend was avoiding me."

Adam couldn't believe what he'd just heard. Sara had called Adam her friend.

Chapter 13

Life had become much better for Adam. He saw Sara at school every day. She made everything better, and life seemed worth living again. Adam no longer dreaded remembering that he existed.

Hopping out of bed, Adam slipped into his clothes and combed his hair in the bathroom. Once his hair looked good, Adam went downstairs. He popped a couple of pieces of bread into the toaster and cracked a couple of eggs into a pan. The sound of sizzling as the eggs hit the metal made Adam's stomach rumble. He picked up a saltshaker and sprinkled a bit into the pan.

He opened the fridge and pulled out a tub of butter. As the toaster snapped up, he spread the butter over the hot bread so that it would melt. He scooped the over-easy eggs out of the frying pan and laid them gently over the toast. He even found some orange juice in the fridge as he put the butter away, completing the meal.

Before sitting down to eat, he wiped up everything and rinsed off the pan. He didn't want to leave any trace of his morning meal. Once he finished, he washed his dishes and went back upstairs to get ready for school.

Later that morning in physics, Sara sat in her usual seat next to

Adam. This time, the other boys followed her back and sat with them.

As the teacher lectured, Adam and Sara spoke quietly to each other. The other boys mostly remained quiet. They were a couple of years older and were only taking the class because it was required. They didn't understand what was happening and just stared blankly as Adam and Sara whispered about the lesson. Occasionally, one of them would intrude with a joke. Sara would giggle sometimes, but mostly she glanced at them politely and promptly turned her attention to the topic of physics.

To try and snatch Sara's attention away from Adam, a boy would sometimes throw in a comment about the lesson. Almost always, Adam would either have to correct them or would add to his statement. Doing so annoyed the commenter trying to impress her but always made Sara smile.

When class ended, they all walked together down the hall. It was nice because Adam didn't have to watch out for Derek for a change. He wouldn't dare to do anything when Adam was with a group of people. For the first time in what seemed like his entire life, Adam could walk through his school without fear. At least for a small part of the day.

They arrived at the intersection where he had to go a separate way. Adam knew it was time to say goodbye. Suddenly, Sara threw her arms around him, pulling him into a tight embrace. She whispered a soft "bye" into his ear as she hugged him. Adam was completely flustered, unable to react. His mind went blank, and he forgot to return the gesture, his arms hanging awkwardly by his sides. Sara released him and left with the other boys, and Adam stood still for a moment before realizing he still had to go to his next class. He looked over his shoulder as Sara walked away with the boys and headed off alone.

*   *   *

Adam had more confidence and was excelling in all of his classes. He was making comments during class now, even the ones without Sara in them. He had more than made up for when he'd fallen behind and was on track to finish the year with a 4.0 GPA. When he started applying to college, Adam was sure to get in.

The future was looking bright again, and Adam knew it. He had the top scores in all of his classes. He was working harder than ever. There were two months left in the school year, and Adam had already finished reading all of his textbooks. At this point, he was just learning the material better than he already had. He was even getting books from the library and learning additional material he didn't need for his classes.

Every day at lunch, Adam stood by the cafeteria door and waited for Sara. When he saw her walk in, he greeted her and they got in line together. The line was long, but Adam was no longer concerned with getting his food and escaping. The days were behind him when he had to hide in the bathroom to eat his food. Now Adam sat in the cafeteria surrounded by a large group and next to Sara.

They all joked and laughed together. Adam ate with a smile on his face, especially as he and Sara looked at each other. Despite the efforts of the other guys, Sara paid a lot more attention to Adam than anyone else.

Once they finished eating, everyone from geometry class walked with Adam and Sara. Even a couple of guys not in the class walked with them until they went their separate ways. Sara and Adam took their seats, and the others sat surrounding them.

Unfortunately, Sara still had to rush to her next class, so she always had to leave Adam behind once geometry ended. His class wasn't in the same direction, and they always parted at the class-room door, saying goodbye for the rest of the day. Sara hugged Adam, and she was gone.

Even without Sara, Adam still enjoyed the rest of the day. He had to avoid Derek again anytime he was traveling alone, but he loved to learn once he arrived at class. He didn't have a single subject he wasn't delighted to study.

His stories in English class were even happier than the one he'd written after meeting Sara. The longer he knew her, the happier his stories seemed to become. Even if they weren't assigned, Adam still wrote stories. He filled his notebook with short stories about love and happiness.

Adam even began a new habit of being productive with his time on the school bus. He kept his notebooks out and studied on the ride. He could only do this on the way home from school, though. If Derek caught up to him on the way to school, he might destroy his notebook. But on the way home, Derek never followed him off the bus.

When he got home that day, Adam went straight for the kitchen. He dropped his bag on the kitchen table and looked around to see what there was to eat. There seemed to be a lot more food in the kitchen than there had been in the past month, and Adam wondered if his father had noticed he'd been eating more. Maybe that was why he was buying more groceries. Adam doubted it. It seemed unlikely that someone who barely said ten words to him in any given week other than drunken ramblings would care if he had enough food to eat. Whatever the reason, Adam was glad to have the food.

He found a bucket of fried chicken in the fridge, picked out a thick breast and a juicy-looking leg, and put them on a plate. He covered the chicken in a damp paper towel to keep it from drying out and put the plate into the microwave.

As he watched the plate spin, he thought about Sara. He pictured her getting a ride home from her mom and studying at her desk in her room. He knew she liked to get her homework done right away so she could take the rest of the night off. After studying, she sat down with her family for dinner, where her two brothers argued over who got the bigger piece of whatever they were having. The eldest brother usually won. Both always finished before her; Sara chewed her food instead of inhaling it. Afterward, Sara always helped clear the table before going back to her room.

Sara liked spending time alone when she was home. At school, she spent the entire day with people talking to her, so when it was over, she enjoyed the quiet. In the evening, she usually sat in her bed and read. Sometimes, she wrote stories. Other times, she drew.

Adam imagined Sara drawing on her bed with her sketchbook resting on her thighs. Her bed had purple sheets and blankets, which Sara found calming. Whenever she had trouble deciding what to draw or write, she stared at the posters on her walls. They were posters of old movies and music. Although Adam had never seen Sara's room or been to her house to meet her family, he felt as if he had for as often as she described her life to him. He even felt as if he already knew her brothers.

Adam worried Sara would notice how one-sided their conversations always were. He never talked about his life. He didn't want to lie to her, so he just avoided the topic. Anytime she asked him about it, he did his best to change the subject. But how long could he keep that up?

The microwave dinged, and Adam pulled out his plate of chicken. With his meal in one hand, he grabbed his backpack with the other. Before Adam could fling the strap over his shoulder and go upstairs, something caught his eye. A speck was moving just outside the kitchen doorway, and he moved closer to investigate.

A spider! It was large and hairy. Adam ran over to squash it, but he couldn't keep up and keep his plate upright, so the spider escaped and whisked down the hallway. Adam began his pursuit. Not wanting to break his line of sight by putting down his plate, he brought it with him, holding it in both hands as he followed.

The creature scurried down the hall and into his father's room. Adam followed it in. The spider was quick and kept moving. It was hard for Adam to trap it under his foot. The chase continued to the other side of his father's bed before Adam finally squashed the beast.

Just as the spider crunched under his foot, Adam heard a bang. The front door smacked into the wall, and Adam listened to the stomping of footsteps coming into the house. The door slammed shut, followed by mumbling. Adam couldn't understand what he was saying, but his father was already angry. Now was not the time to be seen.

Adam crouched behind the bed and hid. Listening, he tried to determine what his father was doing. The kitchen and the living room couch were visible from the front door, which meant there was no way he was going to make it back upstairs unseen. His only hope was to wait for his father to go to the bathroom, which would give him time to get his backpack from the kitchen table.

The mumbling continued, but the sound of clinking empty bottles joined in. Adam knew his father was looking for one that still had some alcohol left in it. Perhaps there were none left and he'd leave the house to buy more.

Adam didn't have such good luck. On the dresser next to his father's bed, he saw a quarter-full bottle of whiskey. He heard footsteps coming down the hall. Adam lay down and scooted under the bed, bringing his plate of chicken with him.

The smell. Adam started worrying that the scent of chicken would alert his father to his presence. He saw huge feet next to him as his father retrieved the bottle.

Please just leave the room, Adam thought as his heart raced with fear. Instead, he watched the bed sink as his father took a seat right above him. He heard him drinking, and then his feet disappeared as he lay down on the bed.

How long would Adam have to stay? There was no way he could sneak out with his father on the bed. Would he have to stay there all night? Or maybe just until he emptied the bottle? Adam hoped the smell of whiskey would at least mask the aroma of his fried chicken.

Adam's stomach began to rumble. He put his hand on it, trying to muffle the sound. He slid the plate up to his mouth and took a bite of the chicken leg. He chewed slowly and quietly, now glad that he'd brought the plate with him.

His father was still lying on the bed when Adam finished the chicken. After sucking every bit off the bones, he wiped the grease on his pants. How much longer was he going to have to stay hidden? He tried to stop thinking about his predicament and instead thought about Sara. She was a much more pleasant thought.

Another hour passed. Adam grew restless and started looking around. He noticed an old dusty book in the corner on the other side of the bed, wedged halfway behind the bed and the nightstand.

Something to read, he thought as he slid close enough to reach the book. *Disgusting.* Dust covered the book after being back there for years. Adam brushed the book off and shook the dust off his hands.

The book had a black hardcover with no title. He opened it and saw empty lined pages. He turned to the very first page and found some handwritten pages. The handwriting was elegant and graceful. He gasped when he realized it was his mother's journal. He flipped through it and came across a day he had long forgotten. He began to read.

Eight-year-old Adam ran through the front door. He hopped onto the couch and sprawled out, hot and tired from playing outside. Mom came in from the other room when she heard him.

"Wash your hands," she told Adam. "I'm making breakfast."

"Okay, Mom," he replied, hopping to his feet and running to the bathroom. When he was finished, he stood in the kitchen doorway and took in the sweet scent of the food cooking. The sound of bacon sizzling snapped through the room. Adam could smell the waffles. He loved waffles.

Suddenly, he felt his feet leave the ground. An arm had wrapped around him from behind and pulled him up into the air. Dad threw Adam over his shoulder and carried him to his chair.

"Did you wash your hands already?" he asked Adam.

"Yes, Dad."

"Alright, good," Dad said as he helped Mom carry the plates of food from the counter to the table.

The three of them laughed together as they ate breakfast. After Adam finished his first plate, Dad piled more food onto it.

"You better eat all that," he told Adam. "You're going to grow up to be big and strong. Gotta get that food into you."

Adam laughed and nodded and pushed a chunk of waffle into his mouth with his fork. He barely managed to force down the last piece.

"Good job," Dad told him, ruffling Adam's hair. "Now help your mom clear the table. I'm going to double-check some stuff so that we can go."

"Yes, Dad," Adam replied as his father left the kitchen.

He handed his mom each plate from the table, and she rinsed them off and put them in the dishwater. Then they cleared the table of leftover food and put it in the fridge. Afterward, she handed him a wet rag to wipe down the table.

"I'm going to go get ready," she said. "Once you finish wiping off the table, you do the same."

Adam acknowledged her with a nod as he ran the rag over the surface of the table. When he was done, he rinsed off his hands and ran upstairs. He didn't have anything to do to get himself ready, so he hopped onto his bed and picked up a toy from his nightstand to entertain himself while he waited for his parents.

"Adam, are you ready?" Mom called as soon as he started playing. "Come back downstairs. It's time to go."

He set the toy back down and leaped off the bed, racing down the stairs. Dad was at the front door, holding it open and gesturing to him to go outside.

"Let's go," he said. "Get in the car."

Adam flew past his father and out the door. As he climbed into the backseat of the car, Mom followed and Dad locked the door behind them. His father didn't head straight for the driver's side door. First, he walked around to the passenger side, opening the door for his wife. Once she was safely in her seat, he closed her door and walked around to get in the car.

As he started the car, Dad turned around and looked at him. "Alright, is everyone buckled up so we can leave?"

"Yes," Adam replied. "As long as you and Mom are."

"Well, good," Dad said as he reached back and tickled Adam.

Adam's body shook as he giggled and pushed the hand away. Dad checked Adam's seatbelt, making sure it was secure before they backed out of the driveway.

Chapter 14

For three hours, Adam hid under his father's bed before he finally heard the sound of snoring. He wondered how long he'd already been asleep without him knowing. It didn't matter. It was too cramped under the bed, and Adam wasn't going to miss his chance to escape.

Slowly and quietly, he crept out from under the bed and snuck out of the room with his plate and his mom's journal. He slipped the journal into his backpack and went upstairs with the plate of chicken bones still in hand, planning on saving the plate and washing it later when his father was gone. He didn't want to risk waking him.

When he got to his room, Adam pulled out his textbooks and studied. After losing hours of study time, it was good that Adam had already finished all of his studies for the school year. At this point, he was only studying for fun and review; he didn't have much else to do. This year, his only schoolwork was assignments he couldn't complete until they were handed out to the class. Having already studied all the material, Adam usually completed them before class had even ended.

As he studied, Adam thought about the breakfast they'd had on that day from his mom's journal. He remembered how good those waffles tasted. Adam loved waffles but hadn't had any since his mom died. He considered cooking them for himself when he could get the ingredients, but he thought they'd take too long to make. Between the bowl and spoon to mix the batter, and the waffle iron, doing the dishes would add more time. He doubted he'd be able to get everything cleaned up in time, especially since he never knew when his father would get home.

The chicken was going to have to suffice for the night. Adam certainly wasn't making any waffles, or anything else. He was already starting to get hungry again, but he'd have to suffer through it until morning.

He studied harder in an attempt to distract himself from his hunger. He'd lost track of how many times he'd solved the same physics problems, but tonight added two more to the tally. He was halfway through solving them for a third time when he finally decided to stop and close his books.

Even though he was tired of resolving physics problems, it was still too early to try and sleep. As his mind wandered back to Sara again, he pulled out his notebook and began to write another short story. This time, he wrote about himself and Sara.

In his story, he and Sara got into the same college far away. They went there together and were married shortly after. From time to time, Sara's family would visit, but other than them, they never saw anyone from here ever again. Adam's father was a distant memory, and as their lives went on, Adam had long forgotten the name of the boy who'd spent so many years tormenting him in school. They lived happily ever after, and Adam never thought about any of them ever again.

As soon as he finished writing, Adam immediately tore the page out of his notebook and ripped it to shreds before throwing it in the trash. He certainly couldn't have Sara or anyone reading it. The mere thought of the embarrassment he would feel was unbearable. Even so, Adam took a moment to imagine Sara reading it and telling him how sweet she found it. Maybe she would tell him that was exactly how she hoped their lives would turn out.

But there was still one more problem, even if Sara did read it and liked it. Adam was still hiding the rest of his life from her. He didn't want her to learn that he was a loser who was bullied constantly whenever she and her friends weren't around. It would be mortifying to have her find out that his goal was to avoid his father as much as possible whenever he was home. What could she possibly think about him if she found all that out? Would she even still talk to him?

Adam thought about that at school for weeks. He was in physics class, showing Sara how to find the change in water pressure as it moved through pipes of different diameters. The other boys with them were also listening, but unlike Sara, they mostly just copied Adam's work onto their papers rather than learning how to do it themselves.

When Sara began solving the problem herself, Adam stared into her blue eyes. Somehow, even in this poorly lit classroom, her eyes seemed to shine as brightly as diamonds on display. How, Adam wondered, would those eyes look back at him if she learned who he really was? How would she look at him if she knew the reality of his life? He wasn't ready to find out.

Sara was the one good thing Adam had in his life. She was the reason he kept going—the reason he wanted to wake up in the morning. He couldn't make it through the rest of high school without her. He wanted to be honest with her, but he couldn't stand the thought of losing her friendship.

Fortunately for Adam, Sara could tell he was timid and didn't like to open up very much. He was reserved, and she found his reluctance to share adorable.

As class was ending, the teacher walked up and down the rows handing out the tests from the previous lesson. *100%* was written in bright red ink at the top of Adam's paper. Sara leaned in and saw it. She smiled and hugged him, whispering, "Good job" into his ear.

Sara showed him her test. Ninety-two percent. Adam had the urge to reciprocate by congratulating her in the same way, but his anxiety got the better of him. Instead, he leaned in and bumped her shoulder with his own. That was the most affection he could muster up the conviction to express. He managed to throw out a "good job" as he pulled back and looked down awkwardly at his test, hoping she would overlook his timidness.

"Looks like we need to spend more time studying!" the teacher yelled over the sound of the ringing bell. "We only had two tests over ninety percent. Other than one in the seventies, the rest were fifty percent or lower. The end of the school year is coming up soon. There's not much time left to get those grades up. You can do it if you try." As Adam and Sara walked past the teacher on their way out the door, she smiled at them and gave them a thumbs-up.

Adam was still thinking about the hug Sara gave him when he walked through the door of his house later that day. He regretted his lack of reciprocation. Instead of making food, he went upstairs, dropped his bag on the floor, and flopped onto the bed.

"You should have just done it, you idiot," Adam said to himself as he lay face down on his bed. "Whatever, it doesn't matter anyway. It's not like someone like her would ever want to be anything more than friends with a loser like you."

Angrily, Adam pulled himself back up and went downstairs to

make food. He knew he had time before his father got home, but he didn't feel like cooking anything. Once again, he slapped some peanut butter onto some slices of bread and went back upstairs with four sandwiches stacked high on his plate, tilted like the Leaning Tower of Pisa.

As he ate, his mind kept switching back and forth between different trains of thought. One second he imagined himself with Sara, the two of them as happy as could be. The next, he was thinking about how she might never talk to him again if they didn't have any classes together next year. What if she didn't even like talking to him? What if she only pretended to because she wanted to have a study partner? It wasn't like any random person would make a good study partner. Was that all she cared about? Or what if she was just waiting for him to make the first move? What if she fantasized about him just as much as he did about her? Or what if she avoided him just as soon as she finished using him to get A's in physics and geometry?

Adam needed a distraction; he couldn't worry about it anymore. His thoughts were bouncing back and forth as fast as his pounding heartbeat. He pulled out his schoolbooks and began to read. At least he tried to. He spent minutes staring at the pages but never managed to get in a single sentence. His head was pulsating with thoughts about Sara. He couldn't concentrate at all.

As he lay on his bed trying to calm down, he remembered his mother's journal, which he'd tucked into the bottom drawer of his dresser, hidden where no one would find it. He hadn't pulled it back out since the first time he'd stowed it away. He would have read it every night since then, but he was too paranoid about his father discovering he had taken it. Sliding off the bed, Adam opened the drawer and took the journal out. He turned back to where he'd left off and continued reading.

Dad drove into an old dirt field and pulled along a long line of parked cars. As Adam unbuckled his seat belt, his dad got out and walked around to the passenger door. He opened the door for his wife and took her hand as she stepped out onto the dead grass.

Following the rows of cars, the three began walking toward a big booth. Overhead was a sign that read COUNTY FAIR. *It had bright-yellow letters surrounded by tiny bulbs that waited to turn on when it got dark. Adam looked up at the sign with a smile on his face. He loved the fair, and the three of them had gone every year for as far back as he could remember. They walked away from the booth with a roll of tickets that would last all day.*

"What should we go on first?" Dad asked.

"The flying pirate ship," Adam said.

"Okay, the flying pirate ship it is, then."

Adam sat between his mom and dad as the ship swung back and forth. His parents smiled as they watched him laughing. They loved nothing more than to see Adam enjoying life.

It was a hot day. The sun was at its highest point, so they went next to the frozen lemonade stand. A few drops of sweat ran down Adam's face as they waited in line, and he grew anxious as the line shortened.

"Two medium frozen lemonades, please," Dad told the cashier when they got to the front. "And what size do you want?" he asked, looking down at Adam.

"Um, a medium, I guess."

"Two mediums and a large," Dad said, knowing that Adam was just being polite. He knew what he really wanted. They sat in the shade under a table with an umbrella, making the lemonades last until the sun wasn't so high overhead.

Adam grew nauseous. He struggled to move, but his body remained pinned to the wall of the Gravitron. He finally managed to sit forward as the ride neared the end and slowed down.

"Can we go on it again?" he asked as he stumbled off the ride, still dizzy

from spinning in circles.

"Again? But we've already been on it three times today. Don't you think it's about time we started to head home?" Mom said, looking at the orange glow of the sun setting over the distant horizon.

"Noooo!" Adam snapped back at such a baffling suggestion. "Can't we stay for just a little bit longer, Mom?"

"Yeah, Mom," Dad said in his defense. "Can't we just stay for just a little bit longer?"

Mom gave Dad a stern look of annoyance. "Oh, alright," she sighed with a moan. "Maybe just another hour."

"Alright, you heard her. Two, three more hours, tops," Dad said, giving Adam a wink.

She glared at his father in anger, although she had a slight smirk hidden under her stern expression. "Fine."

The sun had long gone down by the time they finally left. Adam stared at the brightly lit county fair sign as they pulled out of their parking space and headed home. He couldn't wait until they came back next year.

Adam never went back to the fair again. His mom died just a few months before they would have gone the following year. Adam closed his mom's journal while he thought about all the county fairs he'd missed since. Those days were over. He knew he was never going to have a day like that again.

Chapter 15

Adam's first year of high school was coming to a close. The last day of geometry was almost over. There was no work left to do in class, and everyone was talking about their summer plans. Everyone but Adam. He listened along but avoided sharing his exciting plans to hide in his room all summer so his father wouldn't beat him.

"We're going to drive to the ocean for vacation," Sara told Adam. "I'm not exactly sure when we're leaving. It's sometime in mid-July. We'll be gone for about a week."

"Oh, that sounds like a lot of fun," Adam said. "You'll have to tell me all about it."

That statement worried Adam. Would Sara tell him about it? Did she plan on ever talking to him again after this school year? They didn't have any more classes together after this period, and in two minutes, she could be gone forever and he might not ever talk to her again.

"What about you?" she asked him. "What are your plans for the summer?"

Adam started panicking. He had to think of some response quickly. "I'll probably spend most of it in total silence. Maybe hiding under my bed," was not the response he wanted to give her.

"Oh, you know," he said, "just hanging out. I don't have any plans. I'm just planning on seeing what happens. Just going to go with the flow, you know."

He felt like such an idiot after his lengthy response. He couldn't believe he'd actually started and ended with "you know."

"Oh, that sounds like fun," Sara said to Adam's relief. "It's pretty cool that you don't feel the need to plan the whole thing out like a lot of people here do."

"Yeah, I prefer to just go with it," he told her, happy to use her assumption.

"Earlier, this guy was showing me his plans for the entire summer," Sara continued. "He had the whole thing planned out. Everything he was going to do week by week. It was pretty lame if you ask me. I like that you're not like that."

Before Adam could think of anything to say, the bell rang. His heart sank as he expected Sara to rush out the door to her next class. It was the last day, though, and there wasn't much of a need to worry about making it on time since half the class wouldn't even be there. Instead of rushing away, Sara stayed in her seat, looking at Adam. She had an anxious, eager look on her face that went right over Adam's head.

"Well," he said slowly, not wanting this last moment with Sara to end, "I guess that's it, then."

"Yeah, I guess it is," she said. "Unless you have something else to say before I go?"

"Um, no. Nothing that I can think of."

"Oh," she said, starting to look a little sad. "Alright, I guess I should head to my next class."

They stood up. Adam was hoping she would hug him before she left. He was too afraid to initiate it himself.

"Bye," Sara said. She turned around and left so quickly that Adam didn't even have time to say it back.

He watched as she turned the corner and disappeared. She didn't even walk with him into the hallway. Adam didn't feel like his heart was sinking. He felt like he didn't have one at all. It felt as if someone had ripped his heart out. He had never felt so alone in all his life.

The classroom was empty. Adam stood staring at the open doorway. He might have collapsed back down into his chair, but he didn't even have the motivation to do that. He just stood completely motionless. The one thing that had given him hope had just walked out of his life forever. It was too late to do anything about it now.

When he finally started moving, the hallway was empty. He didn't know if he had been standing there for five seconds or five hours. When he caught a glimpse of a clock in a classroom, he saw it had been about ten minutes. The bell for the next class had already rung. Adam didn't care. He didn't seem to have the ability to move quickly anymore.

On his way to class, he passed the school cafeteria. He moved slowly past it, thinking about all the times he and Sara had eaten lunch together. Those days were over now. Next year, he would be back to hiding in the bathroom stall, eating his lunch on the toilet.

As if the moment couldn't get any worse, Adam felt a jerk on his arm as he crossed in front of the cafeteria doors. Derek and his friends pulled him inside. The lunchroom staff was gone for the year, and Derek and his four friends were using the room to hang out.

Adam held his arms in front of his face as they hit him. He didn't bother to try and escape. He just let it happen. At least this would probably be the last one for the school year, he thought to himself. From them, anyway.

Grabbing Adam by the arms, they dragged him back into the empty kitchen. They threw him to the floor as Miles grabbed a sink nozzle and handed it to Derek. The water used to wash dishes was scalding as it hit Adam in the face. He covered up and rolled away, turning his back to them. By the time they finally stopped spraying him, the skin on his back was bright red.

When the boys finally finished, they walked away, leaving a burned and screaming Adam lying in a giant pool of water. When he was sure they were gone, he got up and continued to class. He thought about not going, but that just wasn't in his nature.

When he arrived, there were only five other kids in class. They were sitting together in a group, laughing and talking about everything that had happened that year. Mrs. Whitmore looked at Adam with the water still dripping from his body and laughed. "I guess water fights are more important than showing up to class on time," she said. "Well, of course, they are. It's the last day of school, and I don't even know why we're here. Class is dismissed. You can all leave."

With that, the rest of the kids got up and walked out the door. Adam turned around, very annoyed. He'd walked all the way there and didn't even get to sit down. With a big sigh, Adam left.

His next class didn't start for a while, and Adam stopped in the hallway, wondering where to go. He couldn't go home until school was over, even if he wanted to. He still had to wait for the bus. Eventually, he decided to walk to his next class. At the pace he felt like moving, it might be time when he got there anyway.

Just as Adam expected from his luck, there were still students in the room when he got to his next class. There were only three or four, but he still felt he should wait until the class was officially over before going in. Instead, he went to the bathroom and hid there until the bell rang.

Finally, the day was almost over, and Adam sat in his final class for the school year. Two other students were sitting on the opposite side of the room and joking among themselves. At this point, the only students left were those who had to wait for the bus. If it hadn't been for the three of them, the teacher would have already left himself. He was sitting at his desk reading a book, constantly looking at the clock and sighing.

Finally, the teacher couldn't take it anymore, and his impatience got the better of him. "You know, it's not like I'm taking roll or anything," he said enthusiastically. "You all can just leave if you want to."

None of the boys wanted to leave, but they all took the hint. The two boys talking got up and left, wondering what to do for the last twenty-five minutes of the day. Adam reluctantly followed. As soon as he exited the room, the excited teacher flew past him and toward the faculty parking lot.

Adam needed to get out of the halls. It was unlikely that Derek was still there, but if he was, the hallway was the last place Adam wanted to be. He just wanted the year to end without any more beatings. Was that too much for him to ask? He went to the nearest bathroom to hide until the school day was officially over.

When he got there, he discovered it had been blocked off for cleaning, so he went to the next closest bathroom but ran into the same problem. When it happened again a third time, Adam realized what was going on. They had already cleaned them and were just leaving them blocked until everyone was gone. He thought about sneaking into one, but he didn't want to risk getting into trouble now in the last ten minutes of the day. The risk was more significant than running into Derek.

Finally, he started heading toward the buses. He decided to take his chances and hope that Derek and his friends were gone. There were only about a hundred kids left in the school. What were the odds one of them was Derek?

When Adam turned the corner to the final hallway leading to the school's front doors, he saw something that stopped him dead in his tracks. He didn't know what to do. Hide, keep going, or turn around and find another route? The choice seemed impossible, and Adam just stood there, unable to move. Before he could make up his mind, he was spotted.

Chapter 16

Sara was sitting on the floor at the end of the hall. Even after all the times he'd talked to her, Adam still found this moment terrifying. He didn't know if she still wanted to talk to him, and he was too shy to just walk up to her. But he also couldn't turn around; she had already seen him. If she did want to talk to him, that would ruin it.

Awkwardly, Adam stood still and stared ahead with a frightened look on his face as Sara looked back at him. A couple of seconds passed, but it felt like an hour. Finally, she waved at him with a big smile on her face. Adam finally drew up the courage to say hello.

"Adam!" Sara jumped to her feet and ran to greet him. "What are you still doing here?" she asked as she excitedly hugged him.

"Oh," Adam said as he waited for his fear to subside, "I was just waiting until it was time to leave."

"Yeah," Sara said. "It's really boring. I've been sitting here for about forty minutes. There wasn't even anyone in my last class, but my mom still couldn't pick me up until after school was over, so I had nothing to do but wait."

"Yeah, it's annoying. My last teacher basically kicked us all out twenty minutes early, so I didn't have anything to do."

Sara giggled. "They don't want to be here any more than we do, I guess. Honestly, I've been ready to go ever since geometry class ended," she said, biting her lower lip. "By the way, thanks for helping me in that class all semester. It definitely made the class easier. And more enjoyable."

"I had a lot of fun studying with you," Adam said. "It made the class way better."

"Well," Sara said, "hopefully next year we'll still have some classes together. Preferably more than two this time."

"Yeah, that would be nice."

"Especially math classes," she said, laughing. "I can't believe how good you are at math. You're so smart."

"Thanks." Adam blushed and looked away shyly. "You're pretty good at it too."

"Definitely not as good as you. I'm not the one who got hundreds on all the tests."

"You still got A's on them. And you got an A in both classes."

"Well," Sara said, "I guess that is what matters, then. Isn't it?"

"I think that's all that matters. You got the same grade I did."

"I think you technically still win, though. Smart boy."

Adam couldn't believe his luck, but he didn't have another response. He stared into Sara's eyes and lost himself in their glow. As terrible as the past couple of hours had been, at least they were ending on a good note. He couldn't think of a better way to end the school year than talking to Sara. They were even alone, and he could finally talk to her without being constantly interrupted by other boys desperately trying to steal her attention.

A blaring sound came from outside. Adam looked behind Sara and saw a car parked by the curb, honking its horn. Sara turned and looked. Adam knew what was coming next.

"Oh, that's my mom," Sara said, just as Adam had known she

would. She was about to walk away, and he wouldn't see her again for the next three whole months. "I guess I have to go, then. It was really nice getting this one last chance to talk to you again. I'm glad we ran into each other."

With that, she hugged Adam, and they both said goodbyes. Adam found it hard to breathe as he watched her walk away. But just before she got to the door, she turned back around. "Do you have a pen?" she asked him. "I didn't bring my backpack today."

"Yes," Adam told her.

"Well," she continued, "can I borrow it?"

"Oh," Adam said flustered, "yes. Of course you can." He swung his backpack out in front of him and pulled a pen from the front pocket. As he handed the pen to Sara, she grabbed the back of his hand.

"Alright," she said, running the pen over the palm of his hand, "this is my phone number. I'm going to give it to you, and in exchange, you have to call me so I can see you this summer. Okay?"

"Okay," Adam forced out with a nod as he swallowed.

Sara had finished writing but still held onto his hand as she looked him in the eyes. "Good. Don't wait too long to call. My summer won't be any fun without you."

Sara's hand slid down Adam's fingers as she finally let go. She turned and walked to the exit doors. As she grabbed the door handle, she looked back and saw Adam still standing there, watching her leave.

"Um," she said, "are you waiting for the bus?"

"Well, yeah," Adam mumbled. "It should be here in like ten minutes."

"Well, come on. I'm sure my mom would be happy to give you a ride. And it'll be faster than the bus."

"Oh, thanks," Adam said as he hurried to catch up to her.

"Who's your friend?" Sara's mom asked when they arrived at the car.

"This is Adam," Sara responded. "Can we give him a ride so he doesn't have to wait for the bus?"

"Adam?" her mom said. It was more of a statement than a question. "We've heard so much about you. Of course, we'd be happy to give you a ride. Get in the car."

Adam wondered what she meant by that as he and Sara piled into the back seat. Were they good things they'd heard? Was it about the weird, shy kid she had met in class? Adam waited anxiously to find out as he buckled his seat belt.

"Sara told us how you helped her study in math," her mother continued. "She says you're the sweetest boy she knows."

Adam was relieved. He realized it was stupid to think it might have been something terrible. Why would she tell her parents what a loser he was and then offer him a ride? He couldn't help it, though. It had become his nature to assume the worst. After all, that was what it usually ended up being.

"Mom!" Sara exclaimed, her face turning red. "You're embarrassing me." She covered her face so he couldn't see how much she was blushing.

"Oh, no, I'm not," Sara's mom said. "He liked to hear that. Look at how much he's blushing. Almost as much as you, Sara."

Adam's face had turned red. He tried to hide it, but he looked terrified. Luckily, Sara couldn't see him through her own hand.

"*Mom*! Stop it!" Sara shrieked in panic.

"Oh, alright," her mom said. "Well, it's nice to meet you, Adam. My name is Olivia. When you come over to visit, you can meet Sara's father, James, and her brothers."

"Nice to meet you," Adam said in a crackling voice.

Adam and Sara didn't say much to each other during the ride.

They were too embarrassed and sat in silence as they drove to Adam's house. They hardly shared a glance. As the car pulled into his driveway, Adam barely managed to crack a smile at her to say goodbye.

"Before you go," Olivia said as Adam opened the door, "take this so that you can call Sara over the summer." She stretched out her hand toward Adam with a piece of paper in it.

"Mom!" Sara shouted. "Come on! I already gave him our number. Stop it."

"Yes, I saw that," Olivia told Sara, "but it would probably be better if he had it on a piece of paper and not written on his hand. Besides, you wrote it on his right hand. So unless he happens to be left-handed, this will save him the trouble of copying it down with his wrong hand."

"Thanks," Adam said as he took the number. "And thank you for the ride."

"Oh, and so polite, too. You sure did find a keeper, Sara."

"Ahhhh," Sara moaned and buried her face in her palms, hiding from Adam as he left the car.

Adam's heart raced as he looked at his hand. He could still feel the pen slightly tickling his palm, with the feeling of Sara's fingers resting on his hand as she wrote. He wished she hadn't ever let go.

Getting a ride home had saved Adam so much time that he found he had an extra hour to himself. He didn't even have his textbooks to study anymore, so he decided he might as well use the time to make food.

Waffles. Adam thought about his mother's journal story and how much he missed waffles. Today was going to be the day he would finally have them again. That would only add to how wonderful this day had already been. If he only had all the ingredients.

He went to the pantry and pulled out an old cookbook. It was his mom's cookbook, and no one had used it since she'd been gone. A recipe for making waffles was likely to be inside. His mom had made them at least once a week.

After finding the recipe, Adam searched the kitchen, looking for the ingredients. In the back of the pantry, he found an old bag of flour. It was dusty, and he wondered if his mom had bought it. He didn't know if it was still good, but he figured he'd try it. It still looked fine, anyway. He was just glad there weren't any bugs in it. Fortunately, the bag was sealed.

Even the mixing bowl was dusty. There wasn't a lot of serious cooking done in the house anymore. Adam washed the bowl in the sink before scooping up the flour. It was a good thing he had so much time since he'd have to do the dishes twice over.

He measured out the flour as precisely as possible. He didn't want to mess up his waffles. Not only did he want to be able to savor his first waffles in years, but he doubted the dusty bag of flour would ever be replaced. He didn't have any money to buy more himself. It would likely be his only bag for the rest of high school.

The sizzle as the batter hit the iron made Adam grin. The batter spilled out over the edge as he closed the lid; he'd forgotten to account for the batter spreading out. The recipe hadn't mentioned how much batter to put on the grill, and he'd used too much. Adam watched in despair as his lost waffles slid down the side of the waf-fle iron and dripped onto the counter. It ran down so slowly that it was almost as if it was taunting Adam with his loss. Sighing, he wiped up the mess.

Adam had just enough batter left to make a second batch. As it cooked, he scrubbed everything except the iron. When they were done, he picked up the searing waffles like a frantic juggler and moved them to his plate. He drenched them in butter and syrup before cleaning up the waffle iron and going upstairs with his double-stacked feast.

Although not quite as fluffy as when his mom made them, the waffles were as delicious as Adam had remembered. He couldn't wait for them to cool down and winced as he tried to blow on pieces already in his mouth. It was the best meal he'd eaten in years.

As he ate, Adam looked at his hand. He'd been careful not to get it dirty so he wouldn't have to wash it and risk losing Sara's number. He still had the written copy tucked safely in his pocket, but he wanted to keep Sara's writing on his palm as long as possible, even if for only a few more hours. He didn't want to wash away the reminder of how good this day had been. He worried it would turn out to be just a dream, and he wanted to keep the proof.

Chapter 17

A week had passed since school ended and Sara wrote her number on the palm of his hand. That same night, he'd picked up the phone to call her, but he got too scared and set the phone back down. All he'd managed to do was to put his finger on the first number, but he never pressed it.

Finally, one week later, Adam dialed her number…and immediately slammed the phone back down as he hit the final digit. He even unplugged the phone from the wall just to be safe.

Today was the day. Adam was determined to call Sara. He was worried it was too late and that she'd already forgotten about him. He couldn't wait any longer; it was now or never. But Adam couldn't stand the thought of never. That idea was even worse than the anxiety he felt when he tried to call her.

Slowly, he dialed. Ten seconds passed between each number pressed. The sound of the ringing pierced Adam's ears like a firing gun. He wanted nothing more than to slam the phone back down. It took every ounce of will he could muster to keep it to his ear.

"Hello?"

"Hello?"

"Hi," he finally said.

"Hi?"

"Um, is Sara there?" he asked.

"This is Sara," the voice answered back. Adam panicked and didn't respond. "Adam?"

"Hi," he repeated.

"Hi!" Sara chirped. "I didn't know if you were ever going to call. I was worried you'd lost my number. Even after my mom gave it to you a second time!" She finished with a giggle followed by a slight sigh. She was still mortified by how embarrassing it had been.

"Yeah, I guess I probably should have called sooner. It's been like a week, I think," Adam said, pretending he didn't know precisely how long it had been.

"That's okay," Sara told him. "I'm just glad you called eventually. The summer just wouldn't have been any fun if you didn't. So, has the start of your summer been fun? What have you been doing all week?"

Adam thought about his week. He'd started each day off hoping his father had already left for work, spending half the day trying to build up the guts to call Sara and the other half dreading the moment he heard his father's car pull into the driveway. He filled his evenings with hours of trying to be quiet in his room and hoping his father never came up.

"It's been pretty fun," Adam lied. "Just been hanging out so far. Haven't done a lot."

"I get that. It's nice to just relax after a long school year. Especially now that we're in high school. It's harder than middle school. Don't you think?"

"There was a bit more work, I guess," Adam said.

"Well, I guess I shouldn't have expected you to think it was hard. You're just way too smart."

"Thanks," Adam said bashfully, not knowing what else to say.

He was hoping Sara would carry the conversation more. He had no idea what else to say.

"So, hey," she started, "do you want to come to hang out at my house?" She had run out of things to say over the phone and thought this would be easier. "My family is playing board games tonight, and you can join us if you want."

"Yeah!" Adam blurted out. "Um," he continued, trying to contain his excitement, "that sounds like fun."

*   *   *

Adam took a long shower, scrubbing thoroughly many times over. After brushing his teeth for ten minutes, he combed his hair until every last strand was perfect, even more so than when he had done it for Sara at school. He applied an excessive coat of antiperspirant. Sara's house was two-and-a-half miles away. It was hot outside, and he didn't want to sweat when walking there. After double-checking that his outfit was straight and his hair was perfectly in place five more times, Adam left for Sara's house.

He walked quickly, but not so fast that he risked overheating. As he went on his way, Adam kept pulling out the paper with Sara's address and looking at it. He had it memorized by now; he just liked looking at it again to remind himself that she'd given it to him. He wished he could have still kept her number written on his hand but figured it would seem odd if she saw it still there a week later.

He turned a corner and looked into the distance, where he saw what he was pretty sure was Sara's house. It was reasonably larger than where he lived. It sat at the end of a long street, right in front of the T intersection, just as Sara had described it. Adam picked up the pace and moved toward it.

As he arrived at the house, he looked around for the house number. He saw one painted on the curb, but that was too worn and faded to tell what it said. He walked up the driveway looking for the house number, then up and down the pathway in front of the porch, but he couldn't find anything.

Suddenly, the front door opened. "Hi, Adam," Olivia said, poking her head outside. "Remember me? I'm Sara's mom. I saw you looking around from the window. Am I correct in guessing you're looking for the house number? It's hiding behind that bush there. It's a terrible place for it. We're going to move it this summer. Probably over the garage. Or just tear up the bush. I don't like it anyway." She laughed. "We haven't decided yet. We're going to repaint the curb, too. There are still a few things to do after moving in. That doesn't matter now. Come in, come in. Sara is just watching TV, I think."

Olivia's long, rambling welcome speech flustered Adam. He walked up the porch and into the house. Inside, it didn't seem as run down as his house. There were no dents in the walls from someone throwing something into it. And there was no smell of bourbon, whiskey, or vodka spilled on the floor.

"Sara!" Olivia called out. "Your friend is here!"

Sara jumped up from the living room couch and ran out to greet Adam. "Hi!" she squealed in a high-pitched voice. "I'm glad you could come over."

"Thanks for inviting me," Adam replied with a nervous crackle.

"So," Sara said, "what do you want to do? I was just watching TV, but we could also play a board game, or chess, or whatever."

"I'm okay with whatever you want to do."

"Okay. Want to play chess?" Sara asked, thinking it would impress Adam.

"Yeah, that sounds like fun," he said, even though the only

thing he knew about chess was how the pieces moved. He hoped he could fake it and that Sara would think he played sometimes.

Sara pulled the box with the chessboard out of the game closet. As she slid it out from under a pile of board games, she subtly wiped off the dust, hoping Adam wouldn't notice. "Here it is. I haven't played in a while," she admitted. "You'll probably have to go easy on me."

"Aright, I'll try," Adam said, hoping he didn't look like a complete idiot when they played.

Adam watched Sara as she set up her side of the board and matched her moves.

"Oh," Sara said as they finished, "your king and queen are backward." She reached over the board and switched them. "They go on the same line as my king and queen, so they reverse on the other side."

"Oh, right," Adam said, trying to brush it off as a simple mistake. "I don't play that much, and it's been a while."

He copied Sara's opening moves as they started, figuring out how to play. It wasn't long before he couldn't do that anymore and had to make up his moves. One at a time, Adam's side of the board grew empty. Move by move, she strategically removed every one of Adam's pieces.

"Checkmate," Sara calmly said, as if she had said it a thousand times.

"Wow, okay," Adam replied as he looked at the aftermath of the massive slaughter he'd just experienced.

"Sorry," she told him sympathetically. "I may have played this a bit more than I led on before we started."

"Yes, I can see that," Adam said with a slight laugh. "I'm guessing a lot more than you let me believe."

"I haven't played in months," she said. "Not since we moved

here. I started playing in the fifth grade. In middle school, someone invited me to join the chess club. I was in it until we moved here. School here doesn't have a club, and I've been busy studying, so I just haven't picked it up again."

"Well," Adam laughed, "that would have been good to know before I got destroyed!"

"Sorry, yeah, I probably should have mentioned that. We can play something else if you want to."

"No, we can keep playing," Adam said. "I know how all the pieces move, but I haven't ever played before."

"Oh my gosh!" Sara exclaimed. "I'm so sorry. I think I just got a little too into it when I finally played again. I definitely should have gone easier on you."

"Well, maybe you can teach me how to play," Adam said.

"That sounds fun. I can do that. You'll have to come over a lot this summer, though."

"Sounds good to me," Adam said. "I don't have much else planned anyway."

Sara started by teaching Adam how to set up the board, after which they played for hours. She taught him strategies, and every half hour they played another game. None of the games ever lasted more than a few minutes. Every time, Sara quickly defeated Adam without difficulty. It didn't bother him at all. He was just having fun playing with her.

"You're starting to improve," Sara told Adam when she finished beating him in two minutes and forty-five seconds.

Adam laughed. "If you say so."

"No, it's true. It may not seem like it, but you weren't making as many obvious mistakes on that one. You're improving. Knowing you, you'll be beating me in no time."

"Well, I doubt that," Adam replied. "You're way better than

me. I don't think I'll ever be able to beat you."

"I'm sure you will someday. You're super smart. I'm sure you'll be great at it."

"Only if you keep teaching me."

Sara's mom called out from the hallway. "Adam, are you staying for dinner?"

"Yes, he is," Sara said as her mom popped her head in through the doorway. Sara looked at Adam with a slight smile. She didn't bother to ask him if he wanted to stay; she simply answered for him. "We have to keep playing chess, right?"

"Yes, of course," Adam said. But even if they weren't playing chess, he still wouldn't want to leave. Sara didn't know it, but Adam just didn't want to go home. He wished he never had to go back there again.

At dinner, Sara's family got to know Adam. He felt awkward with so much attention on him, but it was certainly a lot better than eating at home. Luckily, he had Sara running interference when she could. She was afraid Adam was going to get scared off.

There was so much food on the table that Adam didn't know how they could eat it all. Not wanting to be rude, he planned on sticking to one plate. That plan didn't work out. They kept telling him he could have more, and he started thinking it would be impolite not to have seconds.

Adam tried to hide how nauseous he felt after eating so much food. After dinner, he and Sara went back to the chessboard. Several more hours passed with hardly a break in their playing. Adam could finally survive about ten moves each game before Sara checkmated him.

"See, I told you that you were getting better," Sara said, although Adam still didn't see it.

"Alright, it's getting late," Sara's dad said from the hallway. "It's time to wrap things up."

They packed up the chessboard and put it back in the closet. Then Adam followed Sara to the front door, and they stepped out onto the front porch. Sara shut the door behind them.

"Thanks for coming over," she said. "I had a lot of fun hanging out with you."

"Yes, it was lots of fun. Thanks for teaching me how to play chess."

"Well," Sara said, "I'm not done teaching you yet. You'll just have to come back tomorrow, and we can play some more. I mean, if you want to, that is."

"Yeah, that sounds like fun," Adam said.

"Great! I'll see you tomorrow, then. Come back at like one?"

"Okay."

They said goodnight, and Adam awkwardly turned and walked home.

Chapter 18

Adam felt elated as he headed for home. The sun was starting to set, and his father was sure to be home by now, but it was late enough that he had probably already passed out from drinking. Even if he wasn't, that couldn't upset Adam today. Whatever happened would be worth it.

The sun disappeared behind the distant hills as he walked. Despite his high spirits, he started feeling uneasy. He stopped and looked behind him. The street appeared empty, but he still had a bad feeling. He picked up the pace and kept walking.

Still unable to shake the feeling that something was there, Adam turned around again. Behind him stood a dog. It was large with pure-black fur that looked rough and tangled. He froze as the dog glared at him. Adam's anxiety soared as adrenaline coursed through his veins. Slowly, he began to back up. When the dog didn't move, Adam turned and ran the rest of the way home.

When he got to the front door of his house, Adam looked behind him again. He couldn't see the dog anywhere.

He waited to catch his breath before sneaking inside. When he could breathe calmly again, he peered in through the front window. His father lay blacked out on the couch. Adam saw the empty vodka bottle on the floor and he knew his father wasn't going to wake up for hours. Still not taking any chances, Adam opened the door as quietly as he could and snuck upstairs.

Adam lay on his bed and thought about how fantastic his day had been. He couldn't believe that he'd got to hang out with Sara outside of school. And she even wanted him to come back tomorrow! It was the best feeling in the world. He didn't have much time to think about it, though. Within thirty seconds, his exhausted body gave in and sleep took hold of him.

*   *   *

Adam woke the next morning with a thick film layer on his teeth. Disgusted, he went to the bathroom and brushed his teeth twice as long as usual to make up for not doing it the night before. After, he took off yesterday's clothes, which he'd slept in, and took a long shower.

His stomach rumbled loudly. It was Saturday, and Adam didn't know if it was safe to go downstairs for breakfast or not. He went to the stairs, peeked his head around the corner, and looked through the railing. To his relief, the couch was empty. He went downstairs and found he was alone.

The house remained empty all morning. Adam made an extensive breakfast and lunch before leaving for Sara's house. Today was looking to be as good as yesterday. Adam hoped it didn't end in a terrifying sprint home.

*   *   *

Adam and Sara didn't play chess the entire day like they had before. They played until dinner, and once again, Sara invited him to stay and eat. Adam ate even more this time. After dinner, he and Sara played a board game in the basement living room while her brothers played video games. The brothers occasionally yelled when one of them lost, which was followed by loud laughter.

Just like before, when the day came to a close, Sara's dad popped his head into the room and told them what time it was. This time, Sara said goodbye on the front porch and watched until Adam turned the corner before going back inside.

On his way home, Adam saw the black dog behind him again. His heart raced, but he maintained the same speed. The dog hadn't chased him the night before, so Adam hoped he would leave him alone if he just kept walking. This time, the dog followed him all the way to his house.

Seeing his father asleep on the couch, Adam looked over his shoulder at the dog as he turned the front door knob. Just as he cracked open the door, the dog started barking at him. Adam jumped inside and shut the door.

He quietly went upstairs, wondering whether he was more afraid of the dog charging him or the barking waking up his father. Fortunately for Adam, his father's alcohol-induced coma was way too strong to be broken by a stray dog's yelps.

*　　*　　*

Adam and Sara's routine continued. He spent the day at her house three or four times a week. They always played chess until dinner, and afterward found something else to do. Every time Adam walked home, the dog would come out from wherever he was hiding and follow him until he reached his house. It didn't even bother Adam anymore to have him there. He wasn't going to let anything stop him from seeing Sara.

Each time Adam passed the spot with the dog, he turned around to see if he was coming. After the tenth time, the dog ran right up to him instead of staying back. Adam grew frightened at the big black beast that could rip him apart.

Is today the day he finally attacks? Adam wondered.

This time, the dog wagged his tail playfully and sat down, panting. Hesitantly, Adam reached out his hand and rubbed the dog's head. When he did, the dog jumped back to his feet. Adam jerked his hand away and stepped back, afraid the dog would attack.

Caressingly, the dog stepped forward and rubbed his head against Adam's leg. Adam cautiously put his hand back down and started petting him behind the dog's ear. The dog sat back down and eventually rolled over, exposing his stomach. Adam dropped to his knees and rubbed the dog's belly.

Adam had never had a dog before. He'd always wanted one. His parents had told him he could get one when he turned ten, but that never happened. Now, it seemed, this dog had chosen him.

Not seeing any real reason to go home yet, Adam came up with another idea. He went to the park, and the dog followed. When they got there, Adam sat down and petted his new friend. Then he went searching for a stick. The dog's tail began to wag ferociously when Adam found one under a tree. The dog's eyes shone under the glow of the streetlights as Adam waved the stick back and forth.

Adam threw the stick, and like a bullet, the dog shot after it. He seemed nothing more than a dark blur as he flew through the air to retrieve it. Adam was glad the dog hadn't chased him the first night they met. There was no way he would have made it home.

The dog retrieved the stick, walked it back to Adam, and dropped it at his feet. His fur was dirty and clumped together. He was a stray, yet he was well-trained. Adam wondered what had happened to land this beautiful creature on the street. Maybe he'd gotten too big and his owners didn't want him anymore. Or perhaps they'd moved away and decided to leave him behind. Adam couldn't understand how anyone could do something like that to such a good dog.

For two hours, they continued to play together. The dog loved to fetch and could keep going all night. Adam wished he could stay there with him until it was time to go back to Sara's house, but he had to sleep. He petted the dog for a few more minutes and then started for home, the dog following him.

At his house, Adam was forced to leave his new friend outside. He went upstairs and looked out a window, watching as the dog went back up the street in the direction of where he'd first started following Adam.

Adam wasn't going to Sara's house the next day. On those days, he usually walked to the library and read books for most of the day. When he was on his way, he heard a clapping sound from behind. When he turned, he saw the dog charging down the sidewalk to meet him. Adam reached down as the dog rubbed his head against his legs. Instead of going to the library, the two of them went back to the park.

Adam looked down at his dog's dark-black fur. "I'm gonna call you Smokey."

Chapter 19

Summer vacation was drawing to a close. There was only a week left until the new school year began. While most kids hated the end of summer, Adam preferred the start of the new school year. As much as he enjoyed the break from Derek, going to school gave him more to do than sit in his room and hide from his father, and it was the only way he could keep working toward leaving for college. This year, however, Adam was dreading the end. This summer had been the happiest he'd been in years.

He'd spent the whole summer hanging out with either Sara or Smokey. It was the first time in a long time that he hadn't felt lonely. He was seldom alone except for when he had to sleep. Now he only had a few more opportunities to hang out with Sara at her house, and he would have to start leaving his dog to go to school.

Adam and Sara were sitting on the couch in her living room watching a movie. She had her head resting on his shoulder. While Adam liked that, it also made him nervous, and he sat there totally still, not wanting to move a muscle. As the credits rolled up the TV screen, Sara lifted her head and looked into Adam's eyes. His heartbeat quickened as he looked back into hers.

"So?" Sara asked, finally breaking the silence. "What did you think of the movie?" Her tone sounded sweet and caring.

"It was good," Adam replied. "I liked it. What did you think about it?"

"I don't know," she said. "I mean, it was pretty good, but the first half was kind of lame." Her voice shifted from sweet to annoyed. "Come on. She was throwing signals at him the entire time. It was undeniable! Why did it take him half the movie to finally make a move?"

"Maybe it was just to build up the suspense of the movie," Adam replied innocently.

"I guess," Sara said, squinting at Adam.

"Alright, guys, the movie's over," Sara's dad said, interrupting them. "It's getting late. Time to wrap it up."

"Okay, Dad," Sara said. "Come on, Adam. I'll walk you to the door."

As always, Sara stepped out onto the front porch and closed the door to say goodbye to Adam. She stared at him before she finally spoke. "Well, I guess this is it." She stepped closer to Adam until there were only a few inches between them. "Goodnight."

Adam's chest was pounding, his breath heavy. They had been here dozens of times before, but it was never like this. Was she about to kiss him? Should he kiss her? He had no idea what to do.

"Goodnight," Adam finally mustered.

Sara sighed. "Alright, I'll see you on Wednesday?"

"I'll be here."

"Great," she said unenthusiastically and went back inside before Adam had even started to turn around.

As Adam began the two-mile walk home, he was filled with regret and many questions. Should he have kissed her? Probably. Maybe. What if he'd tried and she pulled away? Did she think of him as just a friend, or was he more? If he tried to kiss her but she only thought of him as a friend, would that ruin everything? Would she keep hanging out with him? Adam wished he had a way of knowing. He wished he had the guts to find out. Either way, the moment had passed.

At least he knew where he stood with Smokey. Adam's dog came sprinting up to him as he arrived at the halfway point, jumping up and down with a wagging tail. Every day without fail, Smokey was always there waiting for him in the morning and as he walked back from Sara's.

Adam wished he could bring Smokey home and keep him there. The only reason Smokey ever went back to his old spot was because that was where he got his food; Adam certainly couldn't afford dog food.

Once, Adam followed Smokey back to where he lived. Adam discovered that Smokey spent his nights sleeping in an alley under an old, rusted car that hadn't moved in years. On the other end of that alley was the back door to a restaurant. Rather than tossing everything into the dumpster, every night at 9:10 p.m., they put that day's leftover food on a crate. At 9:20, someone from the local homeless shelter would pick it up. Smokey knew precisely when to snatch his meals. They never noticed a few pieces missing every night.

For a stray dog, Smokey ate well. He would scarf down his meal and then head over to meet Adam so the two of them could walk back to Adam's house. When Adam went to Sara's house, Smokey followed. Adam wondered how Smokey would deal with the change of routine when school started again.

Now wasn't the time to worry about that, though. Adam was determined to enjoy his time with Smokey. Although it was late, he took Smokey to the park. He wanted to make sure that Smokey didn't forget he cared when he couldn't be around as much.

Adam threw sticks until his arm was so tired he could barely lift them. They stayed out longer than they should have. Adam would have stayed longer if it wasn't so hard to keep his eyes open.

When they got back to Adam's house, Adam hid with Smokey on the side of the house. He wanted to pet him a bit longer before he had to go inside. Smokey lay his head on Adam's lap and fell asleep. Adam looked down at his sleeping dog and felt his own eyes close.

He woke up with a sore hip and shoulder to find himself pinned between the house and Smokey. His whole left side was aching from sleeping on the concrete all night. He got up without waking Smokey, tiptoed to the corner, and peeked around. His father's car was gone. The house was safe, so Adam went inside for breakfast. He made waffles again, just as he had all summer when he had the opportunity. His father had been replacing the empty bags of flour with new ones from the grocery store. Perhaps the first one hadn't been as old as Adam thought.

*　　*　　*

It was the day before school started again. The last time Adam would hang out with Sara, the final chess game they'd ever play this summer.

Adam was playing better than he ever had before. His plan was going perfectly. For the first time, he was going to capture Sara's queen. He moved his piece, checking her king. Behind her king, a few rows away, was her queen. Adam had Sara trapped in an absolute pin. She was forced to move her king out of check, exposing her queen to an attack.

"Nice move," Sara told him. As she knew she had to, Sara saved her king and gave Adam her queen.

"Thank you," Adam replied. "I had a good teacher."

"You've never captured my queen before."

"No, I haven't."

"Well, you did a good job forcing me to sacrifice my queen to checkmate your king."

With that, she moved her rook across the board. Adam's king was trapped in a back rank checkmate with three of his pawns in front of it.

"You played well," Sara said, "but don't be too eager to capture the queen."

"What just happened?" Adam asked.

"I was ready to put you in an easy checkmate," she told him. "I just needed you to move your queen out of the way first."

"Oh, my gosh!" Adam exclaimed. "I can't believe I didn't see that!"

"It was still a good game. At least you managed to force me to sacrifice my queen. I never much liked doing that."

At dinner, Sara's parents asked them if they had any classes together.

"Yes," Sara answered. "We have chemistry together in the morning and trigonometry at the end of the day."

"Oh," Olivia said, "that's nice, now, isn't it?"

"Yes," Sara said. "And having Adam in those classes with me will certainly make them easier."

"I remember that you told us how much he helped you in class last year," James said. "You should study together again this year."

"Oh, most definitely," Olivia added. "It should be a good year for both of you."

"Yes, Sara should certainly get another 4.0 this year," James said. "Won't you, Sara?"

"James!" Olivia shouted. "Don't put so much pressure on her."

"I was just saying she probably will," he responded. "I'm not putting any pressure on her at all."

"I'm sure she'll do just fine," Olivia continued. "Especially since she has a study partner for her two hardest classes. She told us how no one else did very well in the physics or math class you two had together last year. And this year, you have the entire year together instead of just half of it."

*   *   *

Adam left right after dinner. There was school tomorrow, so he couldn't stay as long as he had before. As they got up from the table, Sara walked Adam to the door.

"Well," Sara said, "I guess this is it for the summer."

"Unfortunately," Adam replied. "I'll still see you tomorrow at school, though."

"That's true. This summer was a lot of fun, though. It was great hanging out with you. It sucks that it's over now."

"It does, doesn't it? I had a lot of fun with you, too. It was probably the best summer I ever had."

"Aww, I thought so too."

Sara stepped closer to Adam. She lifted her hand and placed it on Adam's arm. She looked into his eyes and waited on Adam. Adam grew excited and nervous thinking Sara was about to kiss him.

"Sara!" James called from inside before opening the front door. "Come on. You have school tomorrow. It's time to be done. You'll see him tomorrow anyway. Just finish saying goodbye already."

Sara hugged Adam and kissed his cheek. "Bye," she whispered into his ear.

The moment was lost, and Adam left for home. When he

arrived at their usual meeting spot, Smokey was nowhere to be seen. Adam was hours earlier than usual, and Smokey hadn't eaten yet. If he called out to him and brought Smokey home now, he wouldn't eat tonight. Adam decided to just keep walking. If Smokey didn't come home later, he would walk back to get him.

To Adam's disappointment, he saw his father's car in the driveway. He probably hadn't passed out yet, and Adam would have to sneak inside. Hopefully, his last night of summer wouldn't turn out to be the worst one.

Adam saw that the living room and kitchen were empty from the window. He cracked open the door and slipped inside. To his relief, he could sneak up stairs with ease.

Success! Adam made it into his room. Now if his father would pass out by 9 o'clock, Adam could sneak back out to meet Smokey. All he had to do was wait a few more hours.

As quarter to nine rolled around, Adam could still hear the television playing downstairs. Maybe his father was asleep in front of it. Adam snuck to the stairs and peeked down to see his father eating Chinese takeout on the couch with nothing but one bottle of beer on the coffee table. Adam couldn't believe his bad luck. His father had to pick tonight to have something other than hard liquor for dinner.

Adam checked every fifteen minutes until 10 o'clock. By then, there were a few more beer bottles on the table, but his father appeared far from passing out. Adam was stuck in the house. It would be the first time all summer he wasn't out there for Smokey. What if he panicked when he couldn't find Adam? What would he do? Would he come to the house to look for him? Would he just head back to his spot under the old car? Adam hoped Smokey would be alright tonight.

He kept looking out the window to see if he could spot Smokey walking up to the house. As 10:45 rolled around, he heard some barking from outside and ran back to the window. Smokey was standing on the sidewalk looking for him. Adam tried waving from the window but couldn't get Smokey to spot him. He didn't dare open the window and yell down to Smokey with his father awake downstairs. Especially not when he had been drinking.

After a few minutes, Smokey finally gave up barking. Adam watched as he walked over to the side of the house where he would sleep for the night, relieved to know that at least Smokey was safe. He could finally go to sleep himself so he wouldn't be tired on the first day of the new school year.

Chapter 20

Aside from the occasional run-in with his father at home, Adam's summer had been perfect. Although he couldn't avoid the beatings entirely, they'd become less frequent. Given how wonderful the rest of his summer had been, he found it easy not to let them bother him at all.

As his alarm went off, Adam rolled out of bed and started getting ready for school. He had another morning ahead of him where he had to avoid Derek as he got off the bus. He just needed to make it until second period before he could see Sara again. Hopefully, he wouldn't have any classes with Derek.

Adam crept down the stairs. His father was still asleep on the couch. The effects of the alcohol had likely worn off enough, and Adam knew he had to be careful not to wake him.

He made it to the bottom of the stairs. Just as he opened the front door, he heard the squeal of the bus hitting the brakes as it rolled to a stop.

"What are you making so much noise for, you stupid idiot!" Adam's father roared, opening his eyes.

A bottle flew across the room and hit Adam on the shoulder. He looked down and watched it crack when it hit the floor, then ran out the door to avoid any more.

To his surprise and relief, Derek was not on the bus. Adam's shoulder was bruised, but at least he'd make it through the rest of the morning just fine. Who knows, maybe Derek had even moved during the summer and Adam would never have to see him again. He doubted his luck was that good, but then again, his summer had been pretty great. Maybe his luck was finally changing.

Adam took the time he had on the bus to mentally prepare for the new school year. How would things go with Sara now that they had spent the entire summer hanging out? He wondered. He couldn't forget that Derek was likely going to be at school even though he wasn't on the bus.

The bus arrived at school. Taking a deep breath, Adam got up and walked off the bus. As he looked at his school, he actually smiled. He realized that he was happy to be back. He had Sara in two of his classes, he would get to learn new things, and this school year would bring him one year closer to graduating and leaving for college. There was almost a skip in his step as he walked toward the school doors.

He was so happy that he didn't notice Derek coming up from behind. He'd been waiting in the parking lot with all of his friends, who had driven there together, when he spotted Adam. Adam hadn't even bothered to walk quickly, and Derek easily closed the distance.

"Look who it is," Derek said as he put his arm over Adam's shoulder. His friends surrounded Adam. "I missed you this summer, little buddy. Why don't we go somewhere more private and get reacquainted?"

Together, Derek and his friends subtly forced Adam to the side of the school. To anyone who was looking, it appeared as if Adam was going willingly. Once they were on the side of the building, they pushed Adam behind a row of bushes and threw him into the dirt.

Grabbing a handful, Derek rubbed dirt onto Adam's face. Then his friends held Adam down while he pried open Adam's mouth and poured dirt inside. Adam started gagging when he tasted it. Derek even went as far as plugging Adam's nose, forcing him to inhale the dirt before they left.

Adam rolled over, coughing, and vomited. He cried when he thought about Sara seeing him like this. His pants and shirt were covered in dirt. How could he see her now?

Once the retching subsided, Adam picked himself up and went into the nearest bathroom. He looked at himself in the mirror and nearly started hyperventilating. It was worse than he'd thought. His face and hair were a mess. His clothes were a completely different color than they'd started out.

Turning on the sink, he ran his hair under the water and scrubbed his face, still coughing from the dirt in his lungs. He had to wash his ears multiple times to get out all the dirt. Once his head was clean, he unbuttoned his shirt and rang it out in the sink. It was no use, though. The sink wasn't going to clean his shirt, and it probably wouldn't dry before second period started. He gave up and put it in his backpack. Luckily, he'd worn a T-shirt underneath. It wasn't as nice, but at least it was still clean.

After getting his pants as clean as he could, he went to his first class. He was no longer excited about it. Now he sat there dreading the moment he would see Sara again. He wished he could just skip the rest of the day and see her tomorrow. She'd wonder why he didn't show up, though, and Adam wasn't one to skip class for any reason. Plus, the school would certainly call his father if he did. He had no choice but to let her see him looking like this.

Inevitably, second period came around. This time, Adam didn't forget to watch his back. He moved quickly and stealthily as he worked his way down the halls. He wasn't going to let Derek mess him up even more.

When he got to class, Sara was already inside. She waved at him as he walked through the door and gestured at the seat next to her. "Oh, my gosh!" she said, looking at his clothes. "What happened to you?"

"I tripped and fell in some dirt as I was running to catch the bus," he lied. He hated lying to her, but he didn't know what else to do. How could he tell her the truth about how he was held to the ground and forced to eat dirt?

"Oh, no!" Sara exclaimed. "I hope you didn't get hurt."

"No, I'm fine," he assured her, "just a little dirty. It was quite the way to start off the new school year."

"Yeah, I'm sure," Sara giggled. "At least you're okay, though."

*   *   *

When he got home from school, Adam looked for Smokey at the side of the house. The spot where Smokey normally lay was empty. Adam figured he'd probably gone back to the restaurant to find something to eat and would be back by ten tonight. As long as his father was passed out, Adam could sneak out to see Smokey before bed.

That never happened. As the clock hit ten, Smokey was still nowhere to be seen. Adam snuck out the front door to see if maybe he'd missed him and Smokey was already sleeping, but his spot was still empty.

Worried, Adam went looking for Smokey. Eventually, he made it to the alley where Smokey usually got his food. He checked under the old car but still didn't find him. Where could he be?

Adam still had school tomorrow, so after a few minutes he decided to head back home. He checked Smokey's spot again when he got there, but the dog was still nowhere to be found. As much as Adam wanted to wait until he came back, he had to go to bed.

He lay in bed for two hours before finally dozing off. He couldn't stop worrying about Smokey. The end of his day had ended even worse than it started. What if he never saw Smokey again? What if he thought Adam wasn't coming back and ran away?

Adam woke up ten minutes earlier than normal feeling tired. He wanted to check on Smokey again before he got on the bus. He planned on getting up earlier every day from now on so that he could spend some time with Smokey before school.

The spot was still empty. Adam stood staring in despair. He would have to try to find him again after school. He hoped Smokey was okay.

Smokey's spot was still empty when Adam got back from school, so he ate a quick dinner and went to Smokey's alley. He was so worried he practically ran. Smokey had to be there now. If he wasn't, then where could he be? It wasn't like Smokey to just run off like this. It must have been because Smokey didn't know where Adam was when he left for school.

The alley was empty. Smokey was not sleeping under the old car. Adam couldn't find him anywhere.

Suddenly, he got an idea. The park. He couldn't believe he hadn't thought of it before. That was the last place he knew where Smokey could be staying. If Smokey didn't know where Adam was, he might go to their park. Adam went back the way he came as fast as his legs could carry him.

Again, nothing. He walked desperately through the park, checking behind every tree and bush. He yelled Smokey's name as loud as he could, but there was no response. He began to lose hope.

Eleven o'clock rolled around. Adam had been checking outside repeatedly since nine, even though he knew that was before Smokey got his food and he wouldn't be back by then. Even now, well past the time he should have shown up, Adam still hadn't seen him. After sneaking out to make sure he didn't miss him, Adam gave up for the night and went to bed.

Adam looked for Smokey after school every day for a week but couldn't find him. At least he was able to see Sara at school. He never told her about Smokey. He didn't want to have to admit that he'd spent all the rest of his time away from her during summer hanging out with a stray dog. He was afraid she would think it was weird.

On his way to second period, Adam stopped in his tracks. He couldn't believe what he was seeing. Sara was standing next to the door of their chemistry classroom. In front of her stood a boy. Adam looked down and saw their hands together, fingers interlaced. The boy's other hand was wrapped around Sara, holding onto her lower back.

Who was he? Adam was heartbroken. The boy was clearly more than a friend to Sara. They were holding hands. Adam didn't know which was worse—what he was seeing, or that he still hadn't found Smokey. The summer had been the best time of his life. Now, barely a week after it had ended, everything good about it was gone.

Sara turned and saw Adam staring. He didn't even have anything left in him to look away and pretend he wasn't staring. Sara leaned in and gave the boy a kiss on the cheek and hugged him before he walked away.

As the boy turned away from her, Sara looked at Adam again and smiled. She waved him over to come to class with her. As he approached, Adam didn't know whether to ask about the boy or pretend it didn't happen.

"That was Chris," Sara said, taking the decision out of his hands.

"How do you know him?" Adam asked as they entered the classroom.

"He's in my English class. He asked me out last week. We went on a date on Friday, and then again on Saturday."

"Oh," was the only reply Adam had. He'd been wondering why they hadn't hung out over the weekend, even though he'd spent that time looking for Smokey. Sara didn't want to tell him she had a date.

"Yeah, he's really sweet," she continued even though Adam didn't want her to. "I'm not sure how I really feel yet, but it's nice because he actually bothered to make a move. Sometimes guys just make you wait forever to realize they aren't going to."

Adam didn't know how to respond. Was she talking about him? Should he have made a move over the summer? Was it too late now? Maybe he should ask her out before things got serious with Chris.

The bell rang before Adam had a chance to say anything. He wouldn't have the guts to ask her out anyway. Especially now that she was dating someone, even if it wasn't serious yet. Adam definitely wasn't going to make a move until Sara stopped seeing Chris.

As they'd done the year before, Adam had been eating lunch every day with Sara and the other boys who liked to hang out with her at school. Today, Adam sat alone at lunch. He expected Sara to show up, but she never did. Without her, the others didn't bother to sit with him. Adam saw them eating in the far corner of the cafeteria where they thought he couldn't spot them. Fortunately, Adam was sitting in view of the lunch staff, where Derek couldn't do anything to him.

"Where were you during lunch?" he asked Sara as she arrived

at trigonometry. "I waited for you, but you never showed up."

"Oh, my gosh, I'm so sorry," she told him. "I totally forgot to tell you. Chris invited me to lunch off-campus. I didn't mean to leave you waiting."

"That's alright," Adam replied, pretending he wasn't devastated. Of course it wasn't eating alone that was devastating. It was that she went to eat with Chris. "I realized you weren't coming and ate without you. It's fine."

"Well, I really am sorry. I'll make sure to tell you the next time we go off-campus to eat together."

Adam didn't like the ending of that apology. At least she still hung out with him in class. Just like the year before, they sat in the back of the room and went over their notes together. Sara was constantly leaning over to talk to Adam about class. At least he still had his study partner.

After school, Adam continued his routine of looking for Smokey. When he got home, he dropped off his backpack, shoveled down his dinner as quickly as possible, and went looking at Smokey's alley.

"Smokey! Smokey!" he shouted as loud as his lungs could manage. There had never been any reply. Adam was starting to give up hope of ever finding him, but he wasn't ready to give up looking just yet.

He arrived at the alley and snuck over to Smokey's car to look underneath. He was always careful not to let anyone see him. He didn't want anyone to know about the stray dog that lived there. He especially didn't want them to know that he stole food every night. It didn't matter. There was still no sign of Smokey under the heap of rusted metal.

Where could he be? Adam wondered as he kept searching calling Smokey's name. After checking at the park again, Adam called off the search for the day. To his dismay, his father's car was already in the driveway when he got there. Adam had intended to make it home before his father and sneak upstairs, but he hadn't made it back in time.

Peaking in the front window, Adam saw his father rummaging through the fridge and pulling out a bottle of beer. Adam tucked his head back where it couldn't be seen and watched his father's shadow as he walked into the living room and flopped onto the couch. The sound of the TV let Adam know it definitely wasn't the time to go inside.

With nothing else to do, he resumed his search for Smokey. As soon as he was far enough away from his house, he started calling out for Smokey again. He walked the mile between his house and Smokey's alley for an hour, but he never heard an answer back.

"What are you doing out here?" a woman yelled from her front door as Adam walked back to his neighborhood.

"I'm just looking for my dog," Adam told her.

"Well, how long has he been missing?" she asked.

"About a week now."

"A week? Oh, no! Was your dog a big black mangy-looking mutt?"

"Yes!" Adam exclaimed excitedly. "He is! Have you seen him?"

"Yes, I have," the woman said as she approached Adam. "Last week, he was running up and down the sidewalk for hours. He was barking the entire time. I went around and asked everyone if they knew where he'd come from. Nobody had ever seen him before. I'm so sorry. I thought he was a stray."

"Well, did you see where he went?" Adam asked. "I've been looking all week and I haven't seen any sign of him."

"Well, you see," she said, "I called animal control when I thought he was just a stray. The pound came and picked him up."

"The pound?" Adam asked, sounding mortified.

"Yes. He put up a real fight, too. That's one mean dog you have there. I think he even bit one of the men from the pound. You should probably go get your parents and go to the pound if you ever want to see your dog again. In my opinion, though, you should probably just get another dog. That one didn't look like he was really made to be a pet. Way too vicious."

Vicious? Smokey wasn't vicious. He was just defending himself from men he thought were attacking him. He was the sweetest dog in the world. None of this would have happened if Smokey hadn't thought Adam went missing when he went back to school. That was all it was. He had been looking for Adam.

"Excuse me," Adam said after he finished the five-mile walk to the pound after the lady had given him the address.

"I'm sorry, but we just closed for the night," a man at the front desk told him.

"I was told you picked up my dog," Adam continued anyway.

"Oh, alright. Did he have any tags or a tracking chip?"

"No," Adam said, even though he wasn't sure about the tracking chip.

"Okay, we have a book of pictures we take of all the dogs we pick up. When did your dog go missing?"

"Last week."

"Okay. Find your dog and let me know," the man said, handing Adam the book of dog photos.

Turning the pages, Adam found Smokey's picture. He had never seen Smokey like that before. He looked angry as they held him back with a catch pole. Still, Adam recognized his dog.

"That's him!" he exclaimed. "That one there! Can I have him back?"

"Okay, come back tomorrow and I'll get him out for you," the man said. "Of course you'll need to bring one of your parents with you." Suddenly, the man's facial expression changed, and he spoke in a concerned voice when he turned the book to see the picture. "Oh, I'm sorry, kid. Your dog bit one of our guys. We had to put him down."

"Put him down?" Adam asked, feeling like his stomach had jumped into his chest.

"Yeah, you know," the man said, not wanting to say it out loud. "We, uh…you know, gave him a lethal injection."

Adam couldn't believe what he was hearing. He nearly fell to the floor. Smokey was gone forever. Not only that, but he'd found out on the same day he'd found out Sara was dating someone else. The day could not have possibly gone any worse.

Chapter 21

It was almost time for Christmas vacation. Adam hadn't hung out with Sara outside of school since the year began. Even at school, he only saw her in class. During lunch, she always left to go eat with Chris. Adam was back to his old routine of hiding in the bathroom to eat his lunch.

Adam hated seeing Sara and Chris walking together. They were always holding hands. As they passed each other in the halls, Sara always used her other hand to wave at Adam. Adam was forced to smile and wave back as he pretended he wasn't dying inside.

Every day, Adam would show up to school and hope that today would be the day Sara told him she'd broken up with Chris. Every day, he was disappointed. The worst part about it was that she liked to talk to Adam about it. He couldn't tell her he didn't want to hear it. He always just pretended to be interested.

Adam was on his way to chemistry class. He always tried to beat Sara there. Chris always walked her to class, and Adam didn't want to see them together. Today, however, he got held up in his first-period class and wasn't sure if he would get there quickly enough.

They were already there when he got to class, standing outside the room with their fingers interlaced. Adam tried to ignore it, but he couldn't help but look as he drew closer. He wanted to turn around but couldn't.

Suddenly, Sara leaned in closer to Chris. Her beautiful blue eyes closed as she pressed her lips against his. Chris ran a hand through her dark chestnut hair before placing his palm on her cheek and pressing his face against hers. Sara wrapped her free arm around him as they continued to kiss.

Adam was fifty feet away when they started kissing. He walked all the way down the hall and passed them into the classroom, but they still hadn't stopped. He had always assumed they did that, but this was the first time he'd ever had to see it.

He couldn't get the image out of his head of their lips smacking together. The fact that she hadn't come into the classroom yet meant that they were probably still doing it. Adam tried to forget it and control his breathing. He didn't want to be freaking out when Sara came in and sat next to him, but the sight of her kissing him was seared into his mind.

She didn't walk in until after the bell rang. It had been two minutes since they'd started kissing. Were they kissing the entire time? Adam really didn't want to see her right now, but he had no choice.

"Hey, there," Sara said after Adam didn't say anything like he normally would.

"Hey," he said back without making eye contact.

"How's your day going?"

"Fine," Adam lied, pretending it didn't feel like she was shoving her hand into his chest and ripping out his heart. "How is your day going so far?"

"Really good, actually. I got a ride to school with Chris, so we got to hang out for a bit before school started. It was a lot of fun."

"Oh, yeah, that does sound like fun," Adam said even though

he wished she had spent her morning doing pretty much anything else.

During the summer, he often fantasized about them being together once the school year started. He envisioned her meeting him at school and the two of them hanging out until it was time to go to class. He expected it to be him kissing her out in the hallway before class started. How had things gone from good to bad out of nowhere?

"Well, I think we better pay attention," Adam told her, trying to make certain she didn't talk about Chris anymore.

"Oh, yes. Sorry, you're right."

The lesson helped, but it couldn't distract Adam enough to stop him from thinking about Sara kissing someone else. He kept looking at her. She was so beautiful with her long black hair, glowing eyes that seemed to make life a little brighter, and her sweet, soft lips. Every time Adam looked at her lips, he couldn't help but think of someone else kissing them and how she would close her eyes when he did.

Adam couldn't prevent his thoughts from going to the worst places. What if they never broke up? What if, after high school, she left to go off to some other school with Chris? If that happened, he would certainly never see her again.

*   *   *

When he got home that day, Adam needed a distraction. He couldn't stop thinking about Sara wrapping her arm around Chris as he had her face against his. He hadn't even been the one to initiate the kiss. She had.

The whole event had one positive side to it, however. Adam's need for a distraction gave him the motivation to study even harder. At first, it was difficult. He would read a sentence only to realize he had no idea what it said because his mind was blocked by the memory of Sara kissing Chris. But once he got his mind to focus, Adam studied like he never had before.

Hours went by and he never slowed down. There was no time between reading and working on his homework. He couldn't leave any room in his brain for the memory of today to creep back inside. He even pulled out his next book while still reading the one he was on. By the time he was done, he'd finished the entire week's worth of work in one night. He tried rereading the chapters, but that wasn't enough to keep him focused. And as determined as he was, he just didn't have the motivation to read ahead.

Adam looked around for something to do. He didn't have a lot in his room. There was no TV, and that would be too loud anyway. As he searched around for another distraction, he glanced at his dresser and remembered his mom's journal hidden in one of the drawers.

He was hesitant to read any more, but he had nothing else to do, and he couldn't just sit there thinking about Sara kissing someone. As he pulled the journal out of his drawer, Adam felt uneasy about reading it on his bed. What if his father barged in and caught him with it? What would he do?

He sat on the floor between his bed and his dresser. This way, if his father charged into the room, Adam could slip the journal under the dresser where it wouldn't be found. Once he got comfortable, Adam opened the book to a random page and started to read.

About once a month, Mom made a bunch of food and took it to the local homeless shelter when they were serving dinner. As she cooked, Adam played in the backyard. He had his best friend over for the day. The two of them were tossing a baseball back and forth. It was growing rather hot, but they had no intention of stopping. They could do that all day if no one stopped them.

"Adam!" Mom yelled through the kitchen window.

"Yes, Mom?" he answered back.

"It's a little hot out there. I think it's time to come inside."

"But Mom," Adam argued, "we aren't done yet. And it's not even that hot. Just a little bit longer?"

"Fine. Come in and drink some water and then the two of you can go back outside."

Mom kept cooking as the boys came into the kitchen. Adam pulled two cups out of the cabinet and filled them with water.

"Make sure to drink all of it," she told them. "Don't take a sip and then go back outside."

"Of course, Mom," Adam sniped back.

"And when you go back outside, throw the ball under the tree so you're in the shade. You don't need to get a sunburn."

"But Mom," Adam whined, "there isn't enough room under the tree for both of us to throw a ball."

"Oh, there's plenty of room. You'll be standing a little closer together, but it's plenty far enough to toss a ball back and forth."

"Fine," Adam complained.

Adam's mom had them drink the full glasses in the kitchen so she could ensure they finished them. The boys chugged their water, eager to get back outside. Once the glasses were empty, they grabbed their mitts and ran back outside.

Even as his hand grew sore, Adam had no desire to stop throwing the ball. His friend had recently grown to be a bit larger than him, and with his new strength, Adam's hand began to bruise after hours of catching his throws. There was no way Adam was going to admit that, however. He wasn't going to be the one to suggest they should stop; his friend would have to do it.

In the end, neither one of them decided it was time to finally go inside.

"Adam!" Mom called again from the window. "Time to come inside, now."

"Just a little bit longer, Mom?"

"No, it's time to come in. Come on. I made both of you a plate of food. Come and eat."

"Okay," Adam sighed as he and his friend went back inside again.

On the table were two heaping plates of spaghetti. On the counter were two large pots filled with spaghetti, and a large pot of sauce.

"Alright, you two help me carry these to the car and then come back in and eat," Mom told them. "I'm going to take this to the shelter. I'll be back in thirty minutes."

Once she was gone, Adam and his friend grabbed the plates and carried their mountains of spaghetti to the living room where they could watch TV as they ate. They laughed and joked as they ate and watched TV. It didn't take long before both of them had slurped down all the spaghetti on their plates.

Adam and his friend were practically inseparable. During the summer, they hung out every day. During the school year, they were together every weekend. Their teachers even often mixed them up.

Hours passed before they finally stopped watching TV. Once the sun began setting, they went into the backyard to throw the ball again. The temperature was much cooler now, and they could toss the ball all night without any problems. Eventually, their fun had to end.

"Okay, Adam," Mom called from the back door. "It's about time to be done for the night."

"But Mom!" Adam complained.

"No! It's time. You two can play together tomorrow. It's not that big of a deal."

The boys said goodbye and Adam's friend left through the gate and walked home. After he'd gone, Adam continued tossing the ball, practicing his pitch by throwing the ball against the tree. Without a friend, it got boring very quickly, and eventually, he went back inside.

Adam thought back to that day. Life had been pretty good back then. His mother was alive. His father had never beaten him before. Adam enjoyed going to school, too. Nobody bullied him back then.

Now, Adam didn't have any friends to come over to hang out with. He hadn't had a friend over since his mom died. The days of playing baseball in the backyard were over. They were never coming back. Now the most Adam had to look forward to was leaving and never seeing that backyard again.

He didn't even have Sara anymore now that she was with someone else.

Getting ready for bed, Adam's mind went back to the horrible images of the day. He didn't need to go back to how things were years ago. He would have been happy just going back to how they were a few months ago. But just like those days when his mom was still around, the good days of summer vacation were over forever.

Chapter 22

When he woke up the next morning, Adam only experienced a brief moment of peace before he remembered what he'd seen the day before. It distracted him all morning. It was all he could think about, and he barely paid any attention during his first class.

When it came time to go to second period, Adam rushed there as fast as he could. He had to get to chemistry before Sara did. He couldn't see her with Chris outside the door again. Certainly not today.

Although he got there before Sara, it didn't take his mind off it. He sat thinking about how she was probably walking to class now, holding his hand. Once they got there, they would stand around the corner, say goodbye, and then they'd make out again.

Watching the door, Adam waited for Sara to come inside. Once she was in the room, he could know she wasn't kissing him. It wouldn't change anything, but at least for the moment, she would be sitting next to him and not Chris.

Finally, just a minute before the bell rang, she walked through the door. Adam sighed in relief but still imagined she'd been out there kissing him just a moment ago. Why couldn't she just break up with him and tell Adam she wanted to be with him? Why couldn't things just go back to the way they were over the summer?

Still, Adam enjoyed his time with her. Even though Sara had a boyfriend now, she was still so sweet to Adam. They joked around in their classes and compared notes, and Sara would occasionally lean in and whisper in Adam's ear. At times, it was almost enough to make Adam forget she even had a boyfriend.

At least there's no chance of her marrying him, Adam thought to himself. That was the nice thing about high school. There was plenty of time for her and Chris to break up. Maybe it was even a good thing Adam wasn't dating her right now. High school relationships never lasted anyway. Later, the two of them could get together and it would last forever. Adam would just have to be patient. He'd already learned to do that while waiting to graduate. But it would still be really hard.

When the bell rang at the end of trigonometry class, Sara asked Adam to go with her to the library and talk about what they'd gone over in class. Adam was happy to. He was just glad she didn't rush off to go see her boyfriend like she often did at the end of the day. Maybe things weren't going as well between them and she didn't want to see him?

The bus would be leaving soon. As they got to the library, Adam looked at the clock. The bus would be leaving in five minutes. Despite being worried about missing it, Adam had no intention of giving up any time he had to spend with her.

Another ten minutes passed. Adam knew the bus was gone and that he'd have to walk home. As annoying as that was, he didn't really care. Sara had spent time talking to Adam that she could have spent with her boyfriend. Maybe things were actually changing between them.

Suddenly, Sara placed her hand on Adam's. She had reached

over to point at something Adam was writing. She wasn't really holding his hand, but Adam didn't particularly care. It was still nice to have her palm resting on the back of his hand. It was almost as if she was holding his hand. Or at the very least indicating her desire to.

Adam considered placing his other hand on top of hers. He wasn't sure if he had the guts to do it, but he really wanted to take the opportunity to finally make his move. If he let the chance pass him by, how long would he have to wait for another one? Would things get better between Sara and Chris, resulting in him never having a chance again? Maybe he should just try it. It wouldn't be that big of a risk.

"Oh, shoot!" Sara exclaimed as Adam slowly moved his hand, trying to build up the courage to put it on hers.

He put his hand down. "What?"

"I didn't realize what time it was. I was supposed to meet Chris five minutes ago." She pulled her hand away. "He had some stuff to do for a class. I told him I'd meet him twenty-five minutes after class ended. I can't believe it's already been thirty!" She started packing up her bag. "I can't believe you stayed with me this long. Do you have a way to get home? You can get a ride with me and Chris if you want to. I know you normally ride the bus."

"No, it's fine. I have a ride," Adam lied, not wanting to have to ride with her boyfriend. "I'll be okay."

"Okay, good. I'd feel really bad if you had to walk because of me."

Adam didn't tell her that was exactly what he would have to do now. Sara sped out the door and was gone. All of Adam's hopes faded away. She hadn't spent time with him because she wanted to be with him and not Chris. It was because she'd been waiting for Chris and had nothing better to do. Still, the thirty minutes had been great. The way she'd kept her hand on his for so long couldn't have been a bad thing. Unless, of course, she did that with all her friends.

No matter the reason, it didn't change Adam's position. He was stuck at school and would have to walk. He put his trigonometry book and notes into his backpack and left. Despite how it had ended, his time with Sara had been worth it.

Adam walked quickly. The school was miles from his house. It would take over an hour to walk the whole way. He had to get home before his father did. It didn't occur to Adam until he left the school, but he probably wouldn't be able to get any food before that happened, so he'd likely have to go hungry tonight.

It was very cold outside. Adam didn't have anything except a light jacket to keep him warm. He had outgrown all his gloves a long time ago, and his father certainly wasn't going to take him to get new ones. The frigid air made the tips of his fingers sting.

As terrible as it was, the cold helped motivate Adam to get home faster. His fingers and ears froze, and his legs were almost sweating from walking so fast. Just as he was turning the corner onto his street, a car pulled up beside him and Derek jumped out of the passenger seat, followed by his friends.

"Look who it is," Derek said, surprised by his luck in driving past Adam. "Look at the loser walking home from school. Way to miss the bus, you idiot."

Derek grabbed Adam's shoulder strap and pulled off his backpack. Adam tried to take it back, but Brandon and Miles held him back so he couldn't get to it. Derek unzipped the bag and dumped Adam's books and supplies all over the sidewalk as he walked away from Adam, ensuring it was spread out and more difficult to pick up.

"Stop it!" Adam yelled in despair.

"Stop it," Derek repeated in a mocking voice as he finished dumping the bag and threw the backpack into the street. "Shut up! You're so pathetic."

Walking over to Adam, Derek pushed him to the ground. With a swift swing of his leg, Derek kicked Adam's thigh. Derek's friends joined in, kicking the back of Adam's legs. Once he grew tired of kicking, Derek pulled off Adam's jacket and threw it on the ground. Then he took a water bottle from the car and dumped it all over Adam's jacket so it would be too wet to wear.

When he was done, Derek went back and joined his friends as they repeatedly kicked Adam's legs. They were relentless in their beating, not stopping until they saw another car approaching. Once they did, they all piled back into Derek's friend's car, who had waited in the driver's seat so they could leave quickly. Adam watched as the driver laughed and high-fived them all; Adam still didn't know what the driver's name was.

"Try walking home now, idiot," Derek yelled at Adam from inside the car just before they pulled away.

Adam attempted to lift himself onto his feet. On the first try, his legs gave out before he even got off the ground. He fell back down to the sidewalk in agony. During his second attempt, he made it to his feet before his thighs screamed and his knees buckled, causing him to tumble to the ground.

Screaming, Adam grabbed his left elbow as it smacked into the concrete. Blood ran through his fingers. Derek wasn't even here anymore, but he was still managing to hurt Adam.

Finally, on his third attempt, Adam managed to climb to his feet and stay standing. After checking his stability, he looked down at the bloody handprint he'd left in the middle of the square on the sidewalk. He wondered what the people who lived there would think if they saw it before it washed away.

Adam pulled a piece of paper from his backpack and used it as a bandage for his arm. It didn't really do much, but it was all he had. Even once he got home, he couldn't do much for it except rinse it off and wait for it to stop bleeding. Maybe he could use a rag or a paper towel.

Once the bleeding had slowed down enough, he wiped his bloody hand on his pants. He couldn't get any of it on his books. He especially didn't want to have to explain to Sara tomorrow why there was blood on his pages. He doubted she was still truly believing his excuses every time she saw him dirty and beaten. Luckily, neither Derek nor his father wanted the attention a beaten and bruised face would create, so they always stuck to beating him where his clothes would hide it. Sara wouldn't see the bruises on his legs hidden under his pants.

After getting all his books into his backpack without staining them with blood, Adam threw the strap over his shoulder and limped the rest of the way home. His disappointment continued when he got there and saw his father pull in. If it hadn't been for Derek and his friends, Adam would have gotten home with plenty of time to spare. But now it was too late.

Ignoring Adam, his father got out of the car and headed inside. He saw Adam, but he was just getting home from work and wasn't drunk yet. The random beatings usually started after his drinking. Until then, his father generally treated him with mild neglect, as if he simply didn't exist. Still, Adam didn't want to provoke him. He waited until his father was inside before going in himself.

As he entered his room, Adam dropped his jacket and backpack on his bed. His right hand was nearly frostbitten after carrying his wet jacket the rest of the way home. His hands had already been numb before Derek and his friends showed up.

In the bathroom, he used the back of his hand to turn on the sink; his fingers were incapable of turning the handle. He barely managed to get it on and turned to warm so that he could thaw out his hands. He thought about taking a hot shower, but he didn't want the sound to remind his father he was there.

Once his hands were warm and his arm was rinsed of blood, he went downstairs. His father had gone to the bathroom, and Adam used the time to sneak into the kitchen. He grabbed some paper towels for his elbow and a few pieces of plain, untoasted bread for dinner and went back to his room.

Just as he finished making certain the bleeding had stopped, his father came into his room, an empty bottle of gin in his hand. With a swing of his arm, Adam's father threw the bottle at him. As if he had known just where to aim, the bottle struck Adam in the left thigh, exactly where it hurt the worst.

His legs gave out again and he hit the floor. His father walked over and kicked him in the stomach. The pain in his thighs was enough that Adam barely even noticed the pain in his stomach.

After only a single kick, his father left and went back downstairs. Adam snatched up the paper towels and pushed them back into his elbow. Although his beating had been short, the fall had caused his elbow to start bleeding again.

Once everything was over, Adam didn't have a lot of time left that night and only managed to get an hour of studying in before it was time for bed. He already had all his homework done, and there wasn't a lot being assigned right before winter break anyway.

As he lay in bed, Adam wondered if the thirty minutes with Sara had been worth the consequences. Annoyed, he decided he didn't want to think about her tonight.

He pulled out his mom's journal again so that he could think of something else, something before any of this had ever happened. This time he didn't care enough to hide in the corner, so he lay in his bed with the journal and opened it to a random page.

Adam was hanging out with his friend. Mom made them sit at the kitchen table and finish their homework before they could go into the backyard to play. They were in the same class at school and often did their homework together.

Anxious to get back to playing, they tried to get through it as quickly as possible. Adam generally finished first and then helped his friend finish so they could be done. Often, especially with math, his friend would simply copy Adam's homework—whatever it took to get done faster.

Once they finished, the two of them ran out the back door with their mitts to throw the ball around some more. That only lasted until Adam's mom looked over their homework. After finding several mistakes, she called them back inside to finish their homework.

"But we already did it," Adam protested.

"Scribbling a bunch of stuff onto a paper doesn't count as doing it," Mom said. "There are a lot of mistakes here. I know you two would rather be playing, but you have to do it right. Now get back in here."

Annoyed, the boys did as she said and came back inside. After she showed them what was wrong, they redid most of their math homework. Adam didn't have a hard time with math. He always found it easy. But he definitely had other stuff he'd rather be doing.

As much as he didn't want to, this time Adam bothered to do it right. He didn't want to have to come back inside again. That turned out to be the correct choice. Mom didn't let them go back outside until she had checked their work.

"Much better," she told them. "Now you two can go play."

Without a word, Adam and his friend ran out the door again. They didn't care all that much about school. They had crazy plans about playing professional sports and owning a big business together. School was pointless. They didn't know exactly how it would go, but they were going to be rich. The only thing they knew was that they were going to do it all together.

"Okay!" Mom shouted, calling from the door again. "It's time to be done. You two have school tomorrow."

Reluctantly, they stopped playing and put the ball away, and Adam helped his friend pack his backpack up so he could go home.

"Alright Adam," Mom said. "Say goodbye to Derek. It's time for him to go home. You two will see each other at school tomorrow."

Adam closed the journal. It was hard for him to believe that was the way things used to be. The person who tormented Adam every chance he got was once his best friend in the whole world.

Thinking back, Adam thought about how it had all changed. The answer to that couldn't be found in his mom's journal. It happened after she was gone—and Adam knew that if she was still here, the boys would still be friends.

For a while after Adam's mom died, the two of them didn't hang out anymore, but Derek waited patiently for Adam to feel better so they could play together again. Once he was feeling up to it, Adam started coming over to Derek's house. They couldn't play at Adam's house anymore because his father was drunk all the time.

One day, Derek gave Adam an invitation to his birthday party. Adam promised he would be there, but when the day came, he missed it. Before he was able to leave, Adam's father had gotten drunk again and beat him terribly. Instead of going to see his friend on his birthday, Adam spent the night holding his bruised ribs and hiding underneath his bed.

Adam didn't know it, but the three other boys Derek had invited to his party were also unable to go. When Adam didn't show up, a devastated Derek was left sitting at his house all alone on his birthday.

Derek never gave Adam the chance to explain why he hadn't

made it to his party. At school, he started sitting with other kids who eventually became his friends. He and Adam never hung out again.

Chapter 23

In the last weeks of tenth grade, Derek's tormenting of Adam got worse than ever. Before, Derek seemed to bully Adam only when he ran into him, whether in the halls or when he saw him on the bus. He'd never actively looked for Adam. But as the school year came to a close, Derek went out of his way to attack Adam—probably because he knew he wouldn't be able to during the summer.

Derek had been riding to school with his friends. Adam thought that would make the bus ride better. Instead, it only made it worse. Every day when the bus arrived at school, Derek was already there waiting for him. Now Adam could no longer sprint into school before Derek caught up. Because of this, there wasn't a single day of the final month of the school year that didn't start with an attack from Derek.

But summer brought no relief. Last summer had been Adam's best summer. This summer had been his worst. His father began to drink more than ever, and not a day went by that Adam wasn't beaten. Adam spent every night hiding under his bed or in his closet, only for his father to find him anyway. The beatings had become long and brutal. There was no time between them to let his bruises heal. Still, Adam held out hope that eleventh grade would be better. At least it was bringing him one year closer to college.

He hadn't talked to Sara all summer. He thought about calling her, but he was too nervous. They hadn't hung out all year because of her boyfriend. He didn't even know if they'd have any classes together. When the first day of class arrived, he looked forward to running into her, preferably in a few of their mutual classes. If they didn't have any classes together, at least he wouldn't have to see her with her boyfriend. Adam was trying to find the bright side in either possibility. After the past few months, he had to in order to himself keep going.

Adam grew quite anxious on his way out the door. What if Derek would still try hard to find him? Derek rode to school with his friends, but Adam still had to ride the bus. Derek knew when the bus arrived at school, which meant he could wait for Adam as he got off every day if he wanted to. It was possible this entire school year would be as bad as the last few weeks of the last one.

When the bus finally pulled up at school, Adam's heart was pounding. He looked for Derek and his friends. His body was already horribly bruised from his father beating him. He didn't need them to start adding to it.

Adam got off the bus as quickly as he could. He didn't see Derek anywhere but wasn't about to give him the chance to show up. Once he made it inside, he double-checked the room number of his first class and went straight there, managing to make it without running into Derek.

His first-period class was precalculus. There was no way Derek would be in this class, so Adam was safe to wait there until the bell rang. It was also highly likely that Sara would be in this class with him since they were at the same advanced math level. If she was going to be in any class with him, it would be this one.

Adam watched the door for Sara as several other students showed up long before the bell. Generally, people don't make it into precalculus unless they care enough to show up to class on time.

Eventually, the bell rang, but Sara never came. Adam hoped she was just running late, but that was unlikely and definitely not like her. There was only one other precalculus class being held this year. She must be taking that one.

Devastated, it took Adam a few minutes before he could concentrate on the teacher. Luckily, she was only talking about starting the new year and not anything having to do with the class.

Once he regained his focus, Adam opened his notebook and got ready to take notes. He really wanted to excel in this class. He was one of only five juniors in the room; the rest were all seniors. He felt forced to prove something. He also knew that if the others didn't care enough to study, they wouldn't be in this class at all, so it wouldn't be as easy to be at the top of the class as it had been before. He wanted to impress Sara. Even if she was taking the class in a different period, it was still possible they might study together.

He arrived at every class as early as possible and waited for Sara to show up. Each time, he was let down. Five minutes into his last class of the day, Adam knew Sara would not be in any of his classes. He hadn't even seen her in the halls. On the bright side, he hadn't run into Derek all day either.

Only one thing remained in the day: getting home. As the final bell rang, Adam rushed outside and toward his bus. He wanted to finish this day without having seen Derek at all. As he climbed on, he exhaled a sigh of relief. Even though he hadn't seen Sara and had no classes with her, maybe this school year wouldn't be as bad as he worried it might be.

A month into the new school year, Adam hadn't run into Sara a single time. He spent a lot of time in class wondering what she was up to and wishing she was sitting next to him. Precalculus was especially devastating without her. Adam missed his math partner. He had spent all summer assuming they would be in it together and fantasizing about studying with her. He wanted to call her every day after school, but he was always too nervous.

Still, he hadn't seen Derek once. Adam was having a hard time believing his luck. There were seven classes in a day, and at no time had he even passed him in the hallways.

Adam wasn't exactly upset that he could go to school without fear of being forced into a secluded area and getting beaten, or having something thrown on his clothes so that he had to walk around dirty for the rest of the day. Still, he was curious why he hadn't seen Derek. He had seen some of Derek's friends in the halls, but without Derek there, they pretty much pretended Adam didn't exist.

Things weren't perfect, but things at home were better than they had been during the summer. His daily beatings had decreased to weekly beatings. Ironically, while things had gotten worse over the summer because his father was drinking more, they were better now for the same reason. Most days, he was passed out before he could bother trying to find Adam.

One day, Adam heard his father screaming up the stairs as he was coming up, but he never actually made it there. Adam heard him stumbling around on the stairs as he yelled. He braced himself for what was coming next, but then nothing happened and eventually, things got quiet. When Adam came downstairs the next morning to leave for school, he found his father still laying on the stairs.

Astonished, Adam had to hold back his laughter as he thought about how lucky he'd been and how funny his father looked. He had to squeeze past him on his way, careful not to wake him up. Once he closed the door, he ran to the bus in case closing it had made enough noise to wake him.

When he got to school, Adam walked calmly off the bus and into the school. It had been long enough since he'd seen Derek that his vigilance had subsided. He wasn't going to keep up his dash to the doorway if nothing ever happened anymore.

Even in the hallways, Adam walked normally. He had lost the habit of staying away from corners in case Derek was hiding around them. He still walked quickly, but only at a pace necessary to ensure he got to class on time.

As Adam spent more time in the halls, he finally ran into Sara again.

"Oh, my gosh, Adam!" she exclaimed when she saw her friend for the first time in a while.

"Oh, hey!" Adam said as a huge smile came across his face. He thought he would be nervous the first time he saw her again. Instead, he was just happy to finally get to look into those eyes he'd missed so much.

Sara told him she'd been planning on going to class to study before first period, but instead suggested they find a place to sit and catch up. She told him about all the fun things she did over the summer, and Adam tried to make his sound less horrible without lying to her.

"You have precalc first period?" she asked as their conversation moved into the school year. "That sucks! I almost took that one, but I didn't want to study math so early in the morning. We could have taken that together. That class is hard, isn't it?"

Adam pretended it was as the first bell rang, indicating it was time to head to class.

"I'm sorry I haven't been able to eat lunch with you," Sara said as they stood. "Chris takes me out to lunch every day. We need to start hanging out again, though. We can study together. I've missed you." She gave Adam a quick hug and then left for class.

Since Sara ate lunch with Chris off-campus, Adam maintained his habit of getting his food quickly and eating it in the bathroom stall. As gross as it was eating in the bathroom, eating in the cafeteria wasn't worth the risk of running into Derek. He figured if he was going to run into him anywhere, it would be there. At least no one could mess with his food in the bathroom.

Today was pizza day, and Adam grabbed his food and went to the bathroom. He was pretty sure the pizza was specially made to be stale by the time it came out of the oven. He was still going to eat it, of course. Ever since his father's drinking had gotten worse, there wasn't a lot to eat at home, and his school lunch had become his biggest meal of the day.

Adam heard people come into the bathroom and pulled his feet back, hoping not to be noticed. He chewed slowly and quietly, not wanting to let them know he was eating in the bathroom like a weirdo. At least the blandness of the pizza kept it from having too much of an aroma so they were unlikely to smell it.

When they started talking, Adam recognized their voices. Derek wasn't with them, but he could tell that these were his friends. It was odd to see them at lunch without him. Why was he not with his friends?

Even without Derek there, Adam grew nervous. These were the last people he wanted to run into. Of all the bathrooms in the school, why did they have to end up in this one? He had even gone to one far from the cafeteria to avoid the chance of someone coming in during lunch.

"What are we going to do after school today?" Davis asked.

"Not sure," Brandon answered. "Last year, we went to Derek's house because his parents didn't get back for hours, but obviously we can't do that anymore."

Obviously we can't do that anymore? Adam stopped chewing and listened closely, desperate to find out what that meant.

"Yeah, it really sucks that Derek's gone."

Gone? What did he mean gone? Was he gone forever? Had they just stopped being friends? Where was Derek?

"It was dumb that he had to move," Davis continued. "His parents couldn't have just waited until he finished high school to leave?"

Adam couldn't believe what he was hearing. Was Derek really gone forever? Even after hearing them say it, it still seemed too good to be true. He wanted to jump and scream in excitement but had to restrain himself so they wouldn't know he was there.

"I wonder what happened to that kid we used to always pick on?" Miles asked.

"I've seen him in the halls a few times," Brandon answered. "I don't really care anymore. Derek was the one who hated him. I don't actually even know his name. I think Derek said it once or twice, but I don't remember what it was."

They left the bathroom. Adam could barely manage to contain his excitement. He was still hungry, and he didn't want to throw his food all over the floor of the bathroom stall, but with the need to be there gone, he took his food and backpack and went outside. Derek was gone, and his friends clearly didn't care about tormenting Adam without him. There was no need to eat his food sitting on a toilet anymore.

Excitedly, Adam walked down the halls as fast as he could. He was no longer walking quickly out of fear. His days of being afraid were over. Now he was walking fast because he was happy and had too much energy to slow down.

He took in a deep breath of fresh air. It was so much better than the smell of the bathroom, which wasn't cleaned nearly enough. Looking around, Adam chose a spot of grass where he could lean against the wall and sit. As he ate, the food seemed to taste better. It wasn't just that the taste was no longer combined with the smell of toilets. Adam was just happier.

For the rest of the day, he was on top of the world. He strolled to his classes happily. In each class, he found a newly intensified ability to focus. He took tons of notes. Once the teacher was done talking, he burned through his homework while the other kids chatted. By the time the day ended, Adam barely had any work left to do at home. Life was looking better again.

Casually, Adam got up from his seat as the final bell rang. He walked to the bus at a normal pace. Some of the other kids were even passing him in the halls. He had plenty of time to get there and no reason to rush. He was enjoying the walk.

For the first time all year, Adam was sad to see the school day end. Up to now, school was just another place where someone might hurt him, but now it was a place he wanted to be. At home, things would be back to the way they'd always been. Still, that didn't bring his spirits down. All he had to do was make it to the next day.

Chapter 24

dam's newfound spirits didn't fade away. Months passed, and he was still just as motivated every day at school. He studied with Sara a couple of times a week. Derek was gone. He was even eating lunch in the cafeteria again. Without the need to walk all the way to the bathroom, he was finishing much earlier than he had before, which meant he could go to his next class early and use the room to do his homework during lunch.

By the time he got home from school, Adam never had any homework left, but that didn't stop him from using the time to study anyway. By the time Christmas break arrived, he was done learning everything in his textbooks and didn't have anything left for the rest of the school year.

For most kids, Christmas break was their favorite time of the year, with weeks off from school where they didn't have to do anything. For Adam, it was the exact opposite, especially this year. Instead of being able to go to school, he had to stay at home where his father was for weeks. He would also have to spend that time only eating food from home, and there wasn't a lot of that this year.

Anxiously, Adam walked up the stairs when he got home from

school on the first day of the break. He wanted to spend his entire break studying so that he could be done with the whole year by the time he went back to school. When the time came, however, Adam found he was too stressed out to bring himself to study.

Sitting on his bed, he waited, dreading the moment his father would get home. Adam wasn't the only one who got time off during the break. Adam's father also got a few extra days off from work. During this time, he would be home all day. Who knew how that would turn out?

The night wore on, and Adam heard his father come home and turn on the TV like he always did. He listened for the sound of clinking bottles and drunken yelling. But as the hours passed, it never came. Curious as to why, Adam snuck over to the stairs and peeked through the railing.

His father was on the couch, watching TV. He wasn't in his usual slumped posture. He was sitting up and actually paying attention to what he was watching. Usually, he was completely oblivious to what he was watching. With great astonishment, Adam saw the coffee table was empty. There wasn't a single bottle on it, or anywhere else that Adam could see.

Confused, Adam thought back over the events of the last month. He realized he hadn't seen any bottles on the coffee table for weeks. The trash can was normally filled with them, but Adam hadn't seen them in there. What was going on?

Creeping back to his room, Adam lay down on his bed. Was this a good sign or a bad one? How long would it take before his father came in to beat him? Would it be tonight? How much would it happen during the break? Why weren't there any bottles anywhere? Was it because there wasn't any money for alcohol anymore? Did this mean there wouldn't be enough for food? How much would Adam get to eat in the next couple of weeks?

Days passed. Adam managed to study quite a bit. He kept waiting for his father to swing open his door and come in, drunk and screaming, but it never happened. Adam didn't know why, but he was glad about it. But how long would it last?

Then one morning, Adam woke to the sound of his bedroom door handle turning. He opened his eyes and stared into the doorway. Petrified, he stared at his father looking at him from the hallway. Adam wanted to get up and run, but he couldn't move.

"I made breakfast," his father said from the doorway. "Come downstairs and eat."

Adam was confused. Breakfast? His father never made breakfast. This was the last thing Adam expected to happen. Cautiously, he dressed and went downstairs, but his father had already left for work. On the table was a plate of food. It had pancakes, bacon, and eggs.

He double-checked to make certain his father was really gone, and when he knew the house was empty, he approached the plate cautiously, as if it might suddenly explode. Adam had no idea what was going on, and he didn't know how to feel about it.

After getting the syrup and a fork, Adam sat down in front of the plate. He drenched the pancakes in syrup and slowly took his first bite. To his surprise, the food was delicious. Once he started, he didn't stop until he finished everything on the plate. It was the best meal he'd had in a while, especially since he hadn't been eating much during the break.

When he was finished eating, he cleaned his dishes and went back upstairs. He didn't know what he was supposed to do next, so he went back to his normal routine of hiding in his room as often as he could in case his father came back unexpectedly. There he continued studying and working through practice problems.

After staying in his room most of the day, Adam heard his

father come home from work. He crept to his bedroom door and listened, still not wanting to risk opening it even a crack. He waited for the usual sounds of alcohol bottles, yelling, and the TV. To Adam's surprise, he didn't even hear the sound of the TV.

Giving up, he went back to his bed to continue studying. He really wanted to know what his father was doing, but he couldn't risk leaving his room when he had no idea where he was. He wouldn't even risk leaving to go to the bathroom until he heard the television.

"Dinner's ready," his father said, popping his head into Adam's room after an hour.

Startled, Adam nearly threw his precalculus book off the bed as he jumped. "Okay," he finally managed to say after several seconds of trying to comprehend the situation.

Hesitantly, Adam set his books on the nightstand and went downstairs. Did his father expect him to eat at the table with him? Even if he didn't plan on beating Adam, it just seemed like that would be awkward at this point. Why was his father suddenly being nicer?

Whatever the answer, Adam didn't have a choice but to go downstairs and see what happened. He decided he'd rather risk a beating for going to get food than for ignoring his father.

Looking into the kitchen, Adam didn't see his father at the table. As he walked closer, he heard the sound of the television playing in his father's room. He hadn't noticed it before because the volume was set to a much more reasonable level and not screeching like it usually did in the living room.

Adam was still curious as to what was happening, but he was relieved to not have to see his father. On the table was a plate of baked chicken and mashed potatoes with a can of orange soda next to it. He didn't want to risk eating at the table with his father in the next room, so he took everything upstairs to his room.

Adam wasn't very hungry. He'd made sure to eat before his father came home, but he wasn't going to waste the opportunity to eat. He didn't get enough food as it was. Even after he was full, he forced down every last bite. Then, as quietly as he could, Adam snuck back downstairs to clean his plate.

Normally, he would wait until his father had gone to work to bring the plate back down, but today he decided to see how it went. He was also pretty sure today was the last day his father worked until after Christmas, so if he didn't take it back down, the plate would be sitting in Adam's room for the next five days.

When he was done cleaning his dishes, Adam looked in the fridge. There was no alcohol in it, and there wasn't any in the cabinets, either. Was it possible his father had stopped drinking?

For the next few days at dinner, Adam's father made a plate of food and left it on the table for Adam before going back to his room to watch TV. Adam didn't know why he'd stopped, but life was definitely better since his father quit drinking.

On Christmas morning, Adam went into the kitchen and made breakfast. His father was still asleep, and he was careful not to wake him, afraid he might still get beaten if he woke him up. When he finished making his food, he started back to his room but stopped when he saw a tree sitting on the living room coffee table. It was undecorated and looked almost like a branch that had fallen off a tree, but he could tell it was supposed to be a Christmas tree. He hadn't seen one in the house since before his mom died.

Underneath the tree, Adam saw two boxes. He walked over and looked at them. They were unwrapped, nothing more than taped-shut cardboard boxes. The words *To Adam, from Dad* were written on the top of the boxes.

Adam hadn't received a present in years. He didn't even know what to do with them. Should he just take them upstairs now, or should he wait until his father woke up to open them? He decided to leave them there and wait to see what happened.

He spent the rest of the day in his room, waiting all morning to see if his father said anything, but he never did. It wasn't until dinner when his father popped his head into his bedroom door and told him dinner was ready that he found out what was happening.

This time, when Adam went downstairs, his father was sitting at the table eating. Adam looked at the seat next to him and saw a plate of food. Cautiously, he sat down next to his father and started to eat. Adam was beginning to think his father didn't know how to make anything else. The same baked chicken and mashed potatoes weren't as much as most people were probably eating for Christmas dinner, but it was more than Adam had had in years.

Without a word between them, they finished eating their meals. To most people, it would have been considered a very awkward dinner. To Adam, he was just happy his father wasn't beating him anymore. It was probably the longest the two of them had been in the same room together since his mom had died.

"There's some presents under the tree for you," his father said as he left the kitchen and went back to his room.

"Thanks," Adam said, although it took him too long to reply and he wasn't sure his father heard him.

After he finished washing his dishes, Adam went into the living room to get the boxes under the tree. He found the tree moved into the corner of the room. It was still undecorated and so small it looked like an old houseplant sitting in the corner, but to Adam it felt more like Christmas than it had in years. His father wasn't there, and he still felt uncomfortable being down there, so he took the presents up to his room to open them.

Sitting on his bed, Adam tore open a box and found a package of socks. Generally, a teenage kid wouldn't be very happy about getting socks for Christmas, but Adam was excited. Most of his socks were worn down, and he needed new ones. The other box contained a new jacket. He didn't know which present he liked more. He couldn't wait to go back to school wearing his new jacket and fresh socks.

It was the best Christmas vacation Adam had had in a long time. He wasn't beaten once, and he didn't have to spend the entire time hiding in his room. By the end of it, things were starting to become less awkward between him and his father, and the two of them even had a few actual conversations. Adam didn't know why things had changed, but he was glad about it.

As Adam got ready for school on the first day after the break, he was still trying to be quiet, but it wasn't out of fear of being beaten. Now it was just because it would be rude to make a bunch of noise while his father was still sleeping. He was able to do a little more in the morning, though. Before he left for school, he went into the kitchen and made a couple of peanut butter sandwiches for breakfast that he would eat while waiting for class to start.

As he finished sticking the sandwiches in a bag, Adam looked into the living room and saw something sitting on the coffee table. Curious, he stopped and looked at it on his way to the front door. It was a large coin. On the front was a triangle with the words *1 MONTH* written on it.

Adam realized what was going on. He knew why his father was being nicer and why he hadn't seen any alcohol in the house. This was a recovery coin for alcoholics. Adam's father had quit drinking. Smiling, Adam put the coin back on the coffee table, zipped up his new jacket, and left to catch the bus.

Two more months passed by. Things had only gotten better at home. For the first few weeks, Adam and his father talked every night, sometimes for hours. His father talked about his drinking and apologized for all the terrible things he'd done since Adam's mom died. Adam didn't know if this was part of the program or if his father legitimately wanted to make up for everything, but he was happy about the change. His father even bought him all new clothes and school supplies. Adam finally got a new backpack for school. Now he no longer had to fight with the zipper to get it closed.

Every weekend, Adam's father took him out to do something fun. They had gone go-karting, bowling, and to the batting cages. Each weekend, his father surprised him with some new activity. Adam was still a little nervous hanging out with his father, but he couldn't believe how good his life had gotten this school year. Everything had changed.

One day at school, Adam took an early seat in his precalculus class. As he pulled his book out of his backpack, he heard someone sit down next to him. Normally, no one else bothered to come into class this early, and it startled him.

"Hi, I'm Allen," the kid said. "I just moved here. Today's my first day. Do you mind if I sit here?"

"Sure, go ahead," Adam replied.

"I guess not a lot of people bother to show up to class early," Allen said. "What's your name, by the way?"

"I'm Adam."

"Nice to meet you, Adam."

"You too."

"It really sucks moving here in the middle of the semester," Allen said. "Especially since this is my senior year. My father's company decided to move the branch, so we had no choice but to move."

"Yeah, that sounds like it really sucks."

"It is what it is," Allen said. "At least this class uses the same precalculus textbook as my old school. I was having a hard enough time in this class before. I don't think I could have made it if I had to switch books and figure out what was going on. I'm really not looking forward to calculus next year in college. Where are you going to college?"

"Actually, I'm a junior, so I'll still be here next year," Adam said.

"Oh, cool," replied Allen. "You must be pretty smart, then. I certainly couldn't have made it into calculus in high school. Maybe we could study together after school."

"Okay," Adam said.

"Cool. Hey, if you need a ride, I have a car, so I can also give you a ride home if you need."

Chapter 25

Over the course of the next few months, Adam and Allen became great friends. Each day at lunch, they got their meals from the cafeteria and went outside to eat. They hung out together on weekends and spent school days studying together.

Adam also helped Allen study precalculus. When they first met, Allen had been expecting to get a C in the class, but by the end of the year he was aiming for a B. Adam had already finished everything for the year before he'd even met Allen, so he was happy to help his new friend study.

They sat down with their lunches and leaned against the wall, eating and talking about math. Adam generally quizzed Allen on the problems and then helped Allen when he didn't understand something. After a few months of teaching Allen, Adam knew precalculus so well he could probably teach the class himself.

On occasion, Sara would also study with them. Unfortunately, it wasn't as much as Adam would have liked. She and Adam were still close friends, but she was spending more time with her boyfriend than Adam cared for. He was still hoping the two of them would just break up already. He never got to hang out with Sara outside of school anymore.

The school day ended, and instead of going to his bus, Adam waited by the front doors for Allen. When Allen came out, they went to Allen's car. Adam hadn't taken the bus home from school in months.

On the drive to Adam's house, they made jokes and enjoyed listening to the radio. Riding in Allen's car was the first time Adam had listened to music in years. Even if he'd had something to listen to music with, Adam wouldn't have wanted the noise in his house, and he still felt that way even though he no longer had to be so quiet.

Allen always parked on the right-hand side of Adam's driveway so that his dad could still pull into his usual spot. The boys got out of the car and went inside. Adam made sandwiches in the kitchen while Allen sat on the couch in the living room and pulled out his books.

They ate their sandwiches and made jokes as they each went over their homework for the classes they didn't have together. Adam didn't have anything more to do, but he still liked to review the material and double-check his homework before turning it in. It was only about once a week that he actually got new assignments he had to do, and he always finished them quickly.

Once Allen finished his homework, they moved on to precalculus. As always, they started off with Allen looking at Adam's paper as if it had been written in another language. Adam explained it to him a few times before Allen started to understand, and then he did the homework problems on his own paper. They finished by comparing Allen's answers to Adam's, after which Allen would redo the ones he got wrong.

"Hey, you two boys studying again?" Adam's dad asked as he came through the front door.

"Yes, Dad," Adam answered.

"Alright. I'm just going to make some food and then head to my room so that you two can study. It's really good that you study so much. I know I didn't study that much when I was in high school."

From the kitchen, Adam's dad listened as Adam tried to explain how to do the math problem to Allen. He knew Adam was going to get into a great college and really make something of his life. He knew that Adam had kept up his grades despite how terrible his home life was, and he'd spent the year trying to make it up to him.

Once he finished making a plate of food, Adam's dad quietly walked from the kitchen and closed the door to his room. Adam heard the TV turn on, but he turned the volume low. He did that every time the boys did their homework.

When they finished their homework, Adam and Allen turned on the living room TV. They usually finished with about an hour left before Allen had to go home, so they often spent the time watching television.

When it was time for him to go, Allen reminded Adam that tomorrow was Friday and they had plans to go out after they finished their homework. When Allen left, Adam went into the kitchen and saw his father already there making more food. "I'm making spaghetti. Do you want some?"

"Yeah, definitely," Adam answered.

"Good, because I'm making a lot, so you better eat a lot," Dad said with a laugh.

Once dinner was ready, Adam's dad called to him to come eat. Adam was upstairs reading a book. He'd started reading for fun and got books from the library. He was reading about one every two weeks since he didn't have a lot of school work anymore. Adam closed the book and went back downstairs.

"Grab a plate," his dad said.

Adam scooped a big pile of noodles onto his plate and drenched it in sauce. Then he went into the living room, set his plate on the coffee table, and sat next to his dad. While they ate, they watched TV.

It was nice not being alone all the time anymore. Adam had gotten used to having company. If he wasn't hanging out with Allen, Adam was spending his time with his dad. They spent time together every night and always went to do something on the weekends. Adam had practically forgotten about how bad life had been for years.

*   *   *

It was the second week of July. Adam had been having a great summer. He had spent nearly every day hanging out with Allen. His father had taken him to the local amusement park three times, and Adam finally got to go to the county fair again. Life was really looking up. Adam only had one year of school left. He still planned on graduating and going to college, but now he planned on coming back home to visit. College had become merely the next stage in his life and not the escape it had signified for so long.

Allen and Adam pulled into Adam's driveway. His father's car was in the driveway. Adam expected to find his father either sitting on the couch watching TV or in the kitchen cooking food. He had really gotten into cooking this summer and spent most of his time in the kitchen. Adam was now used to eating quite a lot of food as his father kept learning to make new things.

The TV was off when they got inside. Adam found that strange. The TV was always on. Even if his father wasn't watching it, he still had it on to watch from the kitchen as he cooked food. Adam brushed it off and guessed that his father was working from home today. His bedroom door was shut, and it was very quiet.

Adam and Allen sat on the couch and turned on the TV. As the sound of the television echoed through the house, Adam heard something in his father's room. He couldn't tell what it was. Assuming the sound of the TV had just startled him, Adam forgot about it and began watching the show.

An hour passed by. Adam was starting to wonder how long his father was going to be in there working. He assumed that once he was done he would come out and say hello and probably start cooking like he always did. He had made three or four dishes every day all summer. Adam figured he must have had a lot of work to do if he still wasn't out.

As two more hours passed, Adam really started to wonder what it was his dad could be working on that it was taking him the whole day to do it. How much longer was he going to be in there? Adam was curious, but he didn't want to bug his father while he was working. He would just have to wait until he came out.

Eventually, the time came for Allen to go home. As he watched Allen leave, Adam looked at the clock. He and Allen had been there for five hours, and his father was still locked in his room. It was nine at night. Adam felt bad for his father that he had to spend the entire day on his weekend working. Usually, he had Saturdays and Sundays off.

Adam decided to keep watching TV while he waited for his father to come out of his room. He assumed it would only be a few more minutes. He couldn't possibly still have much to do after nine. But another hour passed, and he was still locked in his room. It was now past ten. Adam hadn't seen his father all day.

Adam thought it was possible that after working so hard all day, his father had ended up just falling asleep without ever coming out.

If that were the case, Adam didn't want to wake him up.

By this time, Adam was starving. Usually by now, he'd eaten two or three more meals, as his dad brought him food and told him to try it. It was almost always really good, too. Luckily, the fridge was now always full of leftovers. Adam wouldn't have any trouble finding something to eat.

When he finished microwaving his dinner, Adam took his plate upstairs. If his father was sleeping, he didn't want to have the sound of the TV wake him up. He finished the night eating quietly in his room and reading a book until he fell asleep.

Chapter 26

On Saturdays when Adam woke up, his father was usually in the kitchen cooking. It was usually the aroma of the food that woke him. Today, Adam didn't smell anything.

Adam checked the clock and found it was his normal time to wake up. He got dressed and went downstairs expecting his father to be in the kitchen cooking anyway. Adam thought maybe his father had slept in because he'd worked so late the night before. But when he got there, the kitchen was empty, and the door to his father's room was still closed.

Adam listened but couldn't hear anything. It was obvious to him that his father was still asleep. Adam was too hungry to wait for him to wake up, so he took out some more leftovers and heated them up as quietly as he could, the only sound the inevitable beeping of the microwave.

After eating his breakfast in his room, Adam walked quietly downstairs to see if his father was awake yet, worried he'd find him in the kitchen cooking something that Adam would be too full to eat. The kitchen was still empty. His father's door was still closed, and even after pressing his ear against it, Adam still couldn't hear anything. He figured his father must be really tired if he was still sleeping.

After washing his dishes from breakfast and the night before, Adam decided to sneak out to the library. He'd finished the book he was reading the night before and wanted to return it and check out another. His father would probably be awake by the time he got back, and hopefully, Adam would be ready to eat again.

It didn't take Adam long to check out a new book; he had already picked it out ahead of time. He stayed at the library and looked around for a bit before returning home to give his father enough time to wake up.

After an hour, Adam finally went back home. When he stepped through the front door, he still didn't hear anything. It was after noon by now, and his father never slept past nine. Adam was really starting to wonder what was going on.

He guessed that his father was probably awake but in his room working again. He must have had a really big project at work if he had to work on Saturday to finish it. Adam didn't want to bother him, so he snuck up to his room to read his book. He was excited to start reading it.

As he read, Adam stopped occasionally and listened for his father. At two o'clock, he decided to go down to the kitchen for some lunch. He couldn't believe his father still hadn't come out yet.

Quietly, Adam heated up some more food and went back upstairs. With all this sneaking to get his food, it was starting to feel like before his father stopped drinking. But at least the food was better than it had been before, and Adam wasn't sneaking around because he was afraid he was going to be beaten, but because he wanted to be nice. Hopefully tomorrow, his father's workload would even out and things could get back to the way they had been.

Adam got out of bed on Sunday morning and went downstairs, expecting to find his father in the kitchen cooking a massive breakfast. Instead, he found the kitchen empty once again. He snuck down the hallway and listened at his father's door. He could hear him snoring and thought he must have stayed up all night working on some massive project.

Not wanting to wake him, Adam quietly heated up more leftovers and went back upstairs. He ate his breakfast while reading his book. At noon, he figured his father had to be awake by now and went back downstairs only to find the bedroom door still shut. He heard some mumbling inside and left his father be. He didn't know if he was just waking up or still working on that project.

As the day passed, Adam began to worry. Was something wrong with his father? Adam came downstairs to get food several times, and each time, his father never came out of his room. Adam thought he would read his library book for a bit and spend the rest of the day with his father. Instead, he finished the entire book and spent his evening worrying about what was going on.

When Adam woke the next morning, he expected to smell the aroma of his father cooking breakfast. Then he remembered today was Monday and his father was already at work, so he got out of bed and made his own breakfast.

Allen came over at one o'clock and they watched TV. Except for a break to play a board game, they sat in front of the TV all day. When six o'clock rolled around, Adam waited anxiously for his father to come home. Normally, he got home around 5:30.

Finally, at 8:30, the front door opened. The boys watched as it swung inward and smacked into the wall, startling them. Adam's father had a look on his face they couldn't quite distinguish, and a paper bag in his hand. His clothes were rumpled and several buttons were undone on his shirt. He looked like he'd had a terrible day at work. Adam expected him to say hello and head into the kitchen like usual, but instead, he walked into his room and closed the door without a word.

Chapter 27

"What was that about?" Allen asked.

"I have no idea," Adam lied. His stomach was turning as his mind went back to the days when he dreaded his father coming home.

The boys sat awkwardly in silence watching the TV, neither of them knowing what to say. Adam was worried. He kept hoping that his father would come out of his room and go back to his routine of cooking food. That would confirm that nothing was changing, that it wasn't going back to the way things used to be. As an hour passed, however, Adam started to lose hope in that being the case.

Once again, the time came for Allen to head home. Normally, they'd talk a lot as he was leaving, but today neither of them said much. When the TV show they were watching ended, Allen stood up and went to the door.

"You wanna come hang out at my house tomorrow?" he asked Adam.

"Sure," Adam replied, knowing that Allen only wanted to avoid coming back after how weird things had been tonight.

"Cool," Allen said. "I'll come pick you up at like one, and we can head over."

Once Allen was gone, Adam started to get nauseous. He was suddenly extremely worried about his father coming back out of his room. What if things were back to the way they were before and the only reason he hadn't beat Adam when he got home was because Allen was there? Adam ran upstairs and hid in his room.

Even if things were back to the way they were before, Adam was still used to eating a lot more now, and within a half hour, he was starving, and he didn't think he could make it the entire night without eating something.

Silently, he crept back down the stairs. He peeked around the corner to make sure his father was still locked in his room. Once he had confirmed it, he snuck into the kitchen and opened the fridge. He looked for something he could eat cold so he wouldn't have to use the microwave. There was no way he was going to let it beep. Eventually, he gave up and put a pork chop and some mashed potatoes on a plate, then brought them upstairs to eat cold.

It wasn't nearly as good cold, but at least the food filled him up. Once again, he set the plate on his nightstand. He would wait until his father left for work to go downstairs and wash it. He desperately wanted to believe that things weren't going back to the way they'd been before. He hoped that his father was just having another rough work week and that when it was over and he wasn't so worn out, things would get better again. As hard as he wanted to believe, he was still too afraid to act like that was the case. He was already going back to his old habits of hiding from his father.

The next morning, Adam woke quietly. Even though it was past the time his father should have left for work, he didn't want to make any noise until he was certain he was gone. He sneaked out of his room and looked out a window to see if his father's car was gone. To Adam's relief, it was. He went downstairs to wash his plate from the night before and get some breakfast.

He sat down to eat in front of the TV just like he had all summer, and then he changed his mind. What if his father came home for some reason and found him watching TV? Adam picked his plate back up and went upstairs to eat in his room.

When Allen came over to pick him up, Adam was excited to leave the house. He didn't like having that feeling of fear again. He wanted to get out and go somewhere where he knew he was safe, even if it was only for a few hours.

He stayed at Allen's later than he normally would, but inevitably the time came for Adam to go home. He watched the houses go by as Allen drove him, each house bringing him closer to his own, a place he didn't want to go. He took a deep breath when the car pulled up to his house and tried to act like everything was normal, but he was pretty sure Allen could tell it wasn't. It was hard to hide it after Allen had seen how weird his father had acted the night before. Still, Adam was determined to pretend. He said goodbye to his friend and started to get out of the car.

"You want to come over again tomorrow?" Allen asked just before Adam closed the door.

"Sure," Adam replied.

"Sweet. I'll pick you up at the same time tomorrow."

Instead of backing out of the driveway, Allen watched as Adam walked through the front door, almost as if he knew how terrible things in that house had always been for Adam. Even though things seemed to be good the entire time Allen had known Adam, maybe the past just couldn't be hidden.

Adam tried not to make it too obvious with Allen watching, but he opened the door as quietly as he could so his father wouldn't hear. Once he got the door shut, he watched through the window as his friend backed out of the driveway and left. Adam went to his room to hide for the rest of the night.

When he was lying in bed, Adam wondered if there was really any reason to be so worried. His father hadn't started beating him again. What if there wasn't anything wrong? What if things weren't going back to the way they were? The problem was that Adam didn't have any way to find out. He wasn't about to go knock on his father's bedroom door and see what happened. The only thing he could do was to wait until the weekend and see if his father woke him up on Saturday morning for breakfast. Unfortunately, he still had days to worry about before that could happen.

When Saturday finally came, Adam woke up to a banging sound downstairs. He instantly grew worried. He had been hoping to wake up to the smell of waffles. Still, he wasn't ready to give up hope. Maybe after a long work week, his father had gotten up late and the banging sound was him trying to make breakfast.

Quietly, Adam dressed and left his room. As he peeked through the stairway railing, he saw his father sitting on the couch watching TV. Adam felt a small surge of panic at first but decided to go downstairs anyway. His father had been so nice for months. He couldn't possibly be the same person he had been before for so long. Things were different now. Adam wasn't sure he believed it entirely, but he needed to find out.

Getting to the bottom of the stairs, Adam was so nervous that he felt like he was about to pass out. His father was still staring blankly at the TV. Adam didn't know what that meant. On the one hand, he still had not yelled or thrown anything at Adam like he had when he was drinking. On the other hand, the sober version of his father would have greeted him with a smile already. Adam couldn't stand at the bottom of the steps forever, so he went into the kitchen to make himself breakfast.

He tried to make sense of things but couldn't. This wasn't the angry, drunk version of his father, but it also wasn't the sober, kind version. This was somewhere in the middle. Adam walked right past him, and his father didn't even turn his head. It seemed this was yet another version of his father: one who simply pretended Adam didn't exist.

As he made breakfast, Adam struggled with his thoughts and confusion. At least his father wasn't beating him again. But Adam already missed the times when he was able to hang out with his father. Those were really good times. Would things stay like this for another year until Adam left for college? Or would they quickly turn back into regular beatings?

One more year. Adam was at least glad he only had to worry about any of this for one more year. After that, he would finally be leaving for college. If his father went back to his old self, in one year this place would be nothing more than a memory.

Adam tried not to make noise in the kitchen, he couldn't be completely silent. As he left the kitchen for his room with a plate of pancakes, he didn't dare look at his father. The instant his foot touched the first step, it let out a loud creak.

Suddenly, something flew in front of him and smashed into the wall. Adam looked down and saw the pieces of a broken beer bottle at his feet. Without any hesitation, he flew up the stairs and into his room.

Dropping the plate on his nightstand, Adam abandoned his pancakes and leaped over his bed and onto the floor on the far side. He slid under his bed, hoping his father wouldn't find him. Clearly, he wasn't sticking to ignoring Adam. His father was going back to exactly the way he was before. The beer bottle confirmed he was drinking again.

As Adam hid under his bed, he realized he didn't even really know how he got there. It hadn't seemed like a conscious decision.

Even though the past few months had been good, as soon as Adam sensed danger, the instincts he'd developed over the years of abuse instantly kicked in. He hadn't thought at all. He'd just reacted.

Thirty minutes passed and Adam never heard his door open. His father wasn't coming. At least the incident had been nothing more than a thrown bottle that missed him.

Cautiously, Adam climbed out from under his bed and saw the pancakes on his nightstand. He had completely forgotten about them, but he was glad they were there. Not only had he gotten used to eating breakfast in the morning, but the previous adrenaline rush had added to his hunger.

Although they were cold, Adam ate every last bite of his pancakes and even licked up the syrup on the plate. He was still starving, but he couldn't go back down for more food. It was just his luck that the first time this happened again would be on a Saturday. His father didn't work today, so he'd probably be on the couch watching TV for the next twelve hours or more. There would be no chance for Adam to sneak into the kitchen.

Bored, Adam sat on his bed and stared at the wall. He had already finished the book from the library and didn't have anything to do. Allen was busy today, so Adam had the entire day to do nothing. Adam had been used to hiding in his room all day, but after months of living a much better life, doing so made him extremely anxious.

After a couple of hours of sitting on his bed with nothing but his thoughts, Adam got an idea. He didn't have anything to read in his room, but there was plenty to read at the library. He used to hang out there a lot on his days off from school. Not only that, but it was a safe place he could hide every day except for Sunday when it was closed. The library was also open until nine. If his father had really gone back to his old ways, he would likely be passed out from drinking by the time the library closed, so Adam could sneak back home and get some food from the kitchen.

There was only one problem. With his father on the couch, there was no way for Adam to get downstairs without being spotted.

Silently, he snuck out of his room and down the hall to the top of the stairs. Lying on the floor, he peeked through the stairway railing. The one good thing about his father drinking all day was that it shouldn't be long before he had to go to the bathroom. When he did, Adam would rush out the door and disappear for the rest of the day.

When he finally got his chance, Adam ran out of the house, down the street, and around the corner before he slowed down. His father hadn't ever beaten him in public before, but Adam wasn't going to take any chances.

Adam arrived at the library and looked at the hours on the front entrance. He had forgotten that the library closed at seven on Saturdays, not nine. Once it closed, he would have to wait at the park or walk around the block a bunch of times until he could be sure his father had passed out. At least his father had bought him a new watch while he was being nice so Adam could know what time to go home.

Chapter 28

Ever since Adam's father had started drinking again, Adam and Allen only hung out at Allen's house. Adam never actually told Allen what was going on, but it was clear to him that Adam's house was not a place you wanted to be. Adam felt lucky to have a friend to take him away from that place.

It wasn't long before Adam's dad was right back where he was before. If anything, he was even worse. It was as if he was trying to consume all the alcohol he'd missed during the months he'd been sober. Every time Adam left the house, the thought of going home made him feel like crying. He cried himself to sleep every night, listening to the sound of the TV downstairs, his father long since passed out in front of it.

Even though it was summer, Adam wore long-sleeve shirts. Allen never said anything about it, but he knew why. Adam was trying to hide the bruises on his arms; his father was still concerned about leaving visible bruises on his face.

The only thing that kept Adam going was having a good friend and knowing there was only one year left until he left for college. There was less than a month left before the new school year started, and then Adam would only have nine months to go until graduation. After that, he planned to get a job and save up money for his move to college.

There were only a couple of problems facing Adam now. One was that Allen, who was a year older, wouldn't be there. In another week, he'd be gone to college. Adam wished they could have been in the same grade together. He also didn't know if he'd have any classes with Sara. He hadn't seen her at all during summer. He still had hopes that she'd broken up with her boyfriend Chris over the summer and would be in several of his classes. He also worried that neither was true, and he dreaded the day he would see the two of them together again.

For the moment, though, life was pretty good. Adam sprinted down an alleyway. As he reached the corner of the building, he hid. When he thought it was safe, he emerged from cover, only to be assaulted by what seemed like a hundred bullets. He couldn't avoid them. His lifeless body fell to the ground, riddled with bullet holes.

Allen laughed as Adam set down his game controller and the words *GAME OVER* appeared on the screen, followed by an instant replay of the action.

Adam hadn't ever really played video games before he met Allen, and he wasn't nearly as experienced. He'd lost by a score of 25 to 9, a fact that took a bit of the sting away from his last death. It wasn't like he was going to make a comeback anyway. The game had been lost a long time ago—even before it began, he knew he wasn't going to win. But it was still fun to try, especially since he was playing with his friend.

"Good game," Allen said.

"You too," Adam replied with a hint of annoyance in his voice.

After they finished playing, they went to the kitchen and got some food. Allen's family never ate together at the table, but there was always food. Adam felt lucky that they let him eat at their house. Ever since his father had started drinking again, there was barely any food at his own house. He'd eaten fine for a couple weeks until the leftovers from his father's cooking days ran out. For the last few days of those two weeks, a lot of it had gone bad, but Adam ate it anyway. He couldn't afford not to. He still didn't know what he was going to do for food once Allen moved away. There would still be two weeks of summer before he was able to eat lunch at school.

They sat on the couch and watched TV as they ate. Adam stuffed himself like a bear trying to fatten up for the winter. The worst part about not having any food was that he'd spent the summer getting used to having far more of it than he could possibly eat. Adam didn't know if he could survive on even less than the tiny amount he'd had before.

When midnight rolled around, it was time for Adam to head back home. Allen drove him slowly home. Any time they were going somewhere else, Allen was usually a pretty fast driver, but when he drove Adam home at the end of the night, he always drove slowly. It was as if he was trying to keep Adam away from that house for as long as possible.

Inevitably, they made it to Adam's house. His father's car was in the driveway, but at least he would have passed out long ago. Just as he'd expected, Adam's father was asleep on the couch with the TV on when he got inside. As annoying as it was to have to listen to the TV while he tried to sleep, the noise helped make sure nothing he did would wake his father. He could probably hold a rock concert in his room without being noticed. The TV was always so loud Adam was surprised the speakers still worked.

When he got to his room, Adam lay on his bed and imagined being away at college. After all this time, he was now only a year away. It was a good thing he was so close. He expected this year to be worse than all the rest. Even with Derek gone, things at home were absolutely terrible. But he could make it. Just one more year. Not even a year. One school year. Only nine months.

On their last night hanging out together, Adam and Allen played video games together on his couch. Unfortunately, Adam couldn't enjoy the day as much as he had the others. For a normal kid, it would be sad to have their friend move away. For Adam, it was terrifying. Not only would his friend be gone, but he was going to have to spend a lot more time at his own house.

Even the games were no longer fun. Every time Allen shot him and he watched his character fall to the ground, Adam imagined himself falling to the floor as his father beat him. He still laughed to hide it from Allen. He didn't want to ruin their last day together.

He wondered if he'd ever even see Allen again. At best, he wouldn't see him until he came home for Thanksgiving. But even then, he'd only see his friend a few more times. After that, Adam would move away to another state for college. They'd probably never see each other again.

Chapter 29

Allen brought in two big plates of nachos. Adam tried his best not to think about how little he would have to eat tomorrow and concentrated on the show they were watching. The plates were so big that Adam was full by the time he'd finished half of it. But he wasn't about to waste any. Even as he started to feel like he was going to throw up, he kept eating until every last chip was gone.

When they finished eating, Allen switched the TV back over to the video games. He hadn't even bothered to turn the console off. He unpaused the game and chased Adam down across the map. Adam tried his best to escape, but he was also busy trying not to get too excited, still struggling to keep down all the food he'd eaten. If the game made his heart race, he might not be able to keep the nachos down. But as they played on, he began to feel better.

Eventually, the time came for Adam to go home, and Allen once again made the ride last as long as possible. When he set eyes on his house, Adam's stomach turned. He couldn't believe it was over. Even though Sara had been more special to him than Allen, this felt much worse than the last time he'd walked away from Sara's house at the end of the summer. At least then he'd had the hope of hanging out with her at school, even if that turned out not to be true.

They talked in the car in front of Adam's house until finally, it was time to say goodbye. Adam found it difficult to hold back his tears as he looked at his best friend for the last time. He couldn't believe how awful he felt as he got out of Allen's car and walked to his front door.

Walking through the front door, Adam saw his father asleep on the couch and a bottle of bourbon on the coffee table. He didn't bother trying to be quiet; he just didn't care enough to try. *What's the point?* he thought. Being quiet only delayed the inevitable. Maybe his father wouldn't wake up now, but that wouldn't stop Adam from being beaten eventually. It would happen now or later. Who really cared when? What was the difference?

His nose scrunched up as he looked at his father snoring and drooling on the couch. He hated having to come home and see him there every day. He wanted nothing more than to never have to see his face again. Only one more year and that dream would finally become a reality. But that was still nine months of having to come back to this house.

His senior year was only a week away, but that was an entire week where Adam had nothing else going on but hating his life. At least school gave him purpose. Right now, the only purpose Adam had was suffering.

The first thing that popped into Adam's head the next morning was how he had nothing to do all day except dread the moment his father came home, and then hide in his room until his father either passed out or decided to come up and beat him for no reason. Adam wasn't sure if he actually cared which one it was.

Before, Adam used to sneak downstairs to check if his father had actually gone to work. This morning, he didn't see the point and just walked downstairs. The odds were that he wasn't there, and if he was, would it really make a difference? What would one more beating in addition to the thousands he'd already received and the hundreds he was sure to get really matter?

He went into the kitchen and looked for food. He opened the fridge, and even though he was staring right at it, he didn't actually look to see what was inside. What was the point? The fridge never had anything except alcohol in it anymore.

He looked in the cupboard and saw lots of spices and other things that you needed to make food. His father had stocked the kitchen with lots of them when he was practicing his cooking. The problem was that there wasn't any food to put the spices on. There was no meat, no noodles, no rice, no flour or milk. All of that stuff had long since run out. Unless Adam wanted to eat a jar of nutmeg, he didn't know what he was going to do for breakfast. He felt like he was going to have to live on tap water until school started. Then at least he would get to eat lunch at school. If he was lucky, that would amount to a thousand calories—but that was only during the week. He would have to starve on weekends.

He wanted to cry. How long would it take for his body to go back to the way it was before? He grew angry. He was sick of living this way. Why couldn't it just be over? Why couldn't he just graduate already? Why couldn't all this just end?

Pushing stuff around in the cupboards and knocking a couple of bottles over, Adam finally found something: an entire loaf of bread. As he pulled it out, he found another half a loaf behind it. He was so relieved to find something to eat that his anger subsided and almost turned into excitement. Was there anything else he'd missed?

Going back to the fridge, Adam finally actually looked through it. Behind a pack of beer, he found a package of lunch meat. It was even honey-baked ham, which he loved. He continued rummaging through the fridge. Behind several bottles of liquor, he found a quarter-full jar of mayonnaise.

Counting the bread slices, Adam did the math. There were twenty-four slices in the loaf. Really, there were only six days left until school started, so that made four pieces a day. No matter what, Adam would at least have four pieces of bread to eat until school started. He pushed the full loaf to the side so he could bring it up to his room after he made his sandwich. His father was always so drunk he probably wasn't going to notice a loaf of bread missing.

Adam took his sandwich and loaf of bread to his room, hiding the loaf in his closet. He sat on his bed and ate. He was still hungry when the food was gone. He was used to eating massive amounts of food at a time, and it hadn't been enough to fill him up.

His food situation for the week was now slightly better, but Adam still didn't have much of anything to do. He couldn't go downstairs and watch TV for fear his father would come home early. The TV might cover up the sound of his father's car pulling into the driveway, and he wouldn't even know he was home until he walked through the door.

Adam only had two chapters left in his book. He picked up the book and finished it. When he was done, he figured he should have plenty of time to go to the library and back before his father got home, so he left.

Noon was the worst time of day to be walking around outside. Even though the summer was ending, it was still very hot. The sun beat down mercilessly on Adam as he made his way down the side-walk, but he didn't care. He was just glad to have a place to go that wasn't his house.

When he arrived at the library, he dropped his book off in the return slot and walked through the front doors. The cold air conditioning hit him in the face, and he smiled. He went to the drinking fountain and chugged some water before looking for a new book.

Before, Adam always tried to find a book quickly so he could get home and back to his room. He didn't want to get home to find his father's car already in the driveway. Today, Adam took his time. It wasn't even one o'clock yet, and he had over eight hours left before the library closed and he had to leave. Even if he spent two hours just walking around, he still might be able to finish an entire book before he left.

He picked three books to read that day. One was a fiction adventure novel. Adam loved those books because they usually told about someone escaping from their life by running to the other side of the world on some glorious adventure. Soon, he would do that himself, even if his great adventure was only college. The other two were nonfiction books. One was about the 1930s and how it led up to World War II. He also got a psychology book. He knew that he was going to have to take psychology classes in college, so it would be fun to read up on it now.

He found a chair in the back corner of the library. It was nice and cushioned, making it a great place to hang out for the day. It was also right under an air vent so he would stay cool while he read. Today was going to be a pretty good day.

Chapter 30

Adam was finally in his senior year. The last year until he went off to college and left his terrible childhood life behind forever. Already, things hadn't been as terrible as he had expected them to be. Spending time at the library made things so much easier. He got more studying done than ever, and because he was only really home on Sundays, he hadn't been beaten by his father once.

His father had even started buying more food. The only problem was that even though there was more of it, the food was mostly just bread and lunch meat. Alcoholics didn't seem to care too much about variety in their diets. But Adam didn't mind. He was eating four sandwiches every night, and he didn't seem to be getting sick of them. He was certain he could stand to eat them for another nine months.

Things were also going really well at school. Sara was in three of his classes this year. There was only one calculus class in the school, so they had that together. It was right after lunch, so they would eat lunch in the cafeteria together and then head to class. Adam had hoped Sara would break up with her boyfriend Chris over the summer, but at least he was gone for college. Because of that, Adam and Sara started eating lunch together again. They also had earth science together for first period, and English for the second to last period. Adam wished it would have been the last period. It would have been a great way to end the day. Still, he couldn't complain. At least he had three classes with her. It was nice having English together right after calculus because they could walk to their next class together.

Even with everything going well for him this year, Adam frequently felt anxious. After so many years of everything in his life going bad, he couldn't stop worrying about some terrible thing happening. After only a few short months of not hating being home, his father had turned into an even more abusive drunk. Adam had found a dog, only to have him killed by the pound. He'd finally made a new friend, only to have him leave after a mere half a year. He had met the most perfect girl in the world only to have her get a boyfriend shortly after.

What was going to happen now? Maybe Sara would transfer her classes and he'd never see her again. Maybe she'd tell him she got engaged to Chris and any hope of them breaking up would be lost. A lot of people did that in their senior year of high school. It was probably even more likely because he was already in college. Maybe Adam would find out he hadn't been accepted into any of the colleges he'd applied for, and his dream of leaving would be over. Sometimes Adam felt as if he were waiting for all good things to come to an end.

Every day, Adam woke up with those feelings and tried to cover them up. He studied all day to distract himself. If he didn't get into college, it wasn't going to be because of his grades. He even reviewed his classes in his head when he brushed his teeth in the morning.

Even though he loved having classes with her so he could see her, Adam actually hated to think about Sara at any other time. All he could think about was how she had a boyfriend and how he was never going to be with her.

The only thing that kept him from falling into a horrible depression was the thought that this was the last year he had to worry about any of it. If he had to endure any more than that, he wouldn't have been able to keep going. He was only getting by because he knew that in June, it would all be behind him.

If he wasn't distracting himself with studying, Adam was busy focusing on how life was going to be once he got to college. A lot of people complain about having roommates in college. Adam didn't care if he had fifty other people sleeping in the same room as long as he wasn't sleeping in the same place he was now. At least none of those fifty people would be his father.

On occasion, he would even think about meeting a girl at college. A lot of people did, so why couldn't he? Maybe he'd even find someone better than Sara. He didn't really like to think much about that, though. To him, Sara was the most perfect girl in the world. He wouldn't find anyone better because there was no one better. He didn't want to find someone else at college. He wanted to go off to college with her so they could be together.

For now, the only thing he could do was wait and hope that Sara would break up with Chris. Adam wasn't the kind of person to try and push her to. He certainly wasn't the kind to make a move while she had a boyfriend. He wasn't the kind to make a move at all. Waiting wasn't easy, though.

As each passing week brought him closer to college, it also brought him closer to the probability of never seeing or talking to Sara again. He had hoped that being separated from Chris would end their relationship, but the closer they got to the end of the year, the less likely he realized that would be. If they made it until she went off to college with Chris, it would all be over.

It was an incredibly annoying situation Adam was in. The one thing that was giving him hope was also the same thing that was taking it away. Every day that passed brought him closer to his goal of getting to college, but it also brought him closer to never seeing her again. It made him feel awful and only reminded him how everything good in life goes bad. At least he didn't have to spend all day at his house after school. He hoped to spend as little time in that house as possible until he never saw it again.

The day ended, and Adam walked to his bus and got on. As the bus pulled away, he looked around the parking lot at the long line of parents in cars picking their kids up from school, hoping for one last glimpse of Sara before the day ended. If he was never going to see her beautiful face again when the year was over, he wanted to see it as much as he could now.

He smiled when the bus rolled to a stop by his house. He stayed in his seat and waited for the bus to pull away again. He loved knowing that he wouldn't have to go home until after his father was asleep. When the bus pulled up to a stop near the library, he happily got off and went inside.

Ever since the start of the new school year, Adam hadn't picked up a single book from the library. He just sat at the same table every day and spread out his textbooks to study. The people who worked there had practically begun to consider it Adam's table. It was the best table in the library, big enough for all his books but small enough that no one else could sit at it once he had everything out. It was also next to the computers so he could quickly jump on one of them to look something up if he needed to.

Adam was allowed to keep working at his table when the library closed. It took fifteen minutes for them to close everything up, so the people who worked there let him study for ten extra minutes.

Then he would pack his bag and head out the door with them. Adam didn't need an extra ten minutes to study, but he took every second he could get away from home.

He walked home slowly to delay getting there, even though by this time his father would already be passed out on the couch. Still, Adam always felt better when he wasn't there. Being in that house made him sad.

The next day, Adam was sitting in his English class with Sara when the teacher gave them an assignment to write a short story. They could write about whatever they wanted, but the story would be graded on the proper use of all the grammar rules they'd learned.

Adam stared at his empty paper without any idea what to write. He looked over at Sara as she ran her pencil across the page like she was planning on writing an entire novel by the time the bell rang. He watched as she brushed her hair back behind her ear and away from her face, and then he got an idea of what to write.

After twenty minutes, Adam finished his story. The teacher had everyone trade papers and look for mistakes in their partner's grammar. As Adam read Sara's story, he kept looking over at her reading his. He had written about a girl in a terrible relationship who one day realized that she should have been with someone else all along. Adam was afraid that Sara would realize the hidden meaning in his story, but he also hoped she would.

He was so busy worrying about her reading his story that he was too distracted to get Sara's story. He looked for grammar errors, but by the time he finished a sentence, he'd already forgotten what he'd read. Eventually, he just skimmed over her pages, studying the punctuation to see if he could catch any errors.

Adam felt panicked as they turned in their papers. Sara told him she really liked his story, but he had no idea if she understood it was about her. Maybe she had but decided to ignore it. He also still had no idea what she'd written, and he was afraid she'd be upset if she lost points because he hadn't really proofread it like he was supposed to.

Chapter 31

When he got off the bus at the library that day, Adam noticed the parking lot was practically empty, which was odd considering it was usually busy at this hour. He walked up to the door and tried to open it, only to discover it was locked.

"Sorry, Adam," one of the library employees said, sticking his head out the door when he saw Adam trying to get inside, "the library is closed. We had a water pipe burst. We don't think any of the books were affected because they were all on shelves, but half the floor was soaked. It's going to take a while to get it all cleaned up. We haven't even managed to turn the water off yet."

In dismay, Adam turned and started walking home quickly. He wanted to get there as fast as he could. If he had to go home, he might as well try to get there before his father. He had to hurry if he didn't want to get caught in the kitchen when his father got home.

He got home and made his sandwiches as fast as he could, then rushed to get upstairs before his father walked through the door. It was unlikely, but sometimes his father came home from work early. Adam had learned that things in his life go wrong too often to assume today wouldn't be one of those days.

He was leaving the kitchen and headed for the stairs when the front door swung open. His father stood in the doorway with a bottle of beer in hand. Adam turned quickly and tried to leave out the back door.

His father stood in the doorway and chugged his beer like he didn't want to enter the house while he was still sober. He quickly finished the bottle, screamed, and threw it at Adam as he ran away. Adam was lucky he'd kept his backpack on to save time. The empty bottle hit him in the back, but his bag took the blow. All Adam felt were drops of beer hitting him in the back of the neck.

He moved as fast as he could, but he was also trying to balance his plate. He was afraid of his father catching him, but he didn't want to lose his food in the process. Before he made it out of the house, he felt his father grab his backpack and pull him to the ground. Adam fell onto his back, arching backward over his bag. His plate hit the floor in front of him.

As bad as his back hurt, Adam quickly forgot about that pain as his father's fists hit him in the stomach. Adam tried to escape, but he couldn't get his backpack off. Finally, he tried to hide behind his backpack.

It helped, but only partially. Adam's backpack protected him from being kicked, so his father just bent over again and started punching him in the side of the ribs. Adam couldn't do anything but close his eyes and wait for it to be over.

For minutes, the only relief Adam had was when his father stopped hitting him to scream about how everything wrong in his life was his fault. If it wasn't for Adam, his mother would still be alive. If it wasn't for Adam, his father would have gotten that promotion a few months ago. If it wasn't for Adam, everything would be better.

Once the beating finally ended, his father went into the kitchen for another beer, leaving Adam lying on the floor, bruised and crying. Then his father went into his bedroom and slammed the door.

In agonizing pain, Adam slowly slid his backpack off his shoulders and lay there for a minute, unable to move. He wanted to get upstairs as fast as he could, but he was in too much pain to stand up.

As soon as he could, Adam climbed to his feet. He nearly fell back over in pain as he picked up his backpack, but he managed to get it onto his shoulder. Looking down, Adam saw his sandwiches on the floor. The plate was plastic, so it hadn't broken, but the sandwiches were on the floor. It was gross, but he was too hungry to not eat them. He wasn't going back into the kitchen to make more. He put everything back on his plate and went upstairs.

The sandwiches didn't taste bad, and considering all the times Derek had knocked his food onto the ground, Adam was used to eating dirty food. When he finished, Adam forced himself to study until it was time to go to bed.

He lay in bed thinking about how awful today had been. He just wanted this chapter of his life to be over. He wanted to stop being scared all the time. Even as he imagined tomorrow being better because the library should be open again, all he thought about was how eventually he would have to come back to this house.

The next day at school, Sara kept talking about Chris. Adam tried to fake interest, but that was the last thing he wanted to hear. She said Chris had called her yesterday. Of course it had to be yesterday, probably at the same time Adam was being beaten by his father. It was like these things happened at the same time just to make things worse for him.

After school, Adam went straight to the library. This time, the parking lot was even more deserted, with only a couple of vans parked by the front doors. Adam got a terrible feeling as he got closer and his worst fears were realized.

On the metal edge of the glass doors was a note. Adam looked past it and saw people inside. They weren't library workers, though. They were the clean-up crew. Adam saw them cleaning the carpets. There were lights on inside, but not enough to make it look like the library was open. Angrily, he looked at the note on the door.

Closed

Due to a broken pipe, the library has been closed. We expect the library to open back up NO SOONER THAN NOVEMBER 15TH. We apologize for any inconvenience. Drop-off book returns will remain open, but all other functions will be closed.

Thank you for your understanding,
Library Staff

Adam couldn't believe what he'd just read. NO SOONER THAN NOVEMBER 15TH. It was all in caps, like the world was laughing at him. Like it was being thrown in his face that he couldn't go back to the library for such a long time.

He was so upset that he wanted to pry the doors open and go inside anyway. It wouldn't make any difference to him whether it was open or not. He just wanted a safe place to sit and study. Why couldn't he just be allowed to have that? Why did things always have to go so terribly wrong for him? He should have expected this. He knew something bad had to happen eventually.

As fast as he could, Adam headed home. If he couldn't hang out at the library, he was at least going to make it up to his room before his father got home. This time, he wouldn't make any food; he'd go straight upstairs and wait for his father to pass out before coming down to make his sandwiches.

Two hours after Adam got home and went to his room, there was a loud bang downstairs. Adam recognized the sound. He had heard it ten thousand times before. The door was swinging open and smacking into the wall as his father got home from work. Adam's breath quickened, but he tried to put it out of his mind and continue studying.

Once again, the TV clicked on and the sound echoed throughout the house and into Adam's room. It certainly wasn't the first time this had happened either, but today it was worse for Adam. His anger about the library closing made the TV so annoying. He wasn't supposed to be listening to the TV. His father wasn't supposed to be a twenty-second walk away. Adam wasn't supposed to be in this house at all.

With another loud bang, Adam's bedroom door swung open and his father stood in the doorway. Adam couldn't even get his books off his lap before his father grabbed his arm and started pounding on him.

* * *

By the time December rolled around, Adam couldn't believe how bad things were. Barely a day went by without a beating from his drunk father. His body was bruised from the neck down. The only positive side was that the cold winter allowed Adam to hide his bruises without people noticing. He didn't need people talking about him. He just needed this time to be over.

The library was still closed. When Adam had shown up on November 16th, the sign on the door had been replaced with one that read *Closed until further notice.*

Adam couldn't believe how unlucky he'd been this year. It was as if he was never meant to make it to college, never meant to maintain hope all the way through. Now, with so little time left, life was doing everything possible to break him.

Only six months remained until graduation. He should have been excited, but now it just seemed too long. He didn't think he would make it. Not with the way everything was going. When school closed down for the Christmas break, things got even worse. Now Adam didn't have any place to go at all during the day, and the more time he spent at home, the more the beatings increased in frequency. Sometimes, when his father didn't work, Adam was beaten two or three times a day.

Each time he was beaten, Adam climbed into his closet and closed the door. He sat on the floor in the dark and cried. His fear of being heard was stronger than his depression, so Adam opened his mouth to scream, but no sound came out. He felt his screams trying to push their way up and out.

Adam felt something soft on his closet floor. He picked it up and held it in his hands. It was a tie. The same black tie from before. The tie Adam had planned to hang himself with.

Without a second thought, he tied a loop around the end. He stood and hung the tie from the bar the way he'd done before. He was taller now and had to adjust the height. Once it was where he wanted it, Adam held the noose in front of his face.

Chapter 32

Most kids came back from the two-week school break relaxed and ready to start again. When Adam went back to school, he was dead inside. He was completely broken. The only reason he hadn't used the tie in his closet was the faint glimmer of hope brought on by the knowledge he would be graduating in five months.

One thing that helped Adam make it through the break was filling out his college applications. He wasn't just hoping to go off to college, he was actively preparing to do it. He planned to send them in on his first day back before everyone else. That way, when everyone was busy panicking about doing theirs, he could relax knowing his applications were already submitted.

Still, after everything, even turning in his college applications couldn't undo all that was going wrong in his life. It didn't suddenly make him happy. At best, it gave him only a short burst of excitement that briefly distracted him from his misery. On his first day back to class, all he thought about was how the day would soon end and he'd have to go home. Before, it would have made him happy, but now sitting next to Sara just depressed him even more. He didn't want her to have a boyfriend anymore. But like everything else Adam wanted, that was not going to happen.

Before class, Adam and Sara swapped stories about Christmas break. Adam was typically vague, wording things in such a way that he didn't feel like he was lying, but he definitely wasn't letting her know the truth about things. Mostly, he just listened to Sara tell him how her break went.

Just as Adam knew she would, Sara talked about how her boyfriend had come over when he was home for the break, but at least she didn't spend the entire time talking about it. In fact, she hardly mentioned Chris at all aside from that. Adam was glad about that.

As the day went on, Adam felt himself growing more and more anxious. Every second that passed was a second closer to the time that he'd have to go home. He'd given up on the library opening back up. Once the school day ended, he would have no choice but to go home.

After calculus, Adam and Sara walked together to English class. He couldn't quite figure out what it was, but she seemed different today than she had before the break. He didn't spend too much time worrying about it, though. She was probably just feeling better after the break and not so stressed out.

Adam tried not to, but all through English class, he kept staring at the clock. Tick. Tick. Tick. The sound of the ticking rang in Adam's ears like a banging gong. Every second that passed was one second closer to the end of the day. Adam desperately didn't want it to end.

Inevitably, the bell did ring. Now there was just one more class between him and going back to the house where his father lived. Adam almost felt like screaming as he got up from his seat and walked out the door with Sara.

"Oh, by the way," Sara said before they parted ways, "I forgot to mention it. I, uh, broke up with Chris over the break."

A giant smile almost jumped onto Adam's face, and it took every ounce of strength he had to suppress it. He forced a fake look of concern. He really did care if Sara was sad about it, but he was happy she no longer had a boyfriend.

"Oh, really?" he replied. He thought about adding something like "That's too bad" or "Oh, no!" but couldn't bring himself to do it. He didn't think it was too bad and he certainly wasn't sad about it. He was also concerned Sara would take it the wrong way. He wanted to appear concerned. He would have rather screamed "Oh, yes!" than "Oh, no!" Instead, he chose the middle ground: "What happened?"

"He spent the break trying to get me to do something I wasn't ready to do," Sara answered. "I realized he didn't really care about me."

"Oh," was all Adam could think to say.

"Yeah, it's alright," Sara continued. "To be honest, I don't think I was ever as invested in the relationship as I should have been. I'm not even really sad that it's over. I guess it just wasn't meant to be." With that, she gave Adam a kiss on the cheek and said good-bye before heading to her final class of the day.

Adam watched her walk away before turning around and walking to class as fast as he could. He was running a little late now, but every second he spent with Sara was worth it. He couldn't believe how happy he was. Not only had she given him a kiss on the cheek, something she hadn't done in a very long time, but she was single again. He actually stood a chance.

As he sat in his last class, Adam no longer cared about going home. He just wanted to get there, get the beating over with, and let the time pass so he could come back to school tomorrow. He was too excited to see Sara again to care about anything else.

On the bus ride home, Adam had an idea. Maybe the library

was open again. He hadn't checked since the beginning of December. With everything going wrong in his life, he'd simply stopped caring enough to bother. But now he felt good enough that he wanted to go see. If it was open again, that would make today even better.

As the bus pulled away from his stop, Adam grew nervous. If the library wasn't open, he would have to walk home. He would have wasted his opportunity to make some food before his father got home. But either way, it was too late now. All Adam could do was hope for the best.

To Adam's surprise, there were several cars in the library parking lot. There weren't enough cars to be certain the library was open, but still enough to think it might be. Adam found himself growing even more excited than he was before.

As Adam approached the doors, he looked inside and saw that the lights were on. Still, he couldn't see anyone inside. Suddenly, the sliding glass doors opened, letting him inside. He felt a warmth inside of him like things in his life were finally starting to get better again. Maybe he could make it through the rest of the school year until he left for college.

Adam saw people working behind the counter. "Oh, look! It's Adam," one of them said. "Sorry we were closed for so long. We were supposed to open back up in November, but I guess there was a lot more damage than they originally thought. We didn't open back up until yesterday. Nothing has changed, though. We still have your usual table in the same spot."

Adam was happy to see his friends again. They were always so nice to him. He felt like the library was more of a home than his actual house. If he could, he would have much rather slept overnight in a corner of the library than go home. But at least he could stay here until his father passed out from drinking.

Adam sat at his usual table and went back to his routine of spending the rest of the day studying. He couldn't believe how good it felt to sit there reading his textbooks. Most kids would have found it disturbing how much he enjoyed studying calculus, but Adam wished he could stay forever. The only reason he would ever want to leave was to see Sara again.

By Friday, the bruises covering his body were finally healing. It stopped hurting to sit in his chair and feel it pressing against the bruises on his back. By hiding out at the library again, Adam could finally go a day without being beaten. Still, he couldn't go there every day. As the weekend approached, he grew nervous about what he was going to do when the library closed on Sunday. His only option seemed to be to accept the fact that he'd still get beaten one day a week.

On Friday afternoon after school, Adam was walking out to his bus when someone called his name. "Oh, hey, Adam!"

Adam recognized the voice. Turning around, he saw Sara running up to him. She had a big smile on her face. To Adam, it seemed as if a bright light followed her, making her glow.

"I'm really glad I saw you again," she said. "I was wondering if you wanted to come to my house this weekend. It's been such a long time since you've been over. I've really missed seeing you outside of school."

"Yeah, definitely!" Adam practically shouted, unable to contain his excitement.

"Great!" Sara said. "Do you still have my number, or do you need me to write it down again?"

Of course Adam still had her number. The slip of paper was tucked safely away, hidden in the back of his nightstand drawer where it couldn't possibly get lost. Even if he did lose it, he still wouldn't have lost her number. Adam could still feel each line on the palm of his hand where she'd written it all that time ago; could still feel her hand wrapped around his as she wrote it. Besides, he'd spent so much time staring at it and trying to get the nerve to call her for the first time that he couldn't forget the number even if he wanted to.

"Yeah, I still have it somewhere," Adam answered, trying not to sound too obsessed. "What time should I call you?"

"Unfortunately, I'm busy tonight," she told him, "but you can call tomorrow morning. You know, if you want to. Maybe ten, if that sounds good to you?"

"Definitely."

"Awesome! Hey, my mom is picking me up. We could give you a ride if you want."

"Thanks, that sounds good," Adam said. "I was going to the library and not my house, though."

"Oh, that's okay. I'm sure my mom won't mind."

Adam opened the doors for Sara, and they walked to the parking lot together. He couldn't believe how happy he was. Not only had Sara broken up with her boyfriend and the library opened again, but now he was actually going to hang out with Sara at her house again. His entire life had turned around this week. On Sunday, he'd been wishing he was dead. On Friday, he felt as good as he had that wonderful summer with Sara.

Chapter 33

"Oh, my gosh! Look, it's Adam," he heard from inside the car as they got in. "It's so good to see you again. We haven't seen you in forever. You used to come over practically every day. What happened? Probably because Sara started going out with that other guy. That's okay. She's not seeing him anymore. We always liked you better anyway."

"Mom! Oh, my gosh!" Sara nearly shouted as her face turned bright red.

The entire way to the library, Sara's mom never stopped talking. Sara was mortified. Adam didn't mind. He liked listening to her ramble on. He used to hear it all the time when he would hang out with Sara, and it reminded him of spending time with her. He was glad he was doing that again.

"Bye," Sara said as Adam got out of the car at the library. "Don't forget to call me tomorrow."

At exactly ten the next morning, Adam called Sara. He would have called sooner if he didn't think it would make him seem desperate. As the phone rang, he suddenly grew extremely nervous. Each ring felt like a lifetime. He had called her many times before, but now he felt like it was the first time ever.

It ended up being a rather short phone call. Sara's brother answered, told him he'd tell Sara he was coming over, and then hung up. Adam didn't know if that was really the right thing to do, but he didn't feel like arguing. Hopefully, her brother would actually tell her, and hopefully, Sara would be ready for him to come over. Adam had been ready to leave for an hour, so he snuck out the door without waking his father and left.

When he got to Sara's house, things were just as he remembered them. Sara's mother gave him a long greeting, and then he went to see Sara. Once again, the two of them played chess until it was dinnertime. Adam ate with Sara and her family, and then they watched a movie until it was time for him to go home. It was as if no time had passed since the last time he was there.

On the porch, Sara gave Adam a hug and kissed him on the cheek. They said goodbye, and Sara invited him to come back tomorrow. Not only would he get to see her again, but he could avoid being home on the one day of the week he expected to be. He could go an entire week without being beaten by his father.

Months passed. Things were better than ever between Adam and Sara. They were seeing each other every day of the week. They saw each other at school and then hung out every day on weekends. Adam even got to go to Sara's house once or twice during the week so they could do homework together. Life was pretty good for Adam. He had only a couple of months left until graduation.

March was coming to an end. Adam checked the mail every day for letters from the colleges he'd applied for. He didn't want to risk his father bringing in the mail and not bothering to tell him he got anything. It would be just Adam's luck to not get into college because he never responded to any acceptance letters.

Looking in the mail, Adam found a large envelope. He pulled it out and saw his name on the front. He couldn't believe he was finally holding a letter from a college in his hands. The day had finally come. He wasn't leaving yet, but he was going to confirm the possibility.

Closing the mailbox, he left the rest of the mail inside. He didn't want to bring in his father's mail. Even though it would be the nice thing to do, bringing it inside would only give his father a reminder that Adam was there. So he simply took the letter upstairs and hid it under his bed. He had told Sara the two of them would open all of their acceptance letters together, so he couldn't open it until he went to her house on the weekend.

Once he had the acceptance letter safely hidden, Adam crept out the door and walked to the library. He hadn't gone there straight from school because he wanted to get home before his father could check the mail. The extra fifteen minutes of walking was definitely worth it.

That Sunday, Adam had his acceptance letters from all ten colleges he'd applied to. He put all the letters in his backpack and walked to Sara's house. Not only was he going to Sara's house, but he was going to find out which colleges he could go to. Adam was ecstatic. He practically skipped the whole way there.

When he got to Sara's house, she was waiting with her parents and brothers. Adam was nervous to open the letters with all of them watching, but since they were going to watch Sara open her letters, and since Sara wanted to open hers with Adam, he had no choice but to have an audience.

Adam set his ten envelopes down on the coffee table in the living room of Sara's house. Sara set the envelopes from the fifteen colleges she'd applied to in a pile next to his. Seven of each of their envelopes had been sent to the same school, which meant there were seven chances for Adam's dream of going to college with Sara to become a reality.

They had discussed this possibility before. Ever since they'd started hanging out again, Sara often mentioned the idea of the two of them going to college together. The only concern Adam had was that her parents might convince her to go to a school Adam wasn't going to. What if she picked one of those eight that he hadn't applied to? He didn't know if they would get in, but they had applied to three Ivy League schools together. If they both got into one of those, her parents couldn't possibly object to them going away together.

One by one, they opened their acceptance letters. Sara first opened the eight letters that didn't match any of Adam's schools. Adam opened the envelopes from the three that didn't match hers. Both Adam and Sara were accepted into all of their separate schools. When those were out of the way, they opened their letters to their matching schools.

They decided to save the three Ivy League schools for last. Adam couldn't believe how nervous he was. He looked at the first letter and then Sara's. Both began with the word *Congratulations*. Knowing he had at least a chance of going to the same school as Sara, Adam started to relax. He grew more excited with each congratulatory message. Finally, they got to the Ivy League schools. Adam didn't care which school would accept them both. He just wanted them to get into one of them together.

A bright flash blinded Adam as he opened his first Ivy League letter. Sara's mom had taken a picture. He and Sara unfolded their letters and looked at each other's. Once again, both of them had been accepted. By the time they'd finished opening the last of the Ivy League letters, they discovered that neither of them had been rejected by a single school. Adam and Sara could go to any school they wanted together. The only thing left to do was to decide.

After it was all over, they went to the table and celebrated by eating dinner. Adam was used to seeing a lot of food on their table, but this was more than he had ever seen before. Sara's mom had made a giant feast to celebrate.

As they ate, most of the conversation was about which school they would go to. Sara's father pushed the idea of them going to the same school. He knew Adam would help Sara study if they did. He was also pushing them to pick the same major, although they didn't know what they wanted that to be yet.

Adam didn't have any idea what it was he wanted to do with the rest of his life or what major he wanted to pick for college. He only knew two things. The first was that he could go to any college he wanted and would never have to go back to his father's house again. The second was that whichever college he went to, he wanted it to be the same college as Sara.

As the night came to a close, Adam found himself becoming incredibly nervous. He knew what it was he had to do. For months, he and Sara had spent every day together. Now the two of them were planning on going to college together. Tonight, he finally had to find the courage to do what he should have done that summer years ago. He was going to officially ask Sara out.

Just like she always did, Sara stepped out onto the porch as Adam was leaving and closed the door behind them. Adam was so nervous he could barely keep his legs underneath him. He desperately wanted to tell her goodnight like he always did and retreat to his house. But he knew if he did that, he might never get enough courage to ask her.

"So. Uh. Anyway," Adam mumbled, barely managing to get anything out.

"Yes?" Sara asked.

"I was just wondering," he continued, not being able to find the right words. "I was just wondering if you maybe wanted to, uh…"

"Yes?" Sara asked again.

"Do you maybe want to, uh, like, maybe…" Adam said in a massive panic.

Never mind, it was nothing. I should just go home. I'll see you at school tomorrow, he thought about saying.

"I was wondering if you maybe," Adam continued, "…wanted to, like, go out sometime? Like on a date? Like as boyfriend and girlfriend?"

Adam couldn't believe what he had just said. He sounded like such an idiot. He'd mumbled for what seemed like an hour. Had he really just said all that? He wasn't even sure if he had. But it was too late now. It was out there. The only thing he could do now was to wait for Sara's response.

"Yes!" Sara exclaimed, giving him a big hug. "I've been waiting for you to ask me that since I first met you. When you didn't before I thought you didn't like me like that. I thought you just wanted to be friends."

Suddenly, she leaned in and kissed him. Adam was surprised. He couldn't believe how good it felt to finally have her lips against his.

Chapter 34

Finally, after all these years, Adam had everything he'd ever wanted. He was close to graduation. He had gotten into college. He was going out with Sara. And they were going to attend the same college together. He couldn't believe it. He'd always expected his hopes to be crushed. But they weren't. He'd finally made it.

At school, the boys quickly became upset when they found out Adam was dating Sara. Ever since they'd heard she broke up with Chris, they'd been swarming like vultures. Adam was annoyed by everyone constantly trying to get between them. Luckily, Sara had always mostly ignored everyone but Adam. Now he was officially dating her, and maybe they would leave her alone like they had when she was dating Chris.

As time went by, Adam found out he was wrong. The other boys hadn't stayed away from Sara when she was dating Chris out of common decency. They'd done it because they were afraid of Chris. He was older and a lot bigger. None of them cared about Adam, the small nerd who was about to graduate as valedictorian. None of it really mattered, though. It was annoying, but Sara would always just take Adam's hand and they'd go somewhere else.

Finally, graduation day arrived. Being the top two in their class, Adam and Sara sat up front. The entire school could see the two of them together. When Adam sat back down after giving his valedictorian speech, Sara reached over and took his hand.

Sara's parents planned to take the two of them out to dinner once the ceremony was over. The school was hosting a graduation party in the cafeteria, but neither Adam nor Sara wanted to go. As the top two students in the class, they were expected to show up, but they were planning on leaving right after being seen.

At the first opportunity, Adam and Sara left the party and went out through the side door of the cafeteria, where Sara's parents were to pick them up. As they walked out of the school for the last time, Sara turned and gave Adam a kiss.

They expected to see her parents parked on the curb, but they still hadn't arrived. They could see a hundred cars all trying to get out of the parking lot at once. Sara's parents were having a hard time getting through the parking lot to pick them up.

"It's too bad they expected us to show up to that party," Sara said. "We could be leaving the parking lot right now."

Suddenly, they heard a ruckus behind them. A group of boys was following them out through the door. There was alcohol on their breath.

"Well, look who it is," one of them said, pushing Adam in the shoulder. "If it isn't our old friend Andrew."

"It's Adam," Sara said.

The boy might not have been able to remember Adam's name, but Adam knew exactly who they were. Brandon, Miles, and Davis had tormented Adam for years. They were Derek's friends. The ones who'd helped Derek make Adam's life miserable for years.

Brandon laughed drunkenly. "The valedictorian thinks he's so special, but he needs his girlfriend to stand up for him. You know,

I asked her out once. She turned me down. She must like losers. Doesn't want a real man, I guess."

Adam stood between the boys and Sara. Her parents would be there soon enough. Once they pulled up, they could get in the car and leave. Adam wasn't afraid. He had taken hundreds of beatings from these three before. One more wouldn't make a difference. Sara could run to the parking lot and find her parents while Adam kept them busy.

Out of nowhere, Adam found himself lying on the ground. Miles had pushed him from the side while Adam was looking at Brandon. Adam looked up and saw Brandon grabbing Sara's arm.

"Come on baby," Brandon said. "Leave this loser and come back to my place."

Adam jumped up off the ground and tackled Brandon as he tried to pull Sara away. Brandon fell and smacked his head into the concrete. Adam looked down and saw that he was unconscious. The other boys yelled when they saw their friend lying on the ground. They'd never expected Adam to fight back like that. He never had before.

As quickly as he could, Adam got up and stood between the other two boys and Sara. "Run!" he yelled behind him to Sara.

Miles tried to push Adam down again, but this time he stood his ground and didn't budge. With a big swing, Adam's right fist hit Miles in the jaw, and he fell to the ground. Davis screamed in shock.

Adam couldn't believe his luck. He'd knocked down two out of three of them. He'd never thought he stood a chance against them before. But now he had Sara standing behind him. There was no way he was going to let them hurt her.

Adam turned and faced Davis. Suddenly, Davis ran at him, knocking Adam to the ground. He stood over Adam, punching him while Miles got back up and joined him.

Miles held Adam's arms while Davis viciously punched him in the face. With high school over, the boys no longer cared about not leaving visible bruises for the teachers to see. Adam's face bled and swelled, but the punches didn't stop.

As he tried to turn away from their blows, Adam saw Sara running back to him from the parking lot. He was about to yell to her to stop until he saw her father, James, following behind her, hollering at the boys. Miles and Davis saw James coming and took off running, leaving Brandon still unconscious on the ground.

Sara watched in horror as James picked Adam up off the ground and carried him to the car.

"We need to get him to the hospital!" Olivia told them frantically as they helped Adam into the back seat.

"No, no. I'm fine, really. It's not a big deal," Adam replied.

Although this concerned them greatly, it seemed like nothing more than a minor inconvenience to Adam as he wiped the blood from his nose with tissues Sara's mom kept in her purse.

"Well, we should let the paramedics decide."

"Paramedics?"

"Yes, of course. I called the police as soon as Sara told us what was happening."

Adam panicked for a moment but quickly realized he didn't care. High school was over. The bullies wouldn't be able to retaliate.

After the police finished taking their statements, they headed back to Sara's house. Brandon had woken up and run away before the police got there, and since Adam told them he didn't want to press charges, the police didn't take much of their time. They didn't care about what seemed like a short fight between teenage boys, even if Sara and her parents didn't feel the same.

The paramedics tried to convince Adam to go to the hospital, but he refused. A beating that had barely lasted a minute was nothing to him. His face was bruised, but he didn't have any broken bones or even a need for stitches. All he cared about was that high school was over.

Adam thought about how well he had done at fighting them off. He'd lost in the end but managed to knock down two out of three bullies. He wondered if he wouldn't have been bullied so much if he'd done that before; if only he had tried to defend himself as much as he had defended Sara.

Still, he was glad he hadn't risked getting suspended or expelled for fighting. It didn't matter anyway. It was over now. He wasn't going to be bullied anymore. He smiled as they pulled out of the parking lot and the school disappeared behind him for the last time. He would never have to set foot there again.

"I can't believe they did that," Sara said as they arrived at her house. "We really should go to the hospital."

"This is nothing," Adam assured her as he practically laughed at how minor it was to him. "I've had far worse than this, and it's always been fine."

"What do you mean?"

Adam had spent so long trying to hide from her how much he had been bullied. He didn't want Sara to think of him as the loser kid everyone hated. But when he saw the concern in her eyes, he finally broke down and told her everything.

Sara could always tell he was being bullied, but she never knew how bad it was. Adam always did his best to hide it from her, and she didn't want to pry if he preferred not to talk about it. Now she sat in horror as Adam described everything Derek and his friends had done to him over the years. She let out a gasp as he told her all the things his father had done. She knew why they'd never been to his house and only hung out at her place, but she'd never imagined it could have been so terrible for Adam to stay there.

After Adam told her everything, Sara went to talk to her parents. He watched TV for an hour before she finally came back with her mom. Although they were reluctant because Adam was dating Sara, they weren't going to let him go back to his house after everything they'd learned. There were two months to go before they left for college, and Sara and her parents worried about what could happen in that time. Until then, Olivia told Adam he could stay in the guest room they had in the basement.

Even after all the time he had spent with them, Adam still didn't know how to feel about their generosity. But he was almost eighteen, and his father probably wouldn't even notice if he never came back. Sara jumped excitedly as Adam accepted their offer. He didn't have much he needed to get from his house. He barely had any clothes to pack. He only wanted two things before he left forever: his mom's journal, and her picture. But those could wait until Monday when his father was at work.

The two months Adam spent in their guest room was the best time of his life. The room was small and little more than a storage room with a bed, but at least he felt safe there. It was far better than staying in his old room.

As Adam hung out with Sara every day, it reminded him of the summer he'd spent with her. She continued to teach him how to play chess. He still couldn't checkmate her, but he would occasionally come close.

This summer, however, Adam wasn't dreading its end. When the day finally came, he was just as happy as the day he'd first agreed to stay. He didn't take the bus to college as he'd always pictured himself doing. Instead, Sara's parents drove them both.

Adam felt weird as they packed the car up and left; it felt to him as if he'd already left two months earlier when he'd walked out the front door of his father's house, knowing he would never return.

Adam looked forward to starting college. He loved learning, and he was going to college with Sara. They were even signed up for the same courses.

They had decided over the summer that after college, they would go to medical school. Sara still hadn't picked a specialty, but Adam wanted to be a pediatrician. He wanted to help children the same way those doctors had helped him years ago when his father had broken his arm.

As they drove out of town, Adam didn't bother to look back as he'd always planned, watching the place that had tormented him so much disappear behind him. Instead, he looked at Sara in the seat beside him. He couldn't believe how happy he was. He had finally made it. He had everything he could have hoped for.

About the Author

Joshua Jumper began his journey by serving in the United States Army right after high school, where he developed a strong sense of discipline and commitment. Following his active-duty military service, he continued serving in the Reserves while pursuing higher education at Utah Valley University, earning his bachelor's degree and laying the groundwork for his future endeavors.

Today, Joshua is a medical student at the Spencer Fox Eccles School of Medicine at the University of Utah, where he is part of the class of 2028. His diverse background and dedication to learning inform his writing, bringing a unique perspective to his work as an author.